MEDIUM OF MURDER

Also from RED COYOTE PRESS

Medley Of Murder (2005)
Map of Murder (2007)

MEDIUM OF MURDER

Edited by

Susan Budavari and Suzanne Flaig

Red Coyote Press
Phoenix, Arizona
www.redcoyotepress.com

Copyright Acknowledgments

"Medium Risk," Copyright © 2008 by Susan Budavari
"Heidegger's Cat," Copyright © 2008 by Warren Bull
"A Favor for the Mayor," Copyright © 2008 by Howard B. Carron
"Evil Comes," Copyright © 2008 by Diana Catt
"Mattie in the Middle," Copyright © 2008 by Virginia Cole
"Texas Toast," Copyright © 2008 by Suzanne Flaig
"The Medium is the Message," Copyright © 2008 by Suzanne M. Harding
"iRomance," Copyright © 2008 by Gay Toltl Kinman
"Hocus-Pocus on Friday the 13th," Copyright © 2008 by Kris Neri
"Quick Draw," Copyright © 2008 by Sarah Parkin
"Murders Off the Wall," Copyright © 2008 by David B. Reddick
"Dead Reckoning," Copyright © 2008 by Gary Earl Ross
"Dead Even," Copyright © 2008 by Frank Scalise
"Art Can Be Murder," Copyright © 2008 by Carole Sojka
"Neither Rare Nor Well Done," Copyright © 2008 by Judy Starbuck
"Emerald Green," Copyright © 2008 by Nancy Streukens
"Rose," Copyright © 2008 by John Randall Williams
"A World More Real," Copyright © 2008 by Rachelle N. Yeaman

This is a work of fiction. All the characters, places, and events portrayed in these short stories are either fictitious or are used fictitiously.

Cover by Jack Hillman/Hillman Design Group
Cover photo of man in tunnel by Bryce Kroll/iStockphoto

ISBN-13   978-0-9766733-4-7
ISBN-10   0-9766733-4-7
Library of Congress Control Number   2008920921

Published by
Red Coyote Press, LLC
Phoenix, Arizona 85082
www.redcoyotepress.com

CONTENTS

CONTENTS

INTRODUCTION

For the third installment of this mystery/suspense anthology series, focus is on the polysemic word *medium*.

In some stories, *medium* is an intermediary between the physical and spiritual world; in others, it is mass communication—newspapers, radio, television or the internet. Likewise, it may refer to materials or methods used in art or biology; or even to the actual method by which the murder is perpetrated.

Each author provides a distinct view of present day life in a big city or small town, or offers an unusual glimpse at a bygone era. In every scenario, the particular connection between the type of medium and the murder determines the outcome of the story.

The array of characters includes psychics, both phony and perhaps...real; gangsters and gypsies, talk show hosts and reporters, dedicated school teachers and techno-wise kids, and even, disgruntled older folks out to even a score.

We hope you find these diverse stories tantalizing and that they whet your appetite for other installments of this series.

Special thanks to Joan Domning for her valued remarks during preparation of the manuscript.

Should you wish to contact us with your comments, we can be reached through the website www.redcoyotepress.com

Susan Budavari and Suzanne Flaig
Phoenix, Arizona

THE MEDIUM IS THE MESSAGE
S.M. Harding

Zoe McClanahan dreamed of struggling against her attacker. In her sleep she pummeled the pillow, fighting against the rosary that dug deeper and deeper into her throat. She surfaced to the reality of her bedroom, then lay curled up in the dreamless part of the night.

At four a.m., the phone shrilled with a call from Ed at the night desk at Channel 7. "A lot of action on the cop band," he said. "Tenth and Capitol. You can meet the crew there."

"Tenth and Capitol? That's Channel 2. Ed—is this another one of the Manifesto's kills?"

"Don't know, Zoe. Just a dead body and a lot of cop chatter so far."

She showered quickly, toweled her curly hair, and was driving downtown in fifteen minutes. She thought of the skeletal facts of the cases. Four murders, strung through the Midwest like the beads of a rosary. St. Louis, St. Paul, Madison, Chicago. All news anchors, all employed by Sterling Media Group stations. All garroted.

A note pinned to the first. "Stop the political spin in news or unanticipated consequences will result. The American people deserve better." A page of typescript on the second, a manifesto on the third and fourth. That's when a Chicago reporter had tagged the killer the "Manifesto Strangler."

Four beads on the first decade of the Manifesto's rosary? Was the death at Channel 2 the fifth? Was he getting impatient with the slow pace of prayer? Would he move on or did he have another target in Indianapolis? Several came to mind, but not me. I don't work for SMG and I'm not an anchor. With the grace of God, I never will be either anchor or victim.

Zoe saw a squad car parked across Capitol Street at Sixteenth with her crew's SUV parked at the side of the street. Her cameraman leaned against the cop car, smoking a cigarette. *Six blocks away? Has to be the Feds. They'd taken over in Chicago, shut down the news.*

Zoe swung the car onto Sixteenth, watched her speed, then continued her southbound route at Scioto Street. She found a parking place and was about to get out and hike to Channel 2 when a dark car pulled up beside her. The passenger's side window powered down. "Need a ride, Zoe?"

The voice was as familiar as her dad's. His best friend since Nam, Homicide Captain Bob Raines. "Do I get to pass go—or is this a jail card?"

He laughed, a deep, rolling sound. "Get in, Zoe."

She locked her door and climbed into the unmarked car. "So what's happening?"

"You're never going to get close to the crime scene," he said. "Feds had us shut it down tight."

"You notified them?"

He shook his head. "They called us a couple of minutes after it came in."

"Shit!"

"My sentiments, exactly," he said, putting the car into gear. "After 9/11, the Feds were supposed to turn over a new leaf, start sharing intel. Sure hope Homeland Security is getting more than local law enforcement."

"Didn't you have a buddy in Chicago PD?"

"Still do. He's going to courier a copy of the files to me. In the meantime, I want another pair of eyes on this one." He slowed, took a right on Fourteenth. "If anyone asks, you're on special assignment to my office."

"Assigned?" Zoe took a long look at him. *Grim. Angry to boot. Pity the first Fed he runs into.* "Don't I need a badge?"

He pulled a laminated clip-on from the inside pocket of his uniform jacket and handed it to her.

"Wow, this is better than the junior detective badge you gave me when I was six."

"You remember that?"

"I still have it." *Made me feel grownup, like I was a part of Dad's world.* "But won't the Feds see through this?"

"Too busy running around in circles to check police personnel," he said, stopping at another roadblock on Capitol. He flashed his badge and was waved through. "I want you to check the crime scene for discrepancies—things that we wouldn't notice because we're not in the business of TV news."

"Do I get to look at the manifesto?"

"I'll see that you get a copy later—so ignore it for now." He pulled up in front of Channel 2 and turned to Zoe. "Word from other law enforcement is that the FBI has gotten nowhere. I'll be damned if that happens here. All I want from you is an insider's view. Keep your eyes open, your mouth shut. This is off the record and will be until I say otherwise."

She opened her door. "Biggest story of the year, off the record? You've got to be kidding."

He grabbed her arm. "Zoe, no going off on your own. With television reporters the target, it's too dangerous."

"Anchors, not reporters. Big difference, Bob." She looked at the front entrance of Channel 2. "I'll let you know if I get any ideas—before I follow up."

He laughed. "Goddamn, you're just like your old man." He got out, walked around the front of the car, leaned in to her. "You get ideas, we do the follow-up."

She got out and followed him into the building.

An hour later he drove back to her car.

"I saw a couple of things you might want to follow up on," she said. "One, Dawson had his broadcast makeup on. Usually everyone cleans up right away. Ask his colleagues about his usual practice and if anyone saw him in the makeup after the late news."

"Never would have thought of that. The second thing?"

"The studio was set up for a taping. Maybe a promo, but it was awfully late for that kind of thing. Maybe they just needed a quick redo. If he slightly flubbed a line, or wasn't in the right position, or even if there was external noise they didn't pick up at the time, they'd reshoot the segment. Could have been anything."

"Don't know why they have commercials for news anyway."

"But the bottom-line is—why was he in that studio so late with makeup on? He might have been lured there by someone who knows the ropes."

"An insider?"

She nodded. "From what I've heard, Mike Dawson was a shark. The kind of anchor who'd do anything to get to the next bigger market. He wanted national news."

"He'll never make it now," he said, pulling up to her car. "You'll be at the station all day?"

"Probably."

"I'll send Chris over with a copy of the note. See if anything strikes you."

She turned to him and in the light from the streetlamp could see his grim smile. "I thought the Feds took the note."

"They did. I had one of the techs photograph it before the Feds arrived."

"Very Silver Fox move," she said, grinning.

"Be careful, Zoe."

She drove to Channel 7 on quiet streets, the blush of dawn perceptible on the eastern horizon. She pulled into her space, took her tote, and walked toward the back door. When she got close enough, she read a hand-lettered sign taped to it: ENTER AT MERIDIAN STREET. *Security's finally doing something.*

"Where the hell you been?" Ed asked as she walked to the assignment desk in the newsroom. "Decide on a little nap first? Your crew—"

"—is stuck at Sixteenth and Capitol. There's a cordon around the whole area. Nobody with a camera's going to get close."

"What's going on, Zoe? Where've you been?"

"Working with, uh, an informant. The Feds have taken over, zipped up everything tighter than a coffin. Better than our security guard who's snoring in the lobby."

"Did you get anything we can use?"

"Don't know," she said, sitting on the edge of the desk. She rubbed the back of her neck. "I've got info, but we may not want to go out on a limb and disclose it until they call a press conference."

"Aw, hell."

"I'll write up what I have and you can take a look. I want to stay off-camera on this one." She stood, shifted her tote, glanced at the clock. "Shouldn't our news director be here?"

"Karl feels lousy, wasn't coming in. When I told him what was going down, he said he'd be here about seven-thirty." Ed leaned back in his chair, clasped his hands and stretched. "Think I may stay around a bit, then. Worth it?"

Zoe nodded. "Manifesto's in town."

"Aw, holy hell!"

It was 7:30 by the time she'd written up the story and sent it to Ed. About five minutes later, Karl leaned into her office and cleared his throat. "So who's your source?" he asked, his voice as husky as a forty-year, two-pack-a-day smoker.

"You sound awful."

"Biggest story we've had in years and I feel like shit. Bet it's a pissed-off cop."

She crossed her arms and stared at him.

"OK, OK. Aren't you glad I finagled you an office? Now you can talk to your cop friends without anybody eavesdropping. Keep your secrets. Even from me." He rumbled into a cough that wouldn't stop.

"Office? Converted broom closet complete with sink." She leaned back in her chair. "Any word on a press conference?"

"Nothing. They're keeping everybody away. Can't get hold of anyone over at 2. You working more sources?"

"Yeah, a buddy up in Chicago is going to Kinko's to fax me his files. But he said not to expect much."

Karl nodded. "Keep me in the loop, Zoe." He started to leave. "Oh, there's a woman waiting for you in the lobby. Chris."

Zoe grabbed her purse and pushed away from her desk. "My breakfast appointment. Be back soon."

She swept through the lobby, collected Chris Noel, and walked quickly to Bean Town. When they were seated with coffee and muffins, Zoe said, "You have something for me?"

Chris leaned toward Zoe. "Captain said to be careful, keep a low profile. And don't use your cell or office phones."

What am I supposed to use? A can and string? "This place is too upscale for cops or journalists. Safe. What are the, uh, Big Brothers doing?"

"Buttoning everything down. Benefitting from our work, but not sharing one damn thing." Chris broke her muffin, put it back down, and leaned closer. "Captain said to slip you the document. Ladies' Room when we finish?"

Zoe nodded.

"He also said not to keep it with your notes or other files about the case. Worried it can be traced back to our office, I think."

"Have you looked at it?"

"Briefly. Looks organized, not just a rant."

"Have the Feds shared a profile on the killer?"

"White male with a grudge against television journalists, maybe a fired employee."

"That's supposed to help?" Zoe finished her coffee, wrapped up the muffin and stuck it in her purse. "Let's go. I need to get back."

When Zoe returned to her office, she closed the door and got the envelope from her purse. She quickly scanned three sheets of typescript, then went back and read more carefully. She reached for the phone, thought better of it. She stuffed the papers in her purse and walked to Karl's office.

"What's up?" he asked.

"I'm going out for awhile." She perched on the corner of his desk. "If I continue working on this, I need cover."

He stared at her for a long moment, then flipped through the file folders on his desk and handed her one.

Zoe headed to her car. She stopped at Aristotle's, a landmark restaurant for reporters. She put in her order at the counter, walked to a phone booth at the back by the restrooms. *Must be the last phone booth with a door in the state.* She held a quick conversation, picked up lunch and drove to Butler University's journalism department.

Her knock on a door with Professor David Kessler's nameplate was answered immediately by a tall, thin man with a fringe of white hair decorating his bald head. "Zoe, good to see you—come in and sit. Did I ever thank you for those guest lectures?"

"With dinner, twice," she said, closing the door behind her. She put the bag from the diner on the desk. "This is going to be a working lunch, David. We've got a situation."

"The death at Channel 2?"

She nodded and sketched out what she'd learned, omitting any reference to Captain Bob Raines. "I managed to get hold of a copy of the letter and there are some phrases in it that sound vaguely familiar." She handed him the letter.

He put on his glasses and began to read. He nodded, his lips moved. He put the pages back together, took off his glasses. "What phrases?"

"The ones I've underlined about change and anticipating change. I should know the source, because bells ring every time he uses them."

"I'm surprised they sound remotely familiar to you," David said, rising and walking to a bookcase that spanned one wall. After a minute scanning the top shelves, he reached up and pulled down an older volume. He returned to his desk and handed it to her.

"McLuhan! I should have known." She sat back in the chair and thumbed through the book, noting the handwritten marginalia. "I had Dr. Kidd at Northwestern and he insisted we at least sample some of the older theories."

"Older, oh, man. I'd just started grad school when *Understanding Media* was published."

"Mind if I borrow this?"

"If it helps catch a killer, be my guest."

"What other impressions do you have of the manifesto?"

"Organized, fluid writing, well edited. This doesn't seem like the rambling thoughts of a demented serial killer."

"I agree. Someone educated and comfortable with writing." Zoe leaned forward. "And the point about the consolidation of newspapers and television stations is important. He's talking like an insider."

"I've had the feeling he knows the news business, too. This began four months ago in St. Louis and guess who was in St. Louis that weekend?"

"You?"

"Along with twenty other journalists speaking at the National Collegiate Journalism Conference." He opened a file folder. "Here's the list—three of them had been fired from stations when SMG took over."

"The starred ones? Rod Karrus, Charlie Lamb and Cynthia Jessup?"

"Yeah, Karrus and Lamb have found other jobs in smaller markets. Lamb and Jessup did stints in the Marines."

"Leaving Cynthia Jessup as a prime suspect."

"I remember meeting her at the conference. Zoe, she couldn't be over five foot two."

"All the better to take someone off guard. I'll have to ask Karl his take on her."

"Are we just going to sniff the aromas or eat lunch?"

"Sorry. Sometimes I forget." She took two foil-wrapped gyros from the bag and divvied up the napkins. "I wonder if the Feds are onto this angle."

"I should hope so," David said between bites.

When they'd finished, Zoe gathered up the detritus and deposited it in the wastebasket with a thump. "It's scary how much sense this manifesto makes."

"Conglomerates gobbling up the old family-owned independents, firing reporters and experienced support staff," David said, nodding. "We're threatened with the Mac-news. But I think the really important part is what this guy says about the aftermath of 9/11. It created a growth medium for fear. And the war in Iraq breeds distrust and paranoia. Distrust of journalists because we did shit covering the buildup to the war. Just spouted the White House spin."

She nodded. "OK if I give the local cops your name?"

"Sure. But before you leave, answer one question for me. If this guy is so news savvy, why hasn't anyone published his manifesto? Surely he's sending copies to all the news outlets."

"That's been bugging me, too, but I don't have an answer. Or the answer to why the Feds are keeping such a tight lid on this."

"Terrorists? Homeland Security?"

"Maybe." She picked up the battered copy of *Understanding Media* and reached for the folded pages on the desk. "Thanks, David."

"Mind if I make a copy of this?" he asked. "It may be smart to have a copy outside your immediate possession."

"Good thought. Will you copy your list for me? Can I use your phone?" She made a short call to set up a meeting with Captain Raines while David went down the hall to make a copy.

Zoe spotted Bob Raines sitting on a bench in White River Park dressed in his civvies, sunglasses and a ball cap from the NRA. "Should I keep on walking or is it safe to sit?"

"Sit. No cop I know has time to stroll through the park for pleasure. Of course, who knows with the Feds? Told them I was going on the street to contact my snitches."

"So now I'm officially a snitch?"

He grinned. "Guess so. What'd you learn?"

She told him. "The reference to McLuhan means you might be looking for an older journalist."

"How old?"

She looked at him with a grin. "About your age."

"That might fit," he said, pointedly ignoring the age reference. "I went over the scene photos with the ME and she thinks it was a professional job."

"A hit-man who writes?"

"Someone who was trained to kill that way—clean, quick, silently. Army Rangers or Navy SEALS, maybe. Your dad ever talk about our training?"

"No. He never talked about the war at all." *I learned that lesson the hard way, pestering until he exploded.* "You think it might be a Viet Nam era vet?"

"Might be since you think he's an older guy."

"You know, you might ask Karl if he can remember anyone who was in Nam and went into journalism."

"Your news director?"

"Yeah." She shifted on the bench. "Going to tell me what you learned?"

"You were dead-on about the make-up and studio set up. Dawson always took his make-up off first thing. We talked to everybody there and no one was planning a redo. So someone must have lured him there. We're checking telephone records, but the killer may have already been in the building."

"I wonder how the killer got in? After the late news, doors are locked and only staff is let through security. At least, that's how it's supposed to work."

"Good question. I also got the files from Chicago, but it's going to take a fine-tooth comb to find anything that'll help us."

She looked at the river, closed her eyes and felt the warm sun on her shoulders. "Question: we know this guy has left a note or written piece at each murder. My guess is that he's mailed copies to other outlets. Why haven't they been printed?"

"Gag order."

"What about freedom of the press? Is this from Homeland Security?"

He nodded. "Stupid, isn't it? My theory is they're trying to frustrate him with the silence, make him unravel, start making mistakes."

"While the body count goes up?"

"Sucks, doesn't it? I remember when people were satisfied with a letter to the editor." He sighed, crossed his arms. "But back then, there wasn't a term remotely like 'road rage.' Can't believe how much has changed."

"That's what McLuhan talked about—the changes no one notices that bring radical structural changes to a society."

"God, you're talking like an academic."

"David Kessler at Butler lent me *Understanding Media*. I hadn't remembered much until I started reading. Conglomerates like SMG snuck up on us, have become so powerful they're very hard to head off."

"Well, this guy's found a way to rattle their glass towers."

Zoe took an envelope from her tote. "Copy of the fax from Chicago. Hope it helps. I need to get back and see what we can put together for the evening news."

"Zoe, you be careful. Stay off the air."

As she walked into the newsroom, Karl waved her over. "Meeting with the station manager. We gotta decide what we're going to do with this story—we got a letter from Manifesto and the Feds are threatening to pull our license if we release it."

She nodded, shifted the book and her tote. "Let me dump this stuff."

"Where'd you get the McLuhan book?"

"I had lunch with David Kessler at Butler. He lent it to me."

"Doing your homework, huh?"

"I've only just begun."

Zoe picked her way across the darkened news set, careful of the cables that snaked across the floor. *Long day.* She pushed the door open. At midnight, the other studio doors were closed and the only light was the exit sign at the end of the hallway. The squeak of her sneakers stopped when she thought she saw a light move under the door to Studio B. It was gone before it full registered. She looked again. Everything dark. *Seeing things. Just jumpy. Need sleep.*

Zoe still fumed at the verdict from station management: more silence. Goddamn bunch of cowards who were putting more lives in jeopardy. She shifted her tote and was about to continue down the hall when she heard a cough from Studio B.

She stiffened. *Too late for any legitimate use. Should call the desk, but security's probably on rounds.* Zoe set down her tote and tip-toed to the door. She stood, listening for sounds from inside the dark studio. Nothing. She pulled open a door, slipped in.

The set lights popped on and a voice from the dark said, "Aw, Zoe, why'd it have to be you?"

"I have to ask you the same thing, Karl."

A laugh came from the dark that quickly turned into a coughing fit.

"It's not just a summer cold, is it?" she asked.

"Got a month, maybe two."

"And you're going to spend the time left to you killing journalists?"

"I haven't killed a journalist yet, Zoe." He stepped out from the darkness. "Don't want to start now."

"Who were you planning to take out tonight? Who of the people you work with everyday?"

He sat on a stool, never taking his gaze from her face. "Not one of us, though I could name a couple who're tempting. Jane Talman."

"You were going to lure the other Channel 2 anchor over here? Is that how you got to Mike Dawson? A hot story we wouldn't cover?"

"Guy was so anxious to get out of Indy to a bigger market, he would have met me anywhere. Greedy, just like the damn shirts who run the business. Who the hell thought news was a *business*? I didn't when I started. Could've done something useful with my life instead of wasting it doing political spin."

"We do good work for this community."

"You graduated from Northwestern wanting to be a print journalist. Why aren't you?"

"With newspapers falling like autumn leaves, I didn't have a choice. I needed to earn a living."

"I rest my case." He stood, took a step toward her. "What gave me away?"

"Other than your cough tonight?" She took a step back and bumped into a camera. "You were at the NCJ conference in St. Louis. And that Canadian fishing trip? Dates coincided with the St. Paul murder. Madison and Chicago are close enough for a day trip, and both were on weekends when you were off."

"Not enough, Zoe. Coincidence."

"What have you always told me about coincidence?" She took a small step to the side. "I did some digging this afternoon. You were a Marine. Special Forces."

"Long time ago. Another lifetime."

"But mainly, it was the writing. Clean, terse, logical. Something an editor would have done—if he had your talent and background. Tell me I'm wrong."

"The McLuhan, eh? Good job, Zoe."

"What happens now, Karl? You've lost the element of surprise and I promise I'll fight with everything I have."

He took another step. "I don't want to kill you, Zoe. I don't want to fight you. Let me walk out of here. You got no evidence. Just a tired old man who wants to go out honorably."

"Honorably!"

She never suspected Karl could move so fast, nor that his fist could connect with her jaw with such strength and surety.

She came to with the insistent sound of someone calling her name and the overwhelming smell of ammonia. She opened her eyes to see the night security guard and Bob Raines hovering. She pushed herself up to a sitting position and rubbed her jaw.

"What the hell happened, Zoe?" Bob asked. "Please tell me it wasn't—"

"Manifesto? Wish I could."

"Talk."

She did and when she was finished, Captain Raines began to bark out orders on his radio. "And Chris, let's keep it in the department." He stopped pacing and turned to her. "What'd you do to get away?"

"Nothing."

"But he knew you'd identify him."

She pushed to her feet and winced. "He just wanted a head start."

"Hurt that bad? We should get you to the hospital, your jaw might be broken."

"It's not my jaw."

"Your heart?"

She nodded. "He used to call anchors hair dryer parrots. Oh, my God! Jane Talman! She was supposed to be—"

"Relax, she's sitting in the lobby. Your security man wouldn't let her in. Afraid she was spying for Channel 2." He leaned against the wall. "What tipped you to him?"

"It was just a notion I kept pushing away, but I couldn't stop digging." Zoe took a tentative step toward the door. "Mainly, the writing. How many reporters write like that today? I went back and looked up some of his early print articles." She put a hand on the door. "McLuhan was right. He defined the medium as the extension of the human mind. One is language. Karl's use of language was the message that gave him away."

iROMANCE
Gay Toltl Kinman

Albert Aguirre took one last look at Tori Sanderson's picture on his monitor, smiled and shut down his computer. In an unusual moment of daring, he had ordered airline tickets to Fallbrook, Minnesota, then sent an e-mail telling her when he'd arrive.

His heart thumped at the thought that she was the woman he was going to marry. Him getting married! No one would believe it. He hardly believed it possible himself. All thanks to the Internet.

It was Halloween, so he had suggested they make dinner together when he arrived. They'd already chatted and e-mailed about menus. They had made up appropriate names for everything—Spooky Salad with Eyeballs; Intestines with Blood Sauce. And, for dessert, something from *Desserticide II aka Just Desserts and Deathly Advice*. They'd laughed over the titles, trying to pick the perfect recipe, but there were so many. Maybe "Death by Turtle" on page twenty-one.

It had been a romance fueled by hundreds of e-mails over six months. They'd exchanged pictures, personal histories, and their thoughts about everything. He was sure he knew more about her than any of his friends had known about their prospective brides.

Bride. His heart thumped again. *His* bride. The Internet was truly amazing. Imagine someone who lived in Southern California meeting someone in Minnesota, falling in love—and neither of them ever leaving their own state!

Tori Sanderson met him at the airport. As beautiful—no, more beautiful—than her Internet picture. Long, brown hair, as tall as he at 5' 8", slender and laughing. They looked at each other for a long minute. Then she slowly put her arms around his neck and planted a kiss on his cheek. Her lips felt cold on his warm skin. "Welcome to Minnesota," she whispered into his ear. He thought he would faint from happiness.

They went outside. He'd forgotten how cold it was in the Midwest in October. No matter, they would be moving to California. As they hurried to her car, the chilly wind that whipped through his unlined raincoat made him feel like he'd been tossed into a freezer.

At her home, they started dinner. Albert was so nervous he could hardly chop the vegetables for the Spooky Salad.

The phone rang. While she was talking, he was ready to cook the sausages. He looked in the refrigerator, but didn't see them.

He had noticed what looked like a walk-in freezer earlier on his way to the bathroom, so he went down the dark passageway, opened the freezer door and took a step inside. A dim light came on.

A man in a wheelchair slumped forward.

Albert froze.

There was frost on the man, but Albert tentatively put his hand out to shake him. The man's arm was rigid.

Albert backed out, the freezer door swung closed. He stood staring, as though he could see the man in the wheelchair through the little frosted window.

"Darling, where are you? I've got the Blood Daiquiris and Body Bits ready."

Albert gagged even though he knew the drinks were made with cranberry juice and the bits were hors d'oeuvres of acceptable food items. He darted to the bathroom across the passageway and threw up.

He rinsed his face with cold water.

He went to the living room. Everything was a blur.

Blood Daiquiris and Body Bits were set out on the coffee table.

"What's wrong, Albert?" Tori asked. She looked concerned.

"Must be something I ate on the plane."

"Oh, Albert, do you want to lie down on the sofa?" She led him to it and covered him with a garish afghan. "I'll get some water."

He felt paralyzed.

How had the man died?

Albert told her that he was in no condition to eat anything and escaped to his room.

When he woke up later, he thought that maybe he'd been hallucinating.

She was a sculptor. He knew she did animals. Was she expanding her repertoire? She hadn't said anything about that. He thought they had told each other everything. But he had to admit that he'd left out a tiny detail about his job. He had only said he was a dispatcher for a medical supply company, which was the truth. The one tiny detail he omitted was definitely not something to bring up during a courtship. Even he had enough sense about that.

He had to go back for another look, to make sure he'd really seen what he thought he saw.

In bare feet, he padded down the carpeted hallway, through the kitchen and into the passageway. There was enough outside light coming through the windows for him to find his way.

He opened the freezer door again. The light came on.

The man in the wheelchair was still there, plus what he hadn't seen before—other men in various poses. He counted five.

Maybe they were all mannequins. Had to be.

But what would mannequins be doing in a freezer? In his thin pajamas, he didn't want to step into the freezer.

Back in bed, he considered that if they were mannequins made of plastic, he could tap on them, and maybe hear a hollow sound.

If the men were real, how could he check that? Break off a finger and let it thaw? No, he couldn't bring himself to do that. He shivered under the duvet. His bare feet were like blocks of ice.

Should he leave and report what he saw to the police? What if the men in the freezer were mannequins? Then he'd lose his true love forever. He didn't want to lose her. He *really* didn't want to lose her.

Without the Internet, he never would have met her, or any woman for that matter. He knew he was too shy. He didn't know how to play the game, whether it was at a church function or at a party. But with the Internet he had blossomed. He had actually courted and proposed to a woman!

He thought of all the time they'd spent on the computer talking to each other and how much fun he'd had. They'd met in a culinary chat room. She'd asked what chicken mole was, and he'd told her he'd teach her how to make it, that there was a trick in preparing the chocolatey sauce. He would never have said that face to face to any woman. But he'd really meant it, he wanted to teach someone who'd never made it before.

Next, they started to e-mail each other. And the rest was history.

But what was that history going to be?

They had talked about marriage—and sex. She wanted them to meet and make sure getting married was what they both wanted. She said she was an old-fashioned girl and didn't believe in sex before marriage. She hoped that was okay with him.

Yes, it was. But then he'd had a panic attack nonetheless. His experiences in that arena had been disastrous. He had to do something about that. He went on the Internet to learn as much as he could about pleasing a woman. He'd even bought a book.

Here he was, about to turn thirty-four. If this relationship failed, would he have the nerve to try another, even over the Internet?

He thought back over their relationship. Maybe she had been too easy to woo. Maybe using the Internet for a romance wasn't such a good idea after all.

He must have dozed for awhile for suddenly he felt hot and threw off the duvet.

He decided to go back into the freezer to figure out if the men were real. He had to know for sure. Some sort of imperfection in the skin, a scar, perhaps. There must be some way he could tell. Set his mind at ease. He knew a lot about body parts, but he'd never seen a dead person before.

He crept down the hallway as quietly as he could. Her bedroom door was still closed.

He went through the passageway to the freezer. If she got up and he was fast enough, he might be able to cross the hall to the bathroom.

At the freezer, he pulled on the door.

It wouldn't budge.

Locked?

He tried again, pulling with all his strength.

Locked.

He went to the bathroom to think. The night light showed a ghostly face in the mirror. His. He'd aged in just a few hours.

He was about to go across the passageway to try the freezer door again, when he saw the beam of a flashlight.

"Albert, what are you doing?"

"I didn't want to wake you, so I thought I would use the bathroom here."

"And I didn't want to wake you, so I used a flashlight." She waved the light over the metal door and glass window. "Here's my freezer. That's where I keep my wax sculptures."

"Wax sculptures? The animals?" He'd almost said 'men.'

The opossum, her latest, was the best, so life-like carrying the babies on its back. She had e-mailed pictures to him.

"I'm trying something new, more realistic. That's what you said you liked about the opossum. People at the gallery liked it, too. I want to do things cast in bronze, outdoor statues, they're very popular now."

"You didn't say anything." Maybe he didn't know her as well as he thought.

"I wanted to surprise you. I wasn't sure if I could do it. If the process would work out, I mean. Or even if anyone would like them. I have some life-size figures in wax in there. I'm experimenting with a new formula, and the ingredients require a freezing temperature. Then I'll cast them in bronze. A friend is letting me use his studio. He has all the equipment for handling big works."

They were wax, that's what she said. He felt so relieved. Garden sculptures, yes, they were popular. Kids playing tag. Mothers sitting on benches watching, Guys doing exercises. He wondered how anyone could make anything so life-like. He admired her talent.

"You'll be famous," he said.

When he awoke in the morning, he was happy. He'd found the woman of his dreams. Last night, he must have been a little delirious with jet lag, the food on the plane that hadn't agreed with him, and then the euphoria of meeting her.

Everything was going to be wonderful.

He showered, dressed and went to the kitchen. He called her name. No answer. Then he looked around the house but she wasn't there. He checked the garage which was attached to the house. Her car was gone also.

He drank some coffee and glanced at the sports section of the newspaper, which she had set out along with breakfast dishes for him. Cereal and fruit. She knew exactly what he liked. He ate. He was starving.

Then he fidgeted. He wondered where she was. There wasn't anything for him to do. He wasn't used to doing nothing. He was always on the computer at work and at home. He told himself he was on vacation. Taking a vacation, something he rarely did. He was starting a new life, time to change his habits. But he was still fidgety.

A chance to try the freezer again.

But why did he want to go in there? he asked himself. She said they were wax, so they must be wax.

He'd use her computer while he was waiting. It was in her home office. He turned it on, clicked on Solitaire. Playing the game helped him think.

He could go on the Internet. Check out garden sculptures. She could sell to those companies. Maybe he could help her.

The good thing was, she could do the sculptures anywhere. He'd even install a walk-in freezer if she wanted it.

He accidentally hit another icon, not the Internet one. And there were some pictures.

The first one was the man in the wheelchair!

He was sure of it—only the man was looking right at him, eyes opened, not slumped forward.

"SLEEP" was the title of the picture.

He wondered if she had used a real wheelchair, and the wax figure of a male model.

As Albert clicked through, he saw pictures of men in various poses. He didn't know if any of the others looked like the ones in the freezer.

And then, there was *his* picture!

The one he had e-mailed her!

He stared at it for a second, then exited the program and shut the computer off.

The cereal and fruit and coffee were churning unnaturally in his stomach. What did it all mean?

Of course, she'd have pictures of her work. Of her models. But why was his picture with them? Was he going to be one of her models?

That would explain why the man in the wheelchair was so life-like. Is that what she'd done with the opossum? But how had she been able to handle the animal? And with the babies on its back?

She was an artist, after all, and obviously a talented one.

He paced the house. Then decided to go for a walk. That could be the beginning of his exercise program.

He realized he didn't have a key. He'd have to leave the door unlocked and just walk up and down the street keeping the house in view.

He opened the door, made sure it was unlocked, and was about to step out when he saw her car parked in front. But there was no one in it. He hesitated, going over the possibilities of why her car was there and she wasn't in the house.

The freezer loomed in his mind.

He went back and walked to the freezer. He heard a faint beating sound.

His heart almost leapt out of his chest. There was a hand in the frost on the window of the door.

He froze in fright. Which one of the figures had come to life?

Then he heard a voice that sounded like it was far away.

Her face appeared.

He tugged at the door, but it was still locked. What was she doing in there? Thoughts tumbled in his mind.

He tried to wipe the window, condensation on his side, frost on hers.

"Key in closet." Even though she looked like she was yelling, the sound hardly came through louder than a whisper. She pointed down the passageway.

It took him a minute to process the information. He ran down the length of the hall and found the narrow utility closet. He opened it and on pegs inside were keys. So many keys. Only a few were labeled. He grabbed the one on the FREEZER peg. The word on the key's tag had smudged, and looked like GEEZER.

He ran back and tried to work it into the lock. He dropped it. Tried again.

She fell out into his arms.

"Oh, thank God. I thought you'd never find me." She was cold as ice. "I pounded and pounded and yelled and yelled."

He was so shocked at the crisis, he barely functioned. He helped her into the living room and wrapped the garish afghan around her.

"I thought for sure I was a goner. Get me another blanket. In the same closet."

As he pulled the blanket out, he looked a little more closely at the multiple sets of keys.

He took the blanket to her.

"Something's wrong with the lock. It's not supposed to lock like that. I made sure of that because I didn't want this to happen." She shook her head, and her whole body shivered. "Let's go out. I want to be in the sunshine. It's such a beautiful day. There's a restaurant we can walk to."

It was a beautiful day. Almost a California one, at least in the mid-seventies. As they walked, he held her hand. But it never warmed up.

Later, in his bed that night, he thought about everything that had happened. He still wanted to inspect the wax statues in the freezer.

She kept insisting he have coffee that night. For some reason she forgot he told her he never drank coffee before going to bed. Why had she been so insistent? Had she put something in it to make him sleep? To keep him from prowling around? To keep him from looking in the freezer?

He didn't drink the coffee, a plant did.

He couldn't sleep.

He went to the kitchen, took the milk out of the refrigerator and found a glass in the cupboard, then sat at the table thinking about the lunch menu for the next day.

Within a few minutes, he saw the flashlight bobbing down the hallway from her bedroom.

"Tori?" he said.

"Albert? Oh, you startled me. What are you doing?"

"I had an idea for lunch and was seeing what things we needed." For a moment, only the flashlight illuminated her face, making it into a ghastly caricature of her features, a person she might be in forty years. She turned on the kitchen light.

"The freezer," she said glancing down the passageway. Maybe she thought he had been in there. She visibly shook. "That was a terrible experience."

"It's a statistic that most accidents happen in the home."

"That's where we spend most of our time. I bet the second place where most accidents happen is on the worksite." She grinned, making her the most beautiful woman in the world.

He laughed. "That's true." He felt good being with her. So comfortable. He was a happy man.

"Tell me what you were planning for lunch," she said, settling onto a chair.

Tomorrow would be All Souls' Day, the day of the dead, so he built a menu around that.

"Mmmm, that sounds wonderful," she said after he'd finished.

"Let's go to the lake tomorrow. I'll show you some of the wonders of Minnesota."

"I also want to see the gallery where your works are displayed, and the studio where you are going to do the statues," he said.

"Okay, but first Minnesota."

The next day had been a glorious one. Maybe the happiest of his life.

The only discordant note was when she insisted that he have a cup of herbal tea before going to bed. It seemed out of character for her to be that forceful, almost demanding, particularly after the day when she had been so attentive and caring.

He switched their cups, although he felt guilty even considering she might be trying to give him something to sleep.

Who was he? The loving fiancé or the man who suspected her of nefarious deeds?

He had to go back into the freezer. He had to know for sure.

In the dead of night, he dressed as he would for the outdoors, including gloves, and slipped down the hall again.

He propped the freezer door open with a kitchen chair to make sure he wouldn't be trapped inside.

He looked at the man in the wheelchair. Eyelashes coated with frost. Another was hunched in the pose of The Thinker. Then he unbuttoned the top two buttons of the man's shirt.

Hair on his chest.

Albert was sure if he unzipped the man's pants, he would find him anatomically correct. Not a detail that a sculptor was likely to include.

One of the five was human. What were the odds the others were also? What were the odds that he was going to be number six?

Although he had never seen a dead body, he knew there was a difference in those who were dead, then frozen, and those who had frozen to death. Though all frozen bodies were pinkish in color, lividity told the truth. The former would be blue-grey, the latter pinkish.

His heart pounding loudly, he gently manipulated the coat and shirt sleeves of the man in the wheelchair. His heart plummeted to the center of the earth as he saw the pink area of the arm that had been resting on the wheelchair.

He had frozen to death. What were the chances that it had happened in this very freezer? Albert didn't check the others. One was enough to clear up that niggling doubt he'd had.

Why did she do it? Was she that serious about her art and wanted to carry realism to the macabre extreme? Or did she lure them here to marry them and drain their bank accounts?

The bodies could be covered with wax as she said, then bronzed and planted on lawns, in parks, in buildings. She would be paid several thousand dollars for each one. It was also a good way to get rid of the body.

Albert knew about bodies. But these had been frozen too long.

Were all these men products of an Internet romance, as he was? Without family, as he was?

Shaking, he left the freezer, and put the kitchen chair back.

He went back to his room to hurriedly pack. He had to get out of there before she woke up. How close he'd come to being a body in the freezer. He'd been spared. He'd often thought of that in his job. Why had one person died and another saved by their death? Was the person saved for a reason. What was that reason? To do some good in the world?

He stopped trembling, straightened his shoulders, stood tall. He had a purpose.

The men could not do anything for him, but perhaps he could do something for them.

Actually, they could help by their presence.

For them, he could seek justice.

A plan formed in his mind.

He slowly opened her bedroom door. She lay on her back, her mouth opened and lightly snoring. He tried to wake her. She didn't respond to his voice or his shaking of her shoulder. He doubted she usually slept that soundly.

Now his question was answered about the sedative in the herbal tea.

He was devastated. All of it too good to be true. She had been too good to be real.

In her room, he found socks, mittens, hat and a fleecy warm-up suit and put them on her. She was slumped forward much as the man in the wheelchair, the sculpture she had titled "SLEEP."

He carried her unconscious body to the kitchen and sat her on the chair he had used. From the living room, he took the garish afghan and tied it around her to keep her upright in the chair.

He moved around the house, wiping his prints off everything. He put his sheets and towels into the washer. While they were swooshing around, he mopped the kitchen floor where he'd trod in his bare feet. He cleaned the bathrooms he'd used. She had her own.

Her computer—he'd have to clear that of his e-mails.

She'd already done it.

He deleted his picture from her "gallery."

Prints in the car. He went out to the garage to obliterate those.

He remade his bed with the clean sheets.

The keys.

He tried to ascertain why there were so many keys and most without labels.

Then he noticed each key ring had emblemed car keys: one an Alpha Romeo, one a Mercedes, another a BMW. His only deduction was that they had belonged to the inhabitants of the freezer. He wondered where the cars were. Had she sold them?

He heard a groan, and quickly went to her. "Go back to sleep, Tori, everything's okay." She stilled, looking about as comfortable as if she were sleeping in a tourist class plane seat on an overnight flight.

He eyed the bodies in the freezer with regret.

He hadn't told Tori what his job as a dispatcher was. Not exactly a turn-on in a romance, but he felt he made a great contribution to the quality of life of many. He was a trafficker in body parts. That's what his boss called him.

His job was to sit at the computer all day and move body parts around the country. Boston needed a heart and California had one. Boston got the heart. Nevada wanted skin and Oregon had it. Nevada got skin. There was a lot more to it. He had an inventory that was ever changing, and never long enough. These bodies he was now looking at would never live up to their potential. Body parts that would never be used to help a person live better. All those corneas, kidneys, livers—

She started to awaken and was groggy. He microwaved a cup of coffee, and helped her drink it. She needed the caffeine to wake her up. He didn't want her to fall back asleep. There would be no justice in that, for she would freeze to death.

"Albert, what are you doing?" Her words were slurred.

He moved her, still on the chair, into the freezer, then slipped her cell phone partway into her right mitten.

"You've got a cell phone," he said.

"What am I supposed to do?" Her eyes barely focused but he could see the alarm in them.

"Call the police."

He closed and locked the door, leaving the key in the lock.

She could introduce the police to her cold friends.

DEAD EVEN
Frank Zafiro

"I need you to talk to this girl Madeline and see what she needs," Angelo said in his velvety tone. It didn't put me at ease. There was always an edge behind that tone. "Someone's leaning on her and I want you to fix it."

"You're kidding me," I said.

"Kidding how?"

I sighed. "Uncle Angelo, this is kinda..." I searched for the right word. 'Ridiculous' is what immediately came to mind, but that wouldn't do. "It's irregular," I finished, settling.

"Irregular?" He snorted. "How you can sit out there in flannel land and talk to me about irregular, I'd like to know."

You sent me out here to Washington, I wanted to say, but I bit my tongue.

"Only thing irregular out there, I'm thinking, is if somebody don't get their latté on time." Angelo chuckled.

I didn't reply. *The Pacific Northwest. Land of apples and pine trees. Thank you, Uncle Angelo.*

He continued. "What's so irregular about doing me a favor?"

"Nothing," I said. "Everything I do out here is for you."

"I'm glad to hear that."

I repressed a sigh. "But River City is different than Jersey, Uncle Angelo."

"No kidding?"

I ignored his sarcasm. "It's a lot smaller here. People notice things. The cops already have me in their sights as an outfit guy. I have to be careful, you know?"

"So be careful."

"No, I know that. I just mean, I gotta weigh the pros and cons of everything. Like what you're asking me to do. I gotta do a cost benefit analysis. Figure it against the risk, right?"

"What, you think I don't know business? Who you think you're talking to?"

"I know, Uncle Angelo. I know."

"You know? Then why you think you gotta tell me these things?"

"I'm just sayin', is all."

"You're just sayin'. Give me a break."

I resisted the urge to sigh. I knew he was going to make me do it. "I'm just tryin' to be careful, is all. I got no protection out here. The cops are clean for the most part. And I got hardly anything in the way of muscle."

"So hire."

"I'd love to. But I can't afford it. I haven't even found a guy to replace Isaac."

"That the kid that got pinched?"

"Yeah."

"He make it down under?"

Six feet under, I thought, remembering the pistol in my hand. I wiped a sweaty palm across my slacks. *We drove out to the Bowl and Pitcher Park near the river and sent him to hell. Just because he might turn.* "Yeah, I heard he did," I said.

"How hard is it to replace one guy?"

"He was smart," I explained. "Muscle isn't so hard to find. It's brains that are in low supply."

"Here, too," Angelo sympathized. "It's a friggin' epidemic, stupidity. Some days I think all I have are *baccalá* around this place."

"I hear ya. I got morons here, too."

Angelo sniffed in a breath. I imagined him straightening his silk tie as he spoke. "Listen Dommie," he said. "I need you to square this, aw'right? This Madeline out there with this problem, she's the little cousin to my *goomah* Gabriella, you know? This Gabby, she's bustin' my balls when she should be... you know what I mean?"

I sighed. His mistress. Great. "I'll take care of it."

"You're a good boy," he told me and broke the connection.

I stood up from my small desk off of the restaurant kitchen, shaking my head. I gotta jump through hoops so that Uncle Angelo can continue to get his weasel greased? Wonderful. I walked through the kitchen and out the back door. I stepped on the cloned cell phone, breaking it. Then I tossed the pieces into the dumpster.

I met Madeline at her apartment. Only the picture postcard of a crystal ball taped under the peephole distinguished her door from the others in the complex.

"Oh, Christ," I mumbled and knocked. This was just what I needed. Some kooky broad to protect. Like women weren't crazy enough already, I gotta deal with one who claims to speak to the dead and know things by magic?

The lock rattled and she swung open the door. I saw immediately why Uncle Angelo would be after her cousin, if they looked anything alike. She had volumes of flowing black hair and huge round eyes. Follow that up with a nice rack and plenty of curves and it ain't so hard to figure why I got a call from Jersey.

She smiled. "Hi. I'm Maddie. And you're Dom."

She said it like I was supposed to be impressed that she knew. Like some other large Italian from Jersey would be knocking on her door, but she knew it was me. Psychic, right?

"Mind if we talk inside?" I asked her.

She nodded and stepped aside.

The outside of the apartment may have looked like all the others, but the inside was another thing entirely. Crystals were everywhere. Some of them hung by fishing line from the ceiling. Candles flickered next to little figurines on most of the shelves. A couple of chairs in the living room and a table draped in a purple cloth stood in the corner. And no lie, she had a crystal ball on the table.

I rubbed my nose and sat down without being asked.

"Would you like some coffee?" she asked. "Or some herbal tea?"

"No, I'm good. But we need to talk, so sit down."

She walked past me, her flowing blue dress rippling in the air. Some blonde hair and she could be Stevie Nicks. I caught a whiff of jasmine perfume in her jet wash. I ignored that and the sway of her ass. This woman was nothing but trouble, I figured.

She sat down and crossed her legs. Her expression remained open, except for the small tension lines at the corners of her mouth. I wondered if her cousin called and gave her certain expectations.

"Let's get something straight," I told her. "I don't believe in this voodoo mumbo jumbo you're selling here. I don't care that you make a buck at it, but let's not fool each other that it's not a scam, aw'right?"

Her smile collapsed into a scowl. "What I do is *not* a scam. I am a medium. I commune with the spirits of the dead. Just because you don't understand—"

I waved her words away. "Drop it, sister. We both know how it works. You get weak-minded people in here, read them cold and tell them what they want to hear. It's easy, because they want to believe it anyway. On top of that, you're nice lookin', so the con job goes down easier."

She stared at me. "Why are you being so...mean?"

I chuckled darkly. "Little girl, you ain't seen the beginning of mean."

Genuine fear flashed in her eyes, but she covered it up pretty quick. You gotta be some kind of actress in her line of work, I guess.

I leaned forward. "I'm here as a favor to my uncle. But don't think that makes you some kind of *goomah*-in-law or whatever. I'll help you out, but you gotta do what I say."

She nodded slowly. "Okay."

"And it ain't free, neither," I said.

"You want me to *pay* you? But Gabriella said—"

"What Gabriella said don't much matter," I told her. "What I say does. Now, I'll help you out with this problem or whatever, but we're going to come to an agreement. This is business."

She regarded me carefully. "What agreement?"

"Nothing extravagant. Twenty percent."

She fingered one of the long silver necklaces that hung from her neck. "Of what?"

"Of everything," I said. "But I've got a cop that'll keep the fraud unit off your back. And I'll steer you some business, too. You'll probably come out ahead."

She pursed her lips. Then she asked, "How about ten percent?"

"This ain't no negotiation. It's twenty."

She bit her lip, then sighed. "All right."

"Good." I picked up one of the small figurines and leaned back in the chair, examining it. "Tell me about this problem, then."

She watched the crystal in my hand with disapproval. "It's the Gypsies."

I shrugged. "So?"

"They've got a spiritual business, too. Palm reading, Tarot cards and medium work."

"Along with about four used car lots," I said. "And a whole lotta fencing."

"I wouldn't know about that. But when they saw my ad in the newspaper, the madam and her goons came to see me." Her eyes teared up. "They threatened me."

I suppressed a yawn. If this was a straight up muscle job, it'd be finished in a day. Not bad, when you include a new revenue stream opening up in the bargain.

"They wanted you to stop scamming?"

She pressed her lips together at the word, but nodded. "The old woman told me that if I didn't give up the business, I'd end up dead."

"You go to the cops?"

She looked surprised. "Are you kidding?"

"No. Why?"

"It's just that a guy like you... I wouldn't think you'd suggest going to the police."

"Cops have their uses sometimes," I said.

"What could they do here?"

I shrugged. "Probably not much. But just reporting it might solve the problem. Maybe a cop goes and talks to them. Now they know the cops know, so they can't touch you without being suspects."

She considered, then shook her head after a moment. "That doesn't sound too foolproof."

"It ain't a force field or nothin', but it might work."

"It's not enough," she said. "I'd rather know for sure that they'll leave me alone."

"You mean you can't see that shit in your crystal ball?"

She shot me a glare.

I laughed and let myself out.

* * *

I figured who better to deal with Romanians than a Russian, so I went to see Valeriy Romanov. Val and I were in the same line of work. Sometimes we'd help each other, if the price was right. Since I knew the Gypsies ran some car lots and that Val dealt in hot cars, I figured there might be a connection.

I found him in his small Russian coffee shop, where he usually spent most afternoons. I didn't know if he owned the shop or not, though it helped me to have the restaurant. A legit business made not-so-legit business easier to hide. Val sat reading the newspaper and sipping from a small cup.

"That *Pravda*?" I asked, sliding into the seat across from him.

He looked up and extended his hand, unsurprised as always to see me. "Does not matter. News is same everywhere. Americans, they like to think they are so different from rest of world, but is not so. Only difference is who pulls strings."

"Guys like you and me?"

Val laughed. "Maybe. But even we are small fish, *nyet*?"

"Medium fish," I said and smiled at my own inside joke.

Val raised his hand in the air and snapped his fingers. "Katya! Bring coffee!"

A thin woman with dishwater blonde hair and Slavic features slid a small cup of coffee in front of me. I didn't want any coffee, especially not the Russian blend Val drank, but I didn't argue. I thanked her.

"*Privyet*," she said in a thick accent.

When she walked away, Val spoke. "So you come see me I think for business, *nyet*?"

"Yeah." I sipped the harsh coffee and leaned forward. "I might need your help with the Gypsies."

The corners of his mouth turned down. "What kind help you need?"

"You have any dealings with them?"

He shook his head. *"Nichego."*

I raised my eyebrows. "Really? I'd have figured you to be in business with them."

"As I say, *nichego*. Nothing." He tapped the ashes from his cigarette into the small ashtray. "Why you think this?"

"They have car lots. You deal in cars. I figured it was a natural fit."

Val regarded me without responding. I met his gaze evenly, sipping at the strong coffee and grimacing.

"You no like?" he asked.

"Just a bit stronger than I usually drink it."

"It is from Turkish blend. You know what Turks say about coffee?"

I shook my head.

"Black as hell, strong as death, sweet as love," he quoted.

"Well, this stuff is the first two."

He smiled and took a sip himself. When he set the cup down, he leaned in toward me and gestured for me to do the same.

I leaned forward. His breath was sour with coffee and cigarettes, but his voice was cold and deadly. "I think maybe we don't talk so much about what business I do. Is safest that way."

I sat back and shrugged. "That's fine. But I figured your people had a history with the Gypsies, too. Maybe you can influence them, even if you don't do business."

Val shook his head. "These Gypsies are Romanian, *nyet*?"

"Hell if I know. But your people had the whole of Eastern Europe under your heel for fifty years. I figure maybe some of that held over."

"Romanians always trouble, even for Soviet government." Val took a deep drag off his cigarette and stubbed it out. "Sometimes when we have military exercise, Romania not even show up. Even the men like you and me, in that country they are difficult to deal with."

"So you can't help me?"

"Sure I help you," he said. "You pay, I help. But I can offer nothing special just because I am Russian and they are Romanian."

"I don't need muscle. I got that. I need influence."

"And I no have that. Not with the Gypsies." He shrugged. "*Kak zhal'*. I am sorry."

I reached out and patted his hand. "Another time, perhaps."

"Of course."

I stood to leave.

"Dom?"

"Yeah?"

"Do not underestimate them."

"I won't."

Val watched me for a second. "I hope not."

"I won't," I repeated, and left.

I made a call to my cop.

"I don't control the fraud detectives," he complained.

"At least keep an eye on the apartment," I said.

"That's not even on my side of town."

"Just do what you can, all right?" I shook my head. "Jesus, what do I pay you for?"

"I'll try."

The Gypsy "storefront" was up in Hillyard, a rough section of River City. Smack in the midst of a residential neighborhood, a statue of some saint stood in the middle of a yard next to a large sign that advertised palm readings, tarot readings and communion with the spirits.

I parked up the street a couple of houses away and sat in my car, thinking. This still seemed like a straight up muscle job to me, but it was times like this that I missed Isaac. The kid had been smart. A little strategy was a good thing. It made matters go smoothly and prevented unnecessary violence. Violence worked, but it could be bad for business, too. It wasn't like I was making a ton of money as it was. I couldn't afford for things to go sideways.

After a few minutes, I realized I wasn't going to come up with a better plan, so I got out of the car and walked to the converted house. As I passed the statue, I could see that it was a woman. Fresh flowers lay at her feet.

A bell rang as I swung the front door open and again when I closed it behind me. The smell of incense hung in the air. The living room was laid out almost the same way as Madeline's. Where Madeline's layout seemed contrived, things in here seemed more natural to me. Older. More real.

A small shiver ran across my shoulder blades. The hair on the back of my neck and forearms tickled and stood on end. Madeline was a fake, for sure, but maybe this old Gypsy had something real going on. Hell, there were stranger things in the world and—

I shrugged away the thought. All that was going on here was that these people were better at theater than Madeline.

The sound of clacking beads announced the arrival of the Madam.

She was a tiny woman in a simple, dark purple dress. The lines in her face spoke of wisdom but not yet old age. She wore her iron gray hair pulled back into a tight bun. Long silver necklaces with charms hung around her neck, clicking and clacking as she approached.

Her open expression faded into suspicion as she drew close. "What do you want?" she asked, her tone guarded.

"Maybe I want my palm read," I said.

She shook her head. "No," she said. "You want something else."

"How do you know?"

She ignored my question. "Say your piece," she commanded. "I have work to do in the back."

I was already tired of this spooky bitch. "Fine. I'm here to ask you to lay off Madeline."

"The şarlatan in the apartments?"

"Call her whatever. Just leave her be. There's plenty of business here in town for the both of you."

The Madam crossed her arms and gave me a disapproving stare. "Are you finished?"

"I don't know," I said. "If you're going to leave her alone, then yeah. Otherwise..."

"Otherwise what?"

I shook my head. "Let's not find out."

She shook her head back. "You do not know who you are dealing with."

"Maybe not," I said. "But then, neither do you."

She smiled secretively. "I know more than you think."

"Whatever."

"I know how you will die, Dominic."

I paused. The certainty in her voice hung in the room like a scent.

"How'd you know my name?"

She smiled and said nothing.

"Fine," I snapped. "You know so much, how you figure I'm gonna die?"

"Alone," she whispered. "An old man, alone and frightened."

"No one can tell the future." I waved my hand dismissively with more confidence than I felt. "Look, there's more than enough suckers around town for both of you to make a living. Just let her be."

She drew herself up. "I cannot."

"Can't? Or won't?"

"Both," she answered. "For my nephews, it is a matter of money. They will not allow someone else to cut into our business. For myself, I can not allow a *şarlatan* to bring disrepute and dishonor to true spiritual guides."

Her eyes flashed when she spoke about the honor of her trade.

"Come on," I said. "Cut the act. I understand about the money, but don't try to sell me on this other crap. If it's a financial matter, I can maybe get you ten percent of her take—"

"Crap?" she asked, almost spitting the word. "Do you tell the priest at your church that his service is *crap*?"

"That's different. Besides—"

She held up her hand. "We are finished here. You may go."

I sighed. "I really hoped we could work something out. Otherwise—"

"Otherwise, perhaps you will drive me out to the woods near the river and bury me?"

I froze.

"What?" I whispered, my mouth dry.

She smiled knowingly. "Go. And never bother me again."

"What did you just say?" I said hoarsely. Waves of cold washed past my face and down to my toes.

"Leave!"

The sound of footsteps filled the room. Three men surrounded me.

"What is it, *mătuşă*?"

The Madam's eyes drifted to my right. "Nothing, Dragos. This gentleman was just leaving."

I tore my eyes from the small woman and met the gaze of each man, letting them know they didn't scare me. Then I turned and walked out of the house.

I cast a quick glance at the white statue in the yard before I hurried to my car.

Back at my restaurant, I sat in the office and mulled things over. I still couldn't see where this was anything other than a straight muscle job. A little pressure and the Gypsies ought to break. I wondered if I should hit the Madam's house or one of the car lots.

The car lot would cost too much money, I decided. They might strike back instead of giving in. I needed to send a message, one that didn't cost much but let them know I was serious. Something simple. Something—

How did she know about Isaac?

"Stop it," I said out loud. "She didn't know. She just took a wild guess and got lucky. That's what people like her do."

"People like who, boss?"

I jumped in my seat.

Joe Bassen stood in my doorway. His scarred face brought me some comfort.

"Christ, Joe!"

He closed the door behind him. "Sorry 'bout that, boss."

I waved his apology away. "Listen. I have something for you to do."

Bassen took a baseball bat to the large plate glass windows in the front of the Madam's house. Then he knocked over the big white sign in the front yard and dumped the statue of the saint right on her ass. I got all of this from him the next morning.

"Good job," I said.

"Now what?" he asked.

"Now we wait for them to respond," I said.

They did. Two days later, I got a call from my cop.

"I think that your psychic got herself killed," he said.

"What? Where were you?"

"Hey, it happened before my shift started," he said. "I can't be everywhere."

"You're sure it's her?"

"Yeah," he answered. "My guy at the scene said she was strangled with a pair of panty hose."

"Damn," I whispered.

He laughed. "Guess she didn't see that coming, huh?"

"Real funny," I said and hung up.

I sat at my desk in the small cramped office off the restaurant kitchen and stared down at my hands. The cell phone chirped on the desk in front of me. I didn't need to look at the display screen to know who it was. I could already hear Uncle Angelo's booming voice coming through the telephone receiver.

He would want to know what went wrong.

He would bluster and threaten and tell me I was never going to earn my way back to Jersey.

He would want their blood.

I knew I couldn't let this stand.

I ignored the cell and picked up the desk phone and called Bassen. I told him to pick me up at the restaurant.

"Come heavy," I said. "And bring some weight for me, too."

A piece of plywood covered the large plate glass window at the Madam's house. The saint and the sign had been righted.

"Bastards bounce back," Bassen grunted.

"It's a talent," I muttered back.

Bassen sniffed and rubbed his nose. "We taking out the old lady?"

I shrugged. I didn't want to, but I wasn't sure how much blood would appease Angelo. Bassen kept looking at me, so I finally said, "Just follow my lead."

We exited the car and made our way up the walk. I didn't see any sign of Dragos or his cousins. The front door was unlocked and we let ourselves in, setting off the bell.

The old lady stepped through the beads and regarded me with disdain. "Dragos!" she said in a loud voice.

The sound of footsteps filled the small house and three men burst into the room. We stared at each other for a brief moment and then all five guns came out at once, including mine and Bassen's. I paused a milli-second, waiting for the first crack of gunfire. If it had come, I'd have drilled Dragos old school, right in his face with my .45. But everyone kept their cool, at least for the time being. All gun barrels stayed pointed at the ground.

"This isn't what I want," I told Dragos firmly.

"What you want is irrelevant," Dragos said. "What you have chosen is at hand."

"I didn't choose this. It just happened."

The old gypsy let out a dry, cackling laugh. "Always you say you do not choose, Dominic. And yet everything you do is a choice."

"Shut up!" I yelled at her. "If you'd minded your own business, none of this would be happening!"

She shook her head, still cackling. "This is happening because it is happening."

"Oh, Jesus," I said. I glanced at Dragos and his cousins, both staring hatred at Bassen and me, their pistols clutched in their hands. The old lady sat in the corner, her laughter sounding like dry, crunching leaves. "How did we get into this mess?"

"Because you are dumb son of bitch," Dragos said.

"Someone has to pay for Madeline," I told him.

"She was a fake!" the old woman shrieked.

"Who cares?" I asked, focusing my gaze on Dragos. "It's all about money, right?"

Dragos shook his head. "No. It is also about honor."

I realized this was not going to end well. I saw the darkness in Dragos' eyes. I glanced at the old woman and held her self-righteous gaze for a long moment. I wondered how she knew the things she knew. Then I remembered her words.

Old and alone, she'd said. That's how I would die.

Fuck it. Forty-three isn't old and I damn sure wasn't alone.

I flicked my eyes to Bassen and he caught my look. In that second, I said everything that needed to be said. A moment later, I raised my .45 and blasted a hole in the chest of the guy next to Dragos. He flew back into the wall with a grunt, his shoulders slapping into the drywall.

There was a blast next to me and Dragos' remaining cousin collapsed to the ground with a gurgle. I turned my .45 on Dragos, but not before he leveled the barrel of his own pistol at my head.

His finger twitched.

I grimaced.

Click.

He stared down at the gun in horror.

I smiled. He forgot to chamber a round. I stepped into him and cracked him across the nose with the barrel of my gun. He crumpled to the ground, dropping his pistol. Bassen scooped it up off of the ground.

Without hesitation, I moved toward the old woman. I grabbed her by the shoulder and jerked her tight to my chest. Then I pressed the barrel of the .45 to her temple.

"Dragos!"

Dragos shook his head to clear it, then turned his eyes upward toward me. As he took in the scene, his jaw clenched and a helpless hate came into his eyes.

I met that terrible gaze with my own fire. "Listen to me," I said. "We can come to an agreement here or I can close her eyes forever. You make the choice."

I saw him struggle with submission, but after a few moments he gave a reluctant nod.

"Good," I said. "You're smart, Dragos. This is business."

"Say your piece," he said through gritted teeth.

"It's simple," I told him. "You killed Madeline. We killed these two here. That's it. We're quits."

He shook his head. "Those are my cousins, you—"

"Who do you think Madeline was? Just some bimbo? She was connected."

He didn't answer, but I saw him calculate my words.

"It's even," I told him.

"It is one for two," he said. "Honor demands that—"

"It's even," I said. "I'll give you a life." I gave the old woman a light shake. "Hers. And yours."

Dragos considered. After a few moments, he nodded. "Yes," he said. "Son of bitch. Yes."

I nodded back. Two dead would appease Uncle Angelo. And I'd never have to see another gypsy fortune-teller again.

"Fine," I said. "Swear it."

Dragos drew himself up. "I swear on my father's name."

Good enough, I thought. I released the old woman. She stepped away from me.

"You'll take care of these?" I asked, pointing my gun at the two dead bodies.

Dragos nodded.

Bassen and I walked carefully toward the door, our guns still trained on Dragos. He followed with his eyes. His gaze was flat and deadly.

At the door, I stopped. "On your father's name, Dragos," I reminded him.

He nodded again. "Is finished."

I slid the .45 into my belt, knowing Bassen would keep his at the ready until we reached the car on the street. "All right," I said. "Goodbye, then."

Dragos nodded, but said nothing.

I turned to go.

"Dominic."

It was the voice of the old woman.

I turned to face her. "What?"

A cruel smile spread across her face. "Remember what I told you. You will die as an old man, alone and frightened."

A chill passed over my shoulder blades, but I waved her words away. "Yeah, yeah."

She laughed then, a measured, cackling burst. "Afterward, Isaac waits for you in hell."

Sheets of coldness washed over me again. I swallowed. "Whatever," I whispered.

"In hell, he waits," she hissed and broke into gales of laughter.

We left, her peals of cruel, joyous laughter and Dragos' deadly stare following us out the door.

"You made those bastards pay?" Angelo asked.

"Two of 'em," I said.

He sighed. "I really wish you could've worked this out in a more business-like manner, Dommie."

"I tried," I told him. "These Romanians are a pain in the ass. Even the Russians can't deal with them."

"No? Well, then I guess you did what you had to do."

"I did."

"So this Gabriella is all pissed off at me now," he said.

"Sorry."

"Ah, women are crazy, anyway. She'll come around. Or she won't."

"Yeah."

"You're all right, though? You didn't get hurt?"

"No, I'm fine. My guy, too."

"Good. That's good."

"Yeah."

"You figure this is over out there?"

"Unless this guy don't care about his father's name, yeah."

Angelo considered. "I'm thinking that's a blood oath for him. You?"

"Yeah."

"All right, then. We're back to even, right?"

"I suppose."

"What's that mean?" he asked. "You *suppose*?"

I thought of the Madam's accusing gaze. I felt Dragos' deadly glare. I saw Isaac rotting under a few inches of earth and a pile of leaves, bullets in his back and behind his ear.

In hell, he waits.

"It don't mean nothing," I said.

"Good," Angelo replied. "Then we're even."

"Yeah," I said. "Even."

But I knew I was wrong about that.

EMERALD GREEN
Nancy Streukens

"I make a habit of studying poisons. It's what I like to do best, though I haven't confessed it to anyone until now," I said, turning to the man sitting next to me.

There's something about traveling on a plane across the country at thirty-thousand feet that makes me loquacious. I talk to everybody—my seatmates, the passengers in front and back of me, the people across the aisle, the stewardess, anyone who will listen. I guess it's just nerves. I hate to fly, but my partnership in an antique gallery requires me to make buying trips several times a year. So I fly and I talk and I probably bore people to death. I'm just a gray-haired old lady who can't keep her mouth shut.

I'd been chatting all afternoon with a very nice young man on the flight home to Seattle from New York City. Such a polite fellow. To his credit he hadn't fallen asleep once during our flight. Neither did he pick up a book. In fact, even though he was wearing a headset with one earphone in his ear, I don't think he glanced more than just a few times at the little movie screen several rows ahead of us. He sat in his seat next to the window with his head resting against the seat back, his eyes shut, nodding his head every few minutes to show me he was listening. Every so often he would make a comment or ask me a question about myself. He was a very good listener.

The flight was almost over and I was winding down, but my tongue couldn't seem to stop. I don't know why I started confessing about my secret interest in poisons, except that I'd run out of other things to say. He seemed to perk up a bit when I mentioned the subject, so I continued with enthusiasm.

"My favorite is an old one called Paris Green or Emerald Green. It's a deadly pigment containing arsenic that once was used in paint and wallpaper...fabric, too. But because it's so lethal it's not used anymore. Which is too bad when you think about it because it's supposed to have been a strikingly beautiful brilliant green color. They say it was often used by Cezanne, Van Gogh, and other artists of their period. It's probably not a coincidence that Cezanne's diabetes, Van Gogh's nervous disorders and Monet's blindness are all symptoms of chronic arsenic poisoning."

"Fascinating," my seat companion said without opening his eyes.

"Yes, isn't it? It's also quite interesting that when in the presence of damp, the pigment is said to give off a deadly arsenic gas. Some historians believe that Napoleon died prematurely because the walls of his house on St. Helena were decorated with wallpaper containing Emerald Green."

I glanced at my companion. "Do you suppose they knew it was lethal and papered his house on purpose?"

"I've absolutely no idea," he muttered.

"Well, wouldn't that be amazing?"

"Amazing," he agreed, finally opening his eyes and giving me an odd look. He was probably tired, poor dear.

He continued to stare at me, yet said nothing else so I went on. "Whether or not one believes that, it's a fact that in the 1890s, medical authorities in Italy were concerned about the unexplained deaths of over a thousand children. The cause turned out to be the green pigment in the wallpaper in their houses coupled with the presence of mildew. They thought that since the children were short and played near the floor, they more easily inhaled the heavy arsenic gas."

"And you study all about this, do you?" he asked.

"I know it sounds a bit odd, but it's such a fascinating subject." I looked past him out the window. The dark-green forests of Puget Sound were coming into view. "I can't believe we're here already. I hope I didn't bore you with all my talk."

"No, not at all. It was very interesting. I didn't know much about antiques before."

I smiled. "Well, you certainly do now, I'm sure. I'm dreadfully sorry to chatter on like that. I don't know what comes over me when I fly. I just can't seem to stop. You've been exceedingly patient."

Our plane headed into the clouds and it was obvious that we were making our final descent into the airport. I knew Rebecca, my daughter, would be waiting for me at the gate, so I began to gather up my things. I didn't want to be the last one off the plane. Rebecca doesn't like waiting. She's quick and efficient, ultra-organized. All of which makes for a very capable business partner, if at times, not a very easy one.

Fiona Sheele's & Daughter sounded like a very good idea at the time. I mean, how many women in the world wouldn't love to have their daughters follow them into a business they loved? I'd owned Sheele's Antiques for ten years by the time Rebecca graduated with a master's degree in Western Philosophy. Since there's not a tremendous call for individuals with a degree in Western Philosophy, it took some searching before Rebecca finally found her niche in life and decided that she wanted to join me in my business. I was thrilled, of course. As I said before, who wouldn't be? But that was almost fifteen years ago, and lately, things haven't been so wonderful.

The problem is Rebecca. She's been insisting for the last several months that I need to slow down and take it easy; that perhaps I should move into a smaller place. But I'm only seventy-nine and I told her that I'm not ready to slow down. I've lived in the same house for forty-five years and I'm not going to leave it. We've been arguing about this continually since she first brought it up back in December. Finally, just to get her to be quiet, I told her we'd talk about it after I got back from New York.

To my surprise, Rebecca didn't begin her nagging again until almost four days after my return. Then she started in one night at my house after dinner.

"Fremont House is a lovely place," Rebecca said, waving a brochure in my face. "You've just got it in your head that it's an old folks' home."

"It's filled with old people so it's still an old folks' home no matter what trumped-up name you give it," I argued. "I'm not old."

"Mother, it's a really nice place. You could have a small apartment of your own. And it wouldn't be any trouble. They have people who come in to clean it for you every week."

"I couldn't bear to leave this beautiful place," I said, looking with pride around my dining room with its white-paneled walls and ornate crown molding. "I love it...the way I'd love a child. Your father and I moved here before you were born. Besides, who would take proper care of it if I wasn't here?"

"I know, Mother, it's a wonderful house. I love it, too. But Dad's been gone for ten years. You just rattle around in it. And I know it isn't easy to keep this place up." Rebecca took a bite of salad and peered at me over the top of her glasses as if daring me to disagree.

I sat back in my chair and took a sip of wine, thinking a bit about what she'd said. She probably had a point. This place, lovely as it was, was too big for me. However, it's a great deal better than that tiny high-rise condominium downtown that she lives in. She says it suits her just fine, but in my opinion it's way too small even for one lonely spinster—which she is, although she claims she isn't.

I smiled at her. "Oh, it might be a little too large for me now with its six bedrooms and everything," I conceded reluctantly. "But I love it. And it isn't that hard to keep up."

Rebecca made a face. "There's dust everywhere, Mother. You should at least get another cleaning lady."

"So I'll get another cleaning lady," I said, throwing my hands in the air. Rebecca seemed so startled at my outburst I relented at once. I calmly clasped my hands together and with elbows on the table, said quietly, "Look dear, it's just that I can't find a good one. I don't know what it is with all of them lately. They don't seem to work out anymore. The last one even had the nerve to make up vicious stories about me. Remember? She said I left the stove on when I went to work and left the water running in the backyard. And when I couldn't find my checkbook she accused me of hiding it. Now why on earth would she say ridiculous things like that?"

Rebecca gave me a studied look. "I have no idea," she said evenly. Then she brightened, "Look, if you're worried about the house, why not sell it to me?"

"You?"

"Of course, why not? You know how much I've always loved it. And I'd take excellent care of it. You wouldn't have to worry about a thing," she replied, turning to admire the crystal chandelier above her head and the oriental carpet at her feet.

There was something about her words and the distinct possessive gleam in her eye that did indeed make me start to worry.

It was only now that I remembered Rebecca had always been a very greedy child—never satisfied—always wanting something more. I knew she cherished the house as I did, but now it was becoming clear that this was all just a clever plot to get me out of my home so she could move in. Before I could say anything, she began to rave on again about the old folks' home.

"And another good thing about Fremont House, you wouldn't have to cook. They have a dining room and a twenty-four hour salad bar. You can have your meals whenever you want, and you'd never have to cook again."

"But I love to cook!"

"Mother, you hate to cook. Besides, they also have a nurse on duty around the clock. If you ever got sick, there'd always be someone to help you."

"I'm never sick. Anyway, if I ever got sick I'd call you and you could come help me."

"What if I'm not home? I'm not always home, you know." She took off her glasses and glared at me. "I've got my life to live, too."

Rebecca pretends she has a busy life, but she doesn't. She's past forty and never been married. I don't think my daughter's had a date in the past ten years. She claims she doesn't have the time what with working at the gallery and keeping watch over me. But I ask you, how hard is that? I certainly don't require babysitting and the gallery always seems to just take care of itself.

She gave me another critical glance. "Mother, this way someone would always be there to see that you're all right."

Sometimes I wonder what Rebecca's thinking when she looks at me. Lately, it doesn't feel very loving. In fact, sometimes it doesn't even feel friendly. She always seems to be frowning.

"And they have activities every day," Rebecca continued. "There's bingo and bridge and movie nights…"

"Why would I want to spend my time sitting around with a bunch of old people?" I asked.

"Well, if you don't want to sit around, there are exercise classes."

"Why would I want to spend my time *exercising* with a bunch of old people?"

"But you wouldn't be alone then," Rebecca said, her green eyes glaring at me.

"I like to be alone! I like my independence. I get enough company at the gallery. I spend all day visiting with our customers. By the time I come home at night I'm happy just to sit and be by myself."

Rebecca cleared her throat. "Well, that's the other thing I think we should talk about, Mother. I think you should maybe cut back on the hours you're spending at the shop." She was smiling, but her eyes were hard.

"You can't run the place all on your own," I insisted.

Rebecca shrugged. "I know that. I thought…well… maybe I could get someone to come in a few days a week. I'm not saying you should quit completely…just maybe cut back a little. I think, eventually, if I can get someone to help me for a few days a week, I should be able to handle things on my own."

I knew in that moment that she was definitely serious about this. First, she wanted me out of my house and now she wanted me out of my business. I was being shoved out the door. She was grasping for everything I'd worked my whole life for. She was sucking the soul out of my life, the life out of my soul. It was then that I came to my decision.

"Mother? Why are you staring at me like that? I'm only thinking of your welfare. You told me yourself that you've been tired lately, and sometimes you forget things. I just think that working at the gallery every day might be getting to be too much for you."

I sighed and gave Rebecca a weary smile. "Oh, dearest, let's not argue. What if I promise to think about it? I mean to really give your suggestions some serious thought."

Rebecca blinked. "Really? You will?"

"Yes, I promise," I replied, getting up. "Now I have a few things to show you from my trip." I went over to the sideboard and returned with a roll of heavy paper. I pushed our plates aside and lovingly spread the paper out over the length of the table. Against a cream-colored background the paper was covered with an exotic floral motif of fanciful blooms and brilliant emerald green leaves and vines entwined down its length.

"It's beautiful," Rebecca breathed. "What is it?"

"It's Italian nineteenth-century wallpaper. I found fifteen rolls of it at the Brady Gallery in New York. Do you like it? I think it's rather pretty."

"Pretty? It's gorgeous," Rebecca insisted. "What are you planning to do with it?"

"Why, I don't know exactly."

Rebecca got that greedy gleam in her eye again. "Mother, I know we haven't always seen eye to eye on things lately, but do you possibly think that I could have it?"

I thought a moment and then smiled. "Why certainly dear, I think the wallpaper would be lovely in your place, especially in the bathroom."

EVIL COMES
Diana Catt

The frenzied beat escalated to a deafening pitch as flames leapt skyward, pushing back the darkness of the African jungle. I saw Mutiso's eyes roll back and her body gyrate as the dance possessed her. Beyond the drums, I heard a voice calling my name.

I awoke with a jolt and sat up in bed, breathing hard and sweating profusely. The dream seemed to follow me into the room until I realized someone was hammering on the front door, yelling my name.

Jet lag and sleep clouded my thoughts, but I remembered where I was and how I got here: the rushed departure from Kenya, the three a.m. arrival at Tucson International Airport, the quick stop at my research laboratory at the Medical Center, then home to bed without even taking time to shave.

Again I heard the resonating "Dr. Goodwin" and recognized Natalie Baker's voice. My clock said 7:15. Why was she here, and at this hour of the morning? I was exhausted but forced myself up to open the window. Below, at the front entrance, I saw my technician's spike of red hair poking out of an orange scarf wrapped several times around her neck. The chilly March air cleared my head.

"I'll be right down, Natalie. Don't wake the whole neighborhood."

She looked up and the morning sunlight glinted off her eyebrow rings, nasal captive bead ring, and bridge post. She raised a hand in greeting, but didn't smile.

I threw on some clothes and thought about why I'd returned from Kenya ahead of schedule—I couldn't accept Natalie's last e-mail with the negative lab results for the Tacazzea plant. The assay I had conducted in the field before shipping it to Arizona had been positive. If Natalie had been able to confirm the result, the plant would be worth its weight in gold.

I'd always trusted Natalie, but the potential value of a positive sample might prove too tempting. With so much at stake, I decided I needed to make an unannounced inspection. Had she read the note I left for her at the lab and come by in person to explain?

I hurried downstairs and opened the door. Natalie was shivering and looked close to tears.

"Come in," I said. "What's wrong? Did my note upset you?"

She shook her head. The black lip gloss contrasted even more than usual with her pale complexion. "Oh, Dr. Goodwin, I didn't know what else to do." Her lower lip was trembling.

"Well, spit it out. What's the problem?"

Natalie tried to speak but nothing came out. She took a deep breath and tried again. "I found a body," she said. "In the freezer."

I was stunned. I half expected a confession of faking results and selling off samples, but not this. "A body? What freezer?"

Then her words came out in a rush. "The minus eighty. I read your note and went to get the samples from the freezer so I could repeat the tests you wanted and there he was."

"Who?"

"I don't know. He was jammed in there face down, covered with ice. I just slammed the lid shut, grabbed my stuff and got the hell out. I'm so glad you left a note telling me you were home."

I could only stare at her. There must be a mistake. Then I had an idea and forced a smile. "It's probably a cadaver or a mannequin. Someone playing a joke."

"Are you sure?"

"No, but it's been done before. I'll call Wilson over at the cadaver lab, see if they're missing one."

Natalie's eyes narrowed and her voice became hard. "That's so wrong. Who would do something that mean?"

"We'll find out," I said. I'd seen that look on her face before. Natalie didn't like to be made a fool of. "Look, why don't you wait in the kitchen. The coffee maker is already set up, just push the button." I pointed her down the hallway then placed the call to Wilson.

I described the situation, and left my number. My explanation of a cadaver prank was lame, of course, but I didn't want to think about an alternative until after Wilson checked it out. Instead, I thought about the problem that compelled me to fly half way around the world. The positive field test versus the negative laboratory test.

The field test was simple. I would grind up a native plant and add it to a specially prepared medium then wait a week. Usually, nothing happened. That's why I was so confident when the Tacazzea plant had exhibited incredibly potent antifungal properties. The Kenyans grind up the Tacazzea root and use it liberally in their native medicines. Although its main benefit could be as a preservative to eliminate moldy contamination, local lore attributed stronger powers to the root, including a cancer cure. In my most optimistic daydreams, I envisioned Natalie's results showing an effect on the tumor cell lines, as well as confirming its antifungal role. This could be the find of the century. A lot of people would be healed and I'd have perpetual research funding.

Then I had received her e-mail about the negative results.

When Wilson called back, the body in the freezer made laboratory errors seem minor.

"Dr. Goodwin?" Wilson said. "I checked your freezer. There's a dead body in there for sure and it's not one of ours. Yours has clothes. Most likely, foul play's involved."

"Foul play?"

"Well, sir, how else would a person end up in the freezer? I've called the police."

"Any idea who it is?"

"Nope. It's a man, I can tell you that much. 'Bout all I can make out is his bald spot. He's face down and I ain't touching him. By the way, I checked all the other freezers in here. Yours is the only one with a body."

"Well, thanks. Tell the police I'm on my way."

I updated Natalie and left her in the kitchen while I headed upstairs to finish dressing. The rhythm of my footsteps on the stairs recalled the African drumbeat of my dream and the prophetic words of Mutiso, the Kikuyu elder and legendary healer; their sangoma. At my parting visit to her hut two days ago, she had me toss the magic bones. Mutiso interpreted meaning in the way the bones lay on the mat and announced, "Evil comes to wazungi and disrupts the continuity. You must restore harmony."

Now there was a dead body in my freezer. Probably a murder victim. Could it get more evil than that? On impulse, I donned a red polo shirt. Mutiso had once said red would please my ancestors. Continuity with the dead was the goal of the Kikuyu elder and I had embraced her teachings. But could I restore harmony?

I followed Natalie's car out of the subdivision, then lost sight of her on the highway. I missed the slower pace of Kenya and refused to readjust. Life before Africa had been both hectic and wonderful, but that time had ended in God-awful pain. Two lives lost forever. Would my daughter have been as daring a driver as Natalie seemed to be? Amber would have been about the same age as Natalie was now. Would she have wanted the piercings and spiked hair?

I smiled remembering my rebellious Amber and my wife, Sarah, and then realized the memories no longer sent me into a debilitating depression. I could thank Mutiso for that. The wizened, old African had opened my eyes to the perception of continuity; the physical presence of all things visible and invisible; and the soul's continuation in the spirit world.

Over the course of my many expeditions into the Kenyan rain forests, my story, my pain, had been released to Mutiso. The sangoma had performed her healing ceremony and I had miraculously mended. Africa was good for me.

The police and an ambulance were parked in front of the research center with lights flashing. The few people at work this early were gathered in the lobby around Dorothy's receptionist desk. Dr. Leon Metzger stepped out from the group and greeted me.

"Arvin, didn't expect you back so soon. What a welcome home, eh?" he said, shaking my hand. "Don't know if you've been notified, but there's someone stuffed in your freezer."

"I heard. Any idea who it is?"

"None. But the coroner's here and they're getting ready to remove him."

"Then I'd better get back there. I'll catch you later, Leon."

I headed straight for the common room where shared equipment, refrigerators and freezers were housed. My freezer was standing open and three men were lifting the body out, with a fourth snapping pictures. An empty ambulance stretcher lay nearby. Natalie was just inside the doorway, speaking to a uniformed police officer. I joined them and introduced myself.

"Who is it?" I asked.

"We haven't ID'd him yet," the detective, named Sharp, said. "Ms. Baker tells me that she went to the freezer this morning on your instructions. Can you tell me what time you were here last?"

"Four-thirty this morning. Just flew in from Kenya. I came straight here, stayed about an hour, then went home to bed."

"What was so important that you came here first?"

"I was excited about some test results and wanted to look them over."

"But why the big rush this morning?"

"It could have waited, I suppose. Guess I'm still operating on Kenyan time."

"And did you happen to look in the freezer while you were here?"

"No. But I did leave a note asking Natalie to locate some samples to retest. That's why she opened the freezer."

Detective Sharp nodded. "I see. Was anyone else in the building while you were here?"

"There was a light in Metzger's lab. I assumed it was the janitor." I glanced across the room. The officers were in the process of placing the body onto the stretcher.

"Who has access to this room?" the detective asked.

"Anyone with a key to the outside door. It's a common equipment room. In fact, it's not even locked during the day. My freezer's another matter, however. It's always locked."

Detective Sharp switched his gaze to Natalie. "Was the freezer locked this morning?"

"Yes. I didn't lock it back up, though." She gave me a worried look. "I'm sorry, Dr. Goodwin, but I was so upset."

I frowned. "We'll need an inventory."

"Why? What's in there?" the detective asked.

"The materials we're testing. All are potential new drugs—worth billions maybe."

"You're saying someone might have wanted to steal the stuff in that freezer?"

"Maybe. Drug development can be very cutthroat. If you are first to patent a compound, the profits can be mind-boggling."

"Motive for murder?"

I thought about the people involved in this project, but couldn't picture a murderer among them. "People kill for much less, I've heard, but yes, the money could certainly be a motive."

"So, a person could gain financially by just helping themselves to your samples?"

I shook my head. "It's not that simple. You would have to know which samples were positive in our assays and be able to locate them in the freezer."

"Who has a key to your freezer?" the detective asked.

"There are only three. I have one, Natalie has one and Leon Metzger's group has one. His lab is involved with phase two of the testing process."

Detective Sharp wrote in his notebook. "May I see your keys?" he asked.

I pulled my key ring from my pocket and pointed to a small bronze one. Natalie reached into the front pouch of her backpack and extracted a set of keys on a ring attached to a black strap decorated with silver studs. She held up her freezer key.

I noticed the EMTs around the stretcher were getting ready to depart with the body. The man had probably been trying to steal from me. I needed to know who he was. "Detective?" I said, pointing toward the stretcher. "Maybe I can identify the guy. I'd like to take a look."

He agreed and I moved toward the body. I was vaguely aware that Natalie was following.

Evil comes to wazungi…

I moved closer and could see that ice crystals had formed on the man's face and clothes. Even so, in this position, the dead man was recognizable. I turned to block Natalie's progress toward the body, but I was too slow.

…and disrupts the continuity.

I heard her gasp of recognition.

"Dad," Natalie cried, then fainted.

I caught Natalie and gently lowered her to the floor. Detective Sharp called to one of the EMTs who produced an ampule of smelling salts. Natalie gagged awake in response and struggled upright.

"Her father?" Detective Sharp asked.

"Yes," I said. "Ethan Baker."

"Does he work here?"

"No. He stops by occasionally for lunch with Natalie."

"When was he here last?"

"I don't know, Detective. I was in Kenya until this morning."

Natalie revived and focused wide pools of liquid brown on my face. "Is it really Dad?" she asked.

"I'm afraid so. I'm truly sorry." She looked like she might faint again. "Let me get you some water."

"No," she grabbed my arm. "Please, don't go."

A police officer carried an ice-crusted wallet over to Detective Sharp and said, "His watch is the type with the date. It's stopped at 8:25 last Friday. Don't know if that's a.m. or p.m."

Sharp nodded. "That seems to let you off the hook, Goodwin, if your story holds up. You couldn't have done this from Kenya." He flipped open the wallet to reveal an Arizona driver's license and read the name and address aloud.

Natalie dropped her face into her hands and began to sob.

"Let's go back to my office," I suggested. "They still have work to do in here."

"Not yet," she said. "I need to see him."

"It's OK," the detective said. "Just don't touch anything."

I helped Natalie to her feet and escorted her to the body. Her father's frozen limbs were curved into a grotesque position. I spotted an ice-covered sample vial clutched in his left hand. Caught in the act.

You must restore harmony.

Natalie reached out tentatively toward her father's face. I cupped my much larger hand over hers and brought it back to her side. "He was here Friday for lunch," she said, barely above a whisper. "He was going to Casino of the Sun for the weekend. What happened?"

I gently turned her away from the body and started toward my office, with the detective trailing behind. Before leaving the equipment room, I paused, allowing Natalie to proceed alone. I turned back toward the detective and spoke in a low voice. "See the sample vial he's holding? That shouldn't be allowed to thaw out. If you must take it for evidence, let me get you some freezer packs."

"We'll keep it frozen, but I need details about what's in it. And, let's keep it our secret for the time being."

"Right. If you can get me the number off its label, I'll check the sample log," I said.

Detective Sharp agreed and turned away.

I settled Natalie into the guest chair in my office. I moved the picture of Amber and Sarah from my desk to the bookcase to make room for Natalie's lab notebooks. Then, I brought in another chair for the detective, who joined us a moment later. He handed me a slip of paper which contained the ID number from the vial.

"You said your dad was here Friday?" I asked Natalie, and hoped the detective caught the time reference.

She nodded and wiped her eyes. "Yes. Me, Erin, Dad and Jimmy went out for lunch."

"How did your father seem on Friday?" Detective Sharp asked.

"Okay. Well, maybe a little more quiet than usual."

"The other two people at lunch, do they work here?"

"Erin does. Her last name is Connelly. She works in Dr. Metzger's lab."

"And Jimmy?"

"No. His name's Jimmy Gluck and he's...was, a high school buddy of Dad's."

"Jim Gluck's been a regular around the center for years," I added. "He's a sales rep for Dash-Line Scientific. You can check with Dorothy, the receptionist, but I think he comes in at least twice a week." I pulled open a desk drawer and rummaged around. "I should have his card here somewhere. Yes. Here it is." I was interrupted by Erin Connelly's appearance at the door.

"Oh, Erin." Natalie began to cry anew. Erin hurried to her side, dispensed a hug.

I used this time to look up the ID number from the vial clutched in Ethan Baker's frozen hand. All the information for that sample—type of plant, collection location and date—was listed in Natalie's lab notebook. I turned Jim Gluck's business card over and jotted down the information.

I had half expected it to be the Tacazzea root since that was on my mind, but it wasn't. I couldn't remember anything remarkable about it and looked for the test results. They were negative. But when I looked closely at the writing, I detected a slight alteration. In fact, it was the same evidence of tampering I'd spotted this morning when I'd examined the Tacazzea results. I made a note of this for the detective as well.

"I'm so sorry, Nat," Erin was saying. "I can't believe it. Any idea what happened?"

Natalie shook her head and closed her eyes tightly. "No. My God, who would do this to Dad? Everybody loved him."

"Can I do anything? Get you anything?" Erin asked.

"I'd really like to go home. I need to call my aunt, and Jimmy."

"Just a few more questions, please," the detective said. "You are Erin Connelly?"

"Yes."

"When did you last see Mr. Baker?"

Erin described the lunch on Friday in more detail than Natalie had. She mentioned that the men were planning a trip to Casino of the Sun for the weekend.

"Ms. Connelly, I understand you work in the Metzger lab and have access to the Goodwin freezer?"

Erin looked uncomfortable. "Yes, that's true."

"Where is your key now?"

"Here." She pulled the key from her lab coat pocket. I noticed her hand was trembling. "It's Dr. Metzger's. We keep it in one of the desk drawers. I've got it this morning 'cause I was supposed to get some samples I need for the phase two tests. But, I haven't yet of course, under the circumstances..."

"Was the key in its usual place this morning?"

She glanced up at me, and then quickly shifted her gaze to the floor. "No. It was in the lower drawer instead of the top one. I find it in there sometimes." She shot a look at Natalie. "It's an easy mistake if you're in a hurry. I might have put it there myself the last time I used it. But, really, anyone could have used it."

Erin was starting to ramble. I wondered if she had an idea who was using their key. Was she trying to protect Natalie's father? Or someone from her lab?

Detective Sharp pulled out a small baggie. "I'll need the key," he said and marked Erin's name on the baggie. "When was the last time you used it, Ms. Connelly?"

"I'll need to check my notebook to be sure, but it's probably been four or five weeks."

"Four or five weeks? That seems like a long time. Maybe someone had better explain this testing procedure."

Erin looked at me with pleading eyes. I knew she was thinking she'd said too much already. Ethan Baker would have needed a key to get into the freezer and steal the samples. Metzger's key was handy.

But how had he ended up literally in the freezer? Could he have tumbled in while reaching deep into the chest to retrieve a sample? He'd never struck me as a klutz. Someone else must have been involved, pushed him in. Shut the lid. Locked it. Returned the key.

I described our tests to the detective. "Every sample that I ship from Kenya undergoes the standard protocol, which includes adding a portion of each specimen to a battery of test media to see what effect, if any, the specimen has on bacteria, mold, viruses, or tumor cell culture lines. Specimens which produce positive results are then used to formulate a novel medium and undergo additional testing. This is where the top security procedures are followed. The formula for this test medium is what our competitors want, and could get, if they had access to my freezer or notebook. If any samples are still positive following the second round of tests, then Metzger's laboratory will conduct a detailed chemical analysis. Clinical trials come later."

"How many samples are we talking about?"

"I send home fifty to one hundred every month. Out of those, only five to ten will show some promise in the initial test. Only about one percent of those will make it to Metzger's lab. To put it simply, I might collect samples for two years before getting one specimen worthy of clinical trials."

"So, we're talking about a rare event."

"Rare, but definitely worth the search."

"Let me see if I'm getting this correct. If someone was trying to steal the next wonder drug from your freezer, he, or she, would need to know the test results?"

"That's right," I agreed. "But even more than that. They'd have to know who would buy it." Would Ethan have known where to sell the samples? Had he asked Natalie? Or Erin? Or Metzger?

"I'm going to need access to the notebooks from your lab and from Metzger's lab for fingerprinting."

I didn't want the notebooks to leave the facility, risk having them fall into the wrong hands, but I was willing to cooperate. "If you can fingerprint them here, then I can go over the content with you myself. You probably won't be able to decipher the data without my help anyway. Could you collect the fingerprints while I drive Natalie home? She has calls to make."

The detective nodded. "I can have my technicians get to your notebooks as soon as they finish with the crime scene."

"I should be back in about forty-five minutes," I continued. "Oh, and here's that card for Jim Gluck and some notes I made. You might want to read them." I met the detective's eyes. I wished I could read his mind.

The ride to Natalie's apartment was quiet. Dark clouds had moved into the area, hiding the sun and bringing a gentle rain shower. I turned on the wipers and heard their jungle beat.

Evil comes to wazungi...

When we reached Natalie's place, I walked her inside. "I'll call your aunt," I offered, "and stay until she gets here. I'll contact Jim when I get back to my office."

Natalie dug out her aunt's phone number then sat on the living room sofa, back rigid, staring into space.

While I was waiting for the aunt's arrival, I asked Natalie about the high school friendship between Jim and her father.

"They played football together," she said, her voice a monotone. "Their senior year Dad was hurt in a car wreck. Jimmy was there and saw it all."

"Was Jim in the accident, too?"

"No, but he was a big help to Dad. They'd talk about it sometimes. A good friend of theirs was killed and they'd reminisce about him."

"Was your dad driving?"

"No, the other boy was. They'd been drinking though, so I got that lecture all the time. I ran across an article about the accident in the paper just last week. You know how they have that historical section where they revive stories from years ago? They reprinted it all, including pictures and eyewitness interviews. I showed it to Dad. He was, like, mesmerized." Her voice trailed off.

"Do you still have the article?" I asked.

Natalie thought a moment, then went to a desk and rifled through a stack of newspapers. She chose one, opened it to the second page, and then handed it to me.

There was a picture of a car crumpled against a tree. An eyewitness, Nathan E. Gregory, had been following the car. Gregory described how the driver had swerved to avoid a deer and lost control. Ethan Baker had been thrown from the passenger side. The driver was pronounced dead at the scene.

"Dad acted like he'd never heard of Nathan Gregory," Natalie continued in a defeated voice, "when I said Nathan was the person Dad should've been grateful to all these years for clearing up the little matter of who was driving. The article never mentioned Jimmy."

"Natalie, I think Detective Sharp should see this."

"Why?"

We were interrupted by the doorbell. I went to the door, taking the newspaper with me, expecting Natalie's aunt. Instead, Jim Gluck was standing on the stoop. He looked surprised.

"Arvin?" Jim said. "Is Natalie okay? Dorothy told me what happened."

Jim's clothes were wet and I didn't see his car in the drive. "What'd you do? Walk here?"

"Never mind," Jim said and pushed past me. "Where's Natalie?"

She appeared in the entryway, looking concerned. "Jimmy? I was going to call. Have you heard?"

"Yes. I've been trying to reach you at work. Ethan didn't show at the casino and didn't return my calls all weekend. Dorothy told me what she knew and I came right over. I'm so sorry."

Natalie's tears began to flow as she described finding the body. I watched the man's face. His shock appeared genuine.

"I'm sorry, Natalie," he said again. "It must be horrible to learn your father was stealing samples."

"What?" Natalie said. "Dad wouldn't steal anything."

"But he was caught red-handed removing a vial."

"Where did you hear that?" I asked.

"Dorothy."

"Dorothy doesn't know that."

Jim Gluck turned toward me and spoke slowly, seeming to struggle with his emotions. "Dorothy knows everything."

His gaze traveled to the paper under my arm and his expression changed from concern to anger. Before I knew what was happening, he pulled a gun from his pocket. I'm a big guy, but I have a healthy fear of a gun being pointed at me. My heart pounded with the rush of adrenaline. Heartbeats. Drumbeats. Evil.

"I'd like that paper, Arvin."

I handed him the paper.

You must restore harmony...

"What was it you told Ethan all those years ago, Jim? That he was the driver and you'd cover for him?"

Jim made a choking noise. "Yeah. He was unconscious for days, never saw the paper. He believed I lied to keep him out of jail."

"What do you mean?" Natalie asked.

"He means," I said, "that he's been blackmailing your father for twenty-five years."

"But, that can't be." Natalie shook her head. "They're friends."

"It wasn't blackmail. I never asked for money. Anything he did for me was done out of friendship."

"Imagine his anger when he realized there was no cover-up," I said. "A perfectly credible witness proved he wasn't driving."

"He was a little steamed at first," Jim said. "But he got over it. We're friends, like I said."

"I don't think so. I think he was going to turn you in for stealing my samples."

"What?" Natalie said, sounding totally confused.

"Someone was stealing from me, Natalie. I'm sure it wasn't you. You didn't bat an eye when I asked for specific tests to be repeated. Someone altered the results in your notebook to mask which samples had been positive. With your dad holding that vial, it looked like he was involved. Now, I don't think so. We have the thief and the murderer right here."

Jim glared and held the gun higher, pointed at my head. "You're too clever, Doc. Ethan only suspected what I was up to."

Jim shifted his gaze toward Natalie. "And if you hadn't found that damn story on the wreck, your father would still be alive."

"Don't blame Natalie," I said. "She had no clue what you were doing."

"How can you even consider yourself Dad's friend?" Natalie spat out the words. "You killed him over some stupid samples that don't even do anything."

"Oh, they do something," Jim said. "Only you never saw it. I changed the results, just like old Doc here suspected. The samples are worth a lot to the right company, and I know who's willing to pay. Ethan was going to ruin everything."

"Why on earth would you do this?" Natalie asked.

"Mega bucks, baby. My lucky streak at the casino's run out big time. Enough talk, we're going for a little ride," he said. "Come on, I'm parked around the corner." He motioned toward the front door with the gun.

We left the house and walked single file toward Jim's car. We had only gone a few yards when the police car turned into the drive. I reacted without thinking and threw myself onto Natalie, knocking us both to the ground. Jim took a shot at the police car before running back toward the house. The front door, however, was locked. When Jim, in a panic, turned back around, two police officers had him in their sights.

I accepted Detective Sharp's help in getting to my feet, then extended my own hand to Natalie. The detective pulled the business card with Jim Gluck's contact information out of his breast pocket and flipped it around between his fingers.

"It took me twenty minutes to get around to reading the note you wrote on the back," he said. "We looked for Gluck at home first. Then someone thought to check with your receptionist. She said he'd called in and was headed over here."

"Better late than never, I always say."

"What's on the card?" Natalie asked, wiping dirt from her knees.

Detective Sharp handed over the card.

She read aloud. "'Check vial in Baker's hand for prints. Suspect Gluck involved. Natalie may be next.' Why didn't you tell me?"

I shrugged. "I didn't want to alarm you. I was going mostly on my gut feelings. I thought bringing you home would be the safest place."

Tears were streaming down Natalie's face. I knew the evil had devastated her.

My thoughts flashed to Mutiso.

You must restore harmony.

"Natalie," I said. "I'm planning to expand the field testing on my next trip to Kenya. Would you consider joining my expedition? There's time to think about it, but Africa's a good place to heal."

MURDERS OFF THE WALL
D.B. Reddick

Scraping murders off my bedroom walls?

Not exactly what I had in mind when my next door neighbor, Matthew Malone, finally talked me into sprucing up my spare bedroom. He'd been nagging me about it ever since I inherited the house from my uncle, William, last December.

"Once we're finished in here, this room is going to look fabulous, Charley," Matthew often boasted. "Then you'll be able to have all your family and friends over on weekends."

But, Matthew, I prefer to spend my weekends alone. Sleeping.

Three hours ago, Matthew turned up on my doorstep in a bright yellow T-shirt, purple bib overalls and a pair of red hightops. His arms were also full of scrapers, sponges, paintbrushes and two large paint cans.

"Ready to get started?" he said, oozing with enthusiasm.

"I suppose."

Matthew insisted on using damp sponges and metal scrapers on the papered walls instead of a steam machine. He said it'd be quicker, but I wasn't so sure. I had more water running down my arms than I do in the shower. But as time went on, I began to get the hang of it. I was actually making progress on my side of the room when I suddenly heard a high-pitched screech. I thought Matthew stepped on the cat's tail.

"What's the matter?" I said, turning around.

"Come and look at this," Matthew said.

"What's up?"

"See," Matthew said, pointing at the wall. He had uncovered a yellowish piece of newsprint.

"Okay, so it's the front page from the old *Indianapolis News,*" I said, after taking a quick look. "Somebody must have wanted to preserve history. What's the big deal?"

"Read the main story."

I moved closer to the wall. The story described how a prominent Indianapolis businessman, James F. Harper, 55, and his wife, Margaret, 52, were found stabbed to death in their bedroom by their four-year-old grandson, who'd been sleeping in a downstairs bedroom.

"Okay, it's about a double murder. Probably scared the hell out of that kid. But the murders happened in 1954. Heck, I wasn't even born yet."

"124 Virginia Street. Don't you recognize your own address?"

I looked again.

"Damn, you're right."

"The murders happened in this house, maybe even in this very bedroom," Matthew said, lowering his voice to a whisper. "Doesn't that creep you out?"

"Not really. The murders happened more than fifty years ago. Hey, you know what? It might be fun to talk about this on my next radio show. 'Hey, listeners, guess how I spent my weekend?'"

"Charley, you shouldn't make fun of this," Matthew said, his eyes getting bigger. "What if the killer is still at large? And, what if he hears you talking about the murders on the radio and decides to come after you?"

I didn't want to burst Matthew's bubble, but if the murderer were still alive, he'd probably have to use a walker to come after me. But I didn't say anything.

"I'm sorry, Charley, but this whole thing is like totally freaking me out. I'm out of here."

Matthew threw down his scraper and ran from the room, taking the stairs two at a time until he reached the front door.

Damn, you just can't keep good help these days.

When I woke up around noon on Sunday, I was torn between going upstairs and working on the spare bedroom, or finding out more about the double murders. My curiosity got the better of me, so I drove over to the city's main library on St. Clair Street.

I explained to the little white-haired woman behind the microfilm counter that I was looking for newspapers from September 1954. She walked to a bank of gray filing cabinets on the far side of the room and pulled a few packets from a file drawer. She then stepped over to a machine and threaded a roll of microfilm for me.

"Just push this button here," the woman said, before walking away and leaving me to figure it out on my own.

I sat down at the machine and began reading. Two hours later, I learned the crime was unsolved. In fact, the cops never found a suspect. They theorized the Harpers may have interrupted a cat burglar, who got spooked and stabbed them. I left the library and made a mental note to check my locks when I got home.

WZMN-AM, the radio station where I work, is housed in an historic five-story brick building on Monument Circle in the center of downtown Indianapolis. My show runs from midnight to five a.m., six days a week, but sometimes I like to go in early to read the wire for stories to talk about on the air, before slipping out for a late dinner and some strong coffee to help me stay awake.

I was two hours into my show on Monday morning when I tried to drum up interest in the Harper double murders. My monologue went over like a lead balloon. Nobody but Evelyn from Indianapolis seemed to remember anything about them.

"Know what's interesting about all of this?" she said at one point.

"What's that, Evelyn?"

"Remember the grandson? His name was Tommy Egan. He's running for governor."

I'd just rolled over in bed on Monday afternoon when I heard my doorbell ring. Who the hell could that be?

I dragged myself to the front door where I found two guys in matching black suits, white shirts and bright red ties. They were also wearing dark shades.

Oh, great, a pair of LDS missionaries.

"Are you Charley O'Brien?" the older man asked.

"Last time I checked," I replied. "Mind telling me who you are?"

"We work for Governor Dunn," the younger one spoke up. "Can we come in and talk to you?"

I waved them into my living room, relieved they weren't with the IRS. After they sat down on the couch, the older one asked me why I'd mentioned the Harper double murders on my radio show that morning. When I asked why he wanted to know, the younger man replied, "We'd prefer you wouldn't do it again. It could become a campaign distraction."

"What? You boys don't believe in the First Amendment?"

Two nights later, my producer, Zach Berman, was waiting for me in the control room when I showed up for work. He handed me a piece of paper. It was a story about the local prosecutor's late afternoon news conference.

"Why's Ben Cummins reopening the Harper murder investigation?" I asked after reading the details.

"That's easy," Zach replied. "He's a Democrat just like Tommy Egan."

The next afternoon, my doorbell rang. I, of course, was still asleep. *Wonder if it's the governor's boys? Maybe they've brought lunch.*

I crawled out of bed and sauntered to the front door. It was two different guys. They didn't look like missionaries either. And they didn't have any lunch sacks in their hands.

"Mr. O'Brien," the taller of the two men smiled and extended his hand. "I'm Tommy Egan. Mind if we come in?"

"Guess who dropped by my place today?" I said to Zach later.

"Who?"

"Tommy Egan."

"The guy running for governor? What did he want?"

"That's just it. I'm not sure. He said he hadn't been inside my house since his grandparents' deaths, so I gave him a quick tour. He also thanked me for helping to reopen the murder investigation."

"How did you do that?"

"I just mentioned the murders on my show."

The next afternoon, the phone rang while I was lying on my couch, munching on a fried baloney sandwich and watching Oprah.

"Charley, it's Z-man."

Jerry "the Z-man" Zimmerman owns WZMN-AM and is also a very successful real estate tycoon in town.

"What can I do for you, Z-man?"

"I just got off the phone with the League of Women Voters. They're sponsoring a gubernatorial debate next Wednesday at Clowes Auditorium. It's going to be broadcast live on public TV stations across the state, and they want you to be the celebrity moderator."

"Me?"

"That's right. Go figure, right? If you ask me, they're caught up in the buzz about Tommy Egan's grandparents' murders, but who really cares why. This is great for WZMN. It'll boost your ratings and ad sales, so consider the offer and let me know if you can do it."

Was this an offer I couldn't refuse, or what?

"Haven't done anything like that since I worked news-side in Tucson, but I guess I could give it a try."

"You're the man," Z-man said and hung up.

What's that old saying: be careful what you wish for? Moderating the gubernatorial debate was beginning to feel like it would bite me in the you-know-what before it was done. The local news media had been all over the double murders since the candidates made it a campaign issue. Even my own listeners got into the act. They flooded me with questions to ask. "Ask them how they're going to fix the lousy public schools." "Have them promise to lower my property taxes." "Tell them we don't want any more stinking gambling riverboats."

"I'm beginning to think moderating this debate is a mistake," I confided to Matthew after he dropped by on Saturday morning with a plateful of freshly-baked banana nut muffins.

"Don't be such a worry wart," he said. "Eat a muffin. You'll do just fine. Besides, Daniel and I've already picked out this absolutely gorgeous tie for you. You're going to look so professional."

I appreciated Matthew's moral support and that of his partner. And I knew I couldn't afford to screw up since the Z-man had put his faith in me. So on Sunday afternoon, I headed back to the library to do some research on Peter Dunn and Tommy Egan. The same white-haired woman from the microfilm room was working at the reference desk. When I told her what I was looking for, she wandered off and came back a few minutes later with some folders full of news clippings.

"This should get you started," she said, placing the folders on the table. "But I'll keep looking."

I began leafing through the folders. There wasn't much to distinguish the two candidates. Both were attorneys. Both had been married for years and each had two adorable and very photogenic kids. Dunn hadn't screwed up during his first term in office, so the local pundits were already predicting he'd easily win re-election.

"Here's something that might interest you," the librarian said, handing me a tattered-looking newspaper clipping.

"You're right," I said, glancing at the clipping. "This is very interesting."

Michael Dunn, the governor's grandfather, had donated his business papers to his alma mater.

After rolling out of bed on Monday afternoon, I drove down to the Lilly Library on the campus of Indiana University in Bloomington, about a good hour south of Indianapolis.

My new best friend, Lois, had called her friend, Margaret, at the Lilly Library and she had Dunn's papers waiting for me.

"Here you go," Margaret said, as I helped her lift the box off a cart and onto the table where I was sitting.

It took me two hours just to get through about half the folders in the box. Lots of dull information about Michael Dunn's business wheeling and dealing. But then I suddenly let out a loud yell.

"Shhh, Mr. O'Brien," Margaret said as she ran towards the table. "What's the matter with you? This is a library. We must remain quiet at all times."

"Sorry," I said. "But I think I just found the proverbial needle in the haystack."

Debate day finally arrived. I thought I'd be more nervous than I was. But I was prepared. I'd written out my questions in long hand the day before and had the Z-man's administrative assistant type them neatly on some index cards. Matthew brought over the tie he'd picked out for me. Strawberry and kiwi stripes. I wasn't sure about it at first, but once I put it on, I had to admit it didn't clash too badly with my white shirt and blue blazer.

When I arrived at Clowes, the TV director explained where the cameras would be positioned on stage and how he'd communicate with me through an ear piece. Since I'd taken part in a televised debate when I worked in Tucson, I wasn't completely unfamiliar with what to expect.

When eight o'clock finally arrived, I looked directly into the main camera and read the rules of the debate as determined by the League of Women Voters. Governor Dunn had won the coin toss backstage, so he got to answer the first question and then it was Tommy Egan's turn. It went back and forth like that for the first half hour, with each candidate repeating some of the same rhetoric he'd used a hundred times on the campaign trail. But then I changed everything.

"Governor, in recent days, your aides have alleged in the media that your opponent had the local prosecutor reopen the Harper murder investigation to gain sympathy with voters. Would you like to comment on that?"

The usually unflappable Governor glared at me for a nanosecond. My question obviously had taken him by surprise, but he quickly recovered, grinned and said, "Everybody knows you can't completely control campaign staff. Somebody will invariably say something without thinking first. But, I'll tell you what. I can see why my staffer said what he said. I mean, don't you think it's more than sheer coincidence that the prosecutor reopened the Harper case a few days after you, Mr. O'Brien, peeled a news story off your bedroom wall?"

I'd glanced over at Tommy Egan. He had been wearing a big wide grin on his face when I first asked my question, but his expression quickly changed as he stood behind his lectern listening to the governor's response. I could tell he couldn't wait for his turn.

"Okay, Mr. Egan. As they say, turn about is fair play, so let me ask you directly. Did you ask Ben Cummins to reopen your grandparents' murder investigation?"

"That's preposterous," Egan said. "I can't believe you'd even ask me that question. My grandparents' murder was a very traumatic experience which took me years to get over. I wish you hadn't decided to remodel your house and bring those frightful memories back to the surface."

Touché.

I nodded when he finished and turned back to the governor with my next question.

"Governor, did you know that your grandfather, Michael Dunn, and James Harper, Mr. Egan's grandfather, were once involved in a secret land deal worth millions of dollars?"

"What?" he said.

"I don't understand," Egan interjected.

"What the hell are you doing?" the TV director shouted in my ear.

I raised my right index finger. I needed another minute.

"And, Mr. Egan, what if I told you that your grandfather may have held back some of the profits when the land was ultimately sold to the state. What would you say about that?"

"I don't know what you're talking about," Egan said, as he raised both hands in the air.

"And, Governor, what if I told you, one of my listeners told me this morning that your grandfather had a hair-trigger temper. What's your reaction to that?"

"What are you talking about?" Dunn stammered. "Grandpa just liked getting his own way. God rest his soul."

"Yes, Governor," I replied. "It's too bad your grandfather passed away a few years ago and couldn't enlighten us on what really happened the night the Harpers were stabbed to death."

"Are you suggesting his grandfather may have murdered my grandparents?" Egan asked, stepping out from behind his lectern and walking towards me.

"Yeah, is that what you're implying?" said Dunn, who joined Egan at center stage.

"I'm afraid so, gentlemen."

"Jesus H. Christ, what are you doing?" the TV director was now screaming in my ear piece. "You're out of control, O'Brien. I'll see to it that you never work again in TV."

"You'd better be able to prove that allegation," Dunn said, raising his voice.

Egan nodded. "Yeah, where's your proof?"

"Take a look at this, gentlemen," I said, pulling a sheet of paper out of my blazer.

The phone lines lit up like a Christmas tree when my radio show began at midnight. And, judging from the regulars, my performance as the debate moderator drew mixed reviews.

"Helluva job," Carl from Beech Grove gushed. "You really put those lying, cheatin' politicians in their place. Ever thought of running yourself?"

But then there was Evelyn from Indianapolis.

"Honest to God, Charley O'Brien, you never cease to amaze me."

"What have I done now, Evelyn?"

"Why did you mention the double murders? What did they have to do with the debate?"

Evelyn had a point. But I guess the old newsman in me hasn't completely died yet.

"It wasn't me who made the murders a campaign issue," I finally responded.

During the network news break at one o'clock, Zach rushed into my studio and told me his uncle was holding on line one.

"Awesome job, Charley," the Z-Man said when I picked up the phone. "I loved how you put Dunn and Egan on the spot, but where did you come up with all that business about Dunn's grandfather killing Egan's grandparents? Unbelievable."

"Dunn's grandfather left his business papers to the IU library in Bloomington," I explained. "In one of the folders, I found an unpaid ticket for parking illegally in front of a fire hydrant at 124 Virginia Street. It was dated the same night the Harpers were murdered."

"Well, I'll be damned, Charley," Z-man said. "Hey, before I let you go, tell me one more thing. Who's going to win the election?"

"I don't know," I replied. "But I bet both Dunn and Egan would love to buy me a one-way ticket to Tucson."

MEDIUM RISK
Susan Budavari

Karen Forster closed her cell phone and pushed through the door to the dimly lit train station bar. She had twenty minutes. After taking a moment to get her bearings, she slid onto a bar stool, leaving one seat between her and the only other patron, a man in his thirties hunched over his drink. She ordered a scotch and soda, sipped some then leaned across to tap the man's shoulder.

He turned his head to her. Pocked-marked face, close-set black eyes with deep circles under them, thin lips. A tight-fitting T-shirt accentuated his muscular physique.

"I'm starved." She pointed to the peanut dish. "Are you going to eat those?"

"No. Take them." He nudged the dish over to her and dropped his gaze to his glass.

She popped some peanuts into her mouth. After a few moments, having gathered her nerve, she said, "You know, I can go back in time and change things."

The man didn't look up.

She raised her voice. "Really, I can change things...so that they never happened."

"Look, lady, I'm not interested."

She laughed. "You're passing up a good opportunity. It's taken me a lifetime to figure it out."

He waved her off.

"Don't get nasty," she said as she tucked a strand of shoulder-length auburn hair behind her ear. "Let's talk a little. You'll learn something...Hector."

He glared back at her then averted his eyes.

"Something pique your interest?"

"You called me Hector."

"I saw the "H" on your belt and took a guess. Is it Hector?"

He nodded.

"Well then, how about it?" She waited a moment. "What would you do differently, Hector, if you could do it over again?" She leaned toward him. "It can be something from a long time ago, or even from yesterday. I've done both."

"Leave me alone." He shook his head and muttered a curse under his breath.

"Come on. What have you got to lose?"

"What you say is impossible."

"A year ago, I thought so, too. 'Things like that can't happen'—I would've said. I'd have thought I was being conned or listening to a flake."

"Which are you?"

She smiled and motioned with her hands as she spoke. "Neither. It's real. At first, I'd think of someone—the telephone would ring and they'd be on the other end."

"So what. You don't hear from someone for a while, so you think about them. They call, you remember. Otherwise, you forget."

"You're trying to explain it away." She smirked. "It grew over time. Not only did I know who'd call, or who I'd run into, I knew what they'd say."

"I've had a few drinks, but I'm not stupid. What's your game?"

"You from Jersey?"

"Yeah."

"Remember the big supermarket in Newark that blew up a few months ago? The building was totaled."

"Yeah. So?"

"You know why no one got hurt?"

"No."

"There was a tip. Police evacuated the building."

"You?"

"It was from me." She nodded. "I didn't think they believed me when I called in. But I guess they were smart enough not to take a chance."

"Didn't read nothing about you in the papers."

"I keep under the radar. Don't want people pestering me."

"Lucky guess."

"You think?"

He nodded.

"Uh-uh. It's much more," she said.

"Where are you going with this?"

"Well, what I can do changes—each time it's more. Since the beginning of the year I've been able to go back in time. And change things that've happened."

The man sneered. "You've got to be kidding."

"I didn't expect you to believe me...not right away, anyhow."

He stared at her lips and then into her eyes. "The next thing you'll do is—"

"Try to prove it." She nodded. "I can prove it."

"Yeah, right," he said, popping an ice cube in his mouth.

"Does the name Ruth Ellen Becker sound familiar?"

He stopped chewing the ice. "Maybe."

"She was the little Berkeley Heights girl who disappeared on her way to school."

"It was on television."

"They found her body last month."

"Yeah?"

"You know why?"

"No."

"I went back in time to the moment when the kidnapper started burying her body in a place that couldn't be seen from the highway."

She saw she'd caught his attention. She continued. "I interrupted him. He had to move her. Ended up leaving her body in a more visible spot. So they found her."

"If you could do that—get the body moved, why didn't you stop him from killing her?"

"That's a good question...with a simple answer," she said. "When I first got the power, I didn't know how to use it—I didn't go back far enough. The little girl was already dead."

"Huh? So why not go back again?"

"Rules of the game. Got to get it right the first time."

He shook his head. "I'm stupid to listen to you." He got off the bar stool, dug into the pocket of his skin-tight jeans and took out his wallet. "You're nuts."

"Am I? Don't you want to test me?" She fixed her eyes on him for a long moment. "I know you have a terrible secret."

"What are you talking about?"

"You know."

"Who are you? Some con artist?"

"Have I hit you up for anything?"

"Not yet. And you're not going to." He started walking toward the bartender.

"Poor Naomi," she muttered.

"The man turned. "What did you say?"

"Look, I feel bad for you. It's hard to be alone." She shrugged. "Well, maybe not for you."

"You're full of it. You found out from someone about my wife going missing two months ago." He pointed a finger at Karen. "I'm warning you. I don't want to talk about it."

"Whoa, fella. Watch your temper." She waited until she saw he was calmer. "Sit down and hear me out."

He glanced over his shoulder. "You been following me?"

"I never laid eyes on you until I walked in here. You're the one who lives in Jersey—not me. I'm from Los Angeles and getting out of here to Trenton on the ten-thirty train."

"Prove it."

"Okay. My name's Karen Forster and I *am* from L.A." She nodded. "Want to see my driver's license?"

"Yeah—to start."

She dug in her purse and held her license up in front of him. As he studied it, she said, "Now don't go peeking at my age." She glanced down at her watch.

"I couldn't care less how old you are...or anything else about you. I just want to see if you've told me your real name."

"Go ahead."

"Okay. Name and city match. So what are you doing in Jersey?"

"I go where I'm needed."

"That's B.S."

"What do I need to do to convince you?"

He scowled. "You can't."

"You read about the teen-age girl they found at the Newark garbage dump? She could've died—drugged and closed up in that plastic bag. But she was alive and you know why?"

He drained the last of his drink.

"I went back in time and made sure the guy dropped her an hour later than he intended to." She grabbed a newspaper clipping from her purse and handed it to him. "Here. This is from *The Star Ledger.*

He scanned the article. "So they found her alive." He thought for a moment. "You want me to think you're like that blonde chick in Phoenix—the medium?"

She shook her head. "I can do much more. She can stop some things from happening. But I can also change things that *have* happened."

"You're crazy." He slid off the stool again. "I'm outta of here."

"Think what you'd like—do what you have to—but I'm telling it how it is."

He stared at her without saying a word.

"Haven't you ever wanted to change something that happened?" She watched as his expression turned dark.

"Sure, who hasn't?" He stared at his reflection in the mirror hanging over the bar opposite them.

"I can tell you're thinking about someone. Who?"

"My mother." There was a tear in his eye. "I wish I'd seen her the day before she died. I was supposed to. But I was tired. I called and told her I'd come the next day. At least, I think I did—I meant to. But she died before I got there."

"That's heavy, Hector." She rubbed her forehead. "We all have those *should've, would've, didn't do's* in our lives. Lucky I'm able to undo some of them."

He snickered.

She fingered the delicate gold chain around her neck. "Now, what're you thinking?"

"You're good. Either you're full of it or I am...because I'm starting to believe you."

"You should."

"Prove it right now."

"How do you expect me to do that? My gift isn't pushbutton. I have to prepare myself to change things."

"There you go. You're full of it," he snapped. "You had me going for a moment."

"Let me think. I'm sure there's something I can do."

He leaned toward her.

She got a whiff of his sour, whisky breath and waved her hand in front of her nose. "Give me some space to think."

"Yeah, think. Come up with some good excuse. I've called your bluff."

She flashed a smile. "I've got an idea. It'll be me calling your bluff." She pushed the bar stool between them out of the way. "Let me have your right hand."

The man hesitated, his eyes focusing on her upturned palm. "Oh, what the hell." He thrust his hand out.

She inspected the top of his hand, then turned it palm up. She grabbed his hand and tightened her grip. Her eyes opened wide. "I know your secret," she said.

"I told you I have no secret." He scowled and pulled his hand away."

"What would you give to change what you did?"

"Nothing. I didn't do anything."

"Yeah, right, but I can see you with her." She held her hands straight up, palms toward him. "Okay, it's your decision, Hector...but, if you want me to save you—"

"I don't need any help from you, bitch." He signaled to the bartender standing by the sink wiping glasses. "I want my check."

"You shouldn't be so quick to leave," she said. "I really can help you."

"You're nuts."

The bartender laid the bill down in front of him. "I've put her drink on your tab. Okay?"

"Yeah, whatever." Hector frowned and took out his credit card.

"I'll ring you up." The bartender moved away.

"Thanks for the drink, Hector," she said. "Last chance. Let me do something for you."

He gave her a dirty look and turned away.

"Okay, as I said, it's your call."

The bartender returned with the charge slip. He rolled the credit card over in his hand. "Mantoa. Name's familiar. You in baseball?"

"Not anymore."

"Now I remember," the bartender said. "You were with the Mets a few years ago. A relief pitcher."

"Ancient history." Mantoa took back his credit card and signed the slip in a large slanting scrawl. "Bye, crazy lady," he said over his shoulder as he hurried out to the concourse.

Karen and the bartender exchanged glances. "I bet you meet all kinds," she said.

He nodded. "Especially on weekends. Be careful when you leave. The station's dangerous on Sunday nights." He walked back to the sink and began wiping glasses again.

After waiting a few minutes, Karen checked her watch, then slipped off the bar stool. She waved to the bartender.

The concourse was deserted and darker than she expected. A chill ran through her. She looked up at the signs and turned left.

A voice came from the shadows. "Aren't you going the wrong way?"

Karen turned her head toward the sound and saw Mantoa lurking in the alcove in front of the men's room. She muttered, "Uh, I'm looking for the ladies..."

He grabbed her and dragged her into men's room. "You see, I *do* believe you." Those were the last words Karen heard before he slipped his belt around her neck.

While paramedics administered oxygen to a semi-conscious Karen, the police cordoned off the area in front of the men's room. Mantoa was led away clasped in handcuffs.

A young patrolman approached the tall, stocky sergeant in charge, who was filling out forms. "Whew. She's lucky you got here when you did. Who called in the 911?"

The sergeant looked up. "There was no 911. The Forster woman phoned me herself. I was in the neighborhood."

"Called *you*? I don't get it."

"She came to town last week and stopped in to see me. Said Mantoa murdered his wife. And that she felt something big would happen tonight."

"She knew the Mantoas?"

"Claimed she never met them. But she was certain he killed his wife."

"A psychic?"

"Who knows? More likely a con artist. Mantoa used to be a big-time ballplayer. That kind of money attracts weirdos."

"So you didn't believe her, Sarge?"

"I wasn't sure. Got the feeling she was playing me...that she'd picked up on my suspicions. I warned her to keep out of it. Told her we had an investigation ongoing."

"You check her out?"

He nodded. "Record's clean."

"Didn't she realize Mantoa might go after her?"

"Must have. She called in a story to get me here tonight. Said a woman was being attacked. Even said where. Didn't give her name, but I knew it was her."

"How's that?" the younger man asked.

"She called my cell phone."

"You never give your number out."

"I gave it to her. Still don't know why I did it. Pretty persuasive dame."

"She timed things real close."

"Bartender said she kept Mantoa talking until he upped and walked out on her."

"Can't believe she followed him. If she was really a psychic, she had to know he'd try to kill her."

"Took a gamble. Wanted Mantoa caught."

"She could be the *real* thing, Sarge...a psychic—"

"A psychic?" The sergeant stared at the woman wrapped in a blanket, oxygen mask to her face and nodding to the paramedic. He dug the point of his pen into his pad, thought some more, then turned to the patrolman. "Yeah...has to be."

QUICK DRAW
Sarah Parkin

"The bus! Quick draw!" Billy shouted. He and Marco simultaneously flipped open their phones and snapped a picture of the bus that had just delivered them to the intersection of 50th and Ray Road. He held his phone up to Marco's, and they compared the time stamps on the photos. Billy grinned at Marco. "Gotcha that time."

Marco shrugged, tilting his head so the streetlight caught the blue-black glint of his hair. He usually won in games of speed.

"We better hurry if we're gonna be first in line." Marco hauled on his backpack with the sleeping bag strapped on the bottom. "I can already feel the Orpheum Gen 3 controller in my hands."

Billy nodded, picked up his gear, and the two thirteen-year-olds lugged their packs toward the Premium Electronics parking lot. Excitement tingled through his body, as he thought about the night ahead, camping out to get the new game system as soon as the store opened. Billy couldn't keep the smile off his face as they began their daring adventure.

As they approached, Billy saw a line already forming in front of the door. Oh, well. They would be twentieth in line. They would still get their systems. He rolled out his sleeping bag right away. "We need to establish our space."

"The Premium Electronics sign. Quick draw!" yelled Marco. Again, they snapped photos and compared times.

Billy settled on the already crowded sidewalk and watched as the line continued to stretch out along the building and eventually turn the corner so he couldn't see it anymore. He mentally categorized the groups of people. Some came in large groups, bringing footballs and Frisbees to play out in the parking lot. Others had fold-up chairs and camp stoves. Some were by themselves and leaned against the wall without blankets. Several groups brought cards or games. Good idea. Too bad he hadn't thought of that. He only had his Game Boy and some snacks.

"The line. Quick draw!" said Marco. Phones flipped. Pictures clicked. Billy laughed. He had taken a picture of the front of the line and Marco had snapped the people behind them. Billy agreed to save their spot while Marco went to take a picture of the line around the side of the building. He rushed back. "They are having a huge party over there. Some guy has gigantic speakers and everybody is dancing. It's crazy 'cause the noise didn't hit me until I went around the corner."

Marco and Billy switched places and Billy went to look for himself. Sure enough, the party music blasted him as soon as he went around the corner. He played for a moment with stepping around the corner and back again, laughing to himself at the noise difference.

Walking back to Marco, Billy noticed the air getting colder. The temperature began to drop and the boys wiggled into their sleeping bags stretched out on the hard concrete. For a few moments, neither said anything, but Billy noticed Marco's forehead scrunching up so he asked the question about the one subject he knew Marco wouldn't bring up. "How's your sister doing?"

Marco looked sideways at Billy. "Marlee? She's gonna be okay. Her cheekbone is broken, and she has some stitches in her ear. I guess she has three broken ribs. My dad wants to kill Nick. He moved all her stuff back home."

"Why did her boyfriend beat her up?" asked Billy.

"I don't know," said Marco. "It all seems stupid."

Billy didn't know what to say. None of it made any sense to him. To break the awkward silence he pulled the Premium Electronics ad out of his pack and read aloud, "Orpheum Entertainment Systems. Redefining the gaming world."

Marco joined in, having memorized the ad. "High Definition Video. Sensory Sound System." Their voices grew louder. "60 Gigabytes of Memory. Get your new Orpheum Generation 3. Available Friday morning at Premium Electronics!"

At the end of their recitation, they were shouting and a few people looked their way, but Billy shrugged and smiled. The fact that the other people were in line overnight meant they were excited about the Gen 3, too.

"Do you think our moms have caught on?" Marco asked. "Do you think they know we're not at either house?"

"No way." Billy held out his phone. "They would have called us."

Marco's eyes lit up. "Oh. Yeah. We tricked our moms!"

Billy tried to keep the conversation light. School, girls, and computer gadgets dominated the conversation as they shared their snacks. After a few hours, Marco stopped responding to conversation. Billy heard a light snore. Amazed anyone could sleep on this hard ground, Billy pulled out his Game Boy and clicked away. He noticed a couple sharing a sleeping bag really moving around a lot and wondered if they were actually doing it. *God, I'm a pervert for watching!* He pulled his head all the way into his sleeping bag and kept playing the game. Occasionally, he poked his head out to see if anything was going on. Too excited to sleep, he alternated between the game and daydreaming about the Orpheum Gen 3.

The beginning of the sunrise caused a glare on the screen of Billy's Game Boy. He snuggled deeper into his sleeping bag and looked around at the long row of people and camping equipment lined up in front of the Premium Electronics Store. Just a few more hours to go before the doors opened and the Orpheum Gen 3 would be in his hands. He glanced at Marco and wondered how he could sleep on the hard concrete. Maybe his sleeping bag was puffier. Next time they did something this crazy, they would plan differently. Bring more stuff. One group had a portable heater. Billy wished he had the nerve to go over to that group so he could get warmer. He might lose his spot, though.

Headlights flashed as a black Hummer rolled into the parking lot and he heard the rumbling of an engine. A man dressed in what looked like a blue Premium Electronics employee shirt climbed down from the passenger side, jingling his keys in his pocket as the Hummer drove away. The people at the front of the line made room for him to get the door open.

Billy reached his arm into the cold air to nudge Marco. "Somebody's here. Wake up."

"What time is it?" Marco yawned.

Billy checked his phone. "Six."

Marco, instantly awake, eased his eyes out from under the covers and asked, "Are they opening up early?"

"I don't know."

A smile of victory spread across Marco's face. "Our moms didn't catch us. They both think we're at each other's houses."

Billy grinned back. "Yep."

"Cool." Billy saw Marco's braces catch the early morning light. Maybe his were shining, too.

The man with the keys turned as if to open the door, but then walked down to the corner of the building to take a look at the line. He observed the party crowd and then swung around to face the crowd at the front of the line. He held out a handgun with a silencer on the end of it.

"I want everybody's cash in here." When the Gun Man held out a pillowcase, Billy realized the man wasn't there to open the doors early.

One lady started screaming. The man pointed the gun at her. Billy hoped someone from the loud party around the corner heard her, but no one appeared.

The line had scrunched away from Gun Man, closer to the door of the store. Billy's hand reached down to his jeans pocket to make sure his money was still there. He wanted that game system.

Gun Man stood between the front group of the line and the corner. He gestured with the gun to the people closest to him. They handed over their cash. One person stated he only had credit cards and offered them to the man. Gun Man lifted his right leg and kicked the man in the chest, knocking him to the ground. The next person in line threw his whole wallet in the bag. People leaned over to help the injured man.

Billy didn't want to give up his money. He glanced at Marco and saw his forehead scrunched up with worry. This was a lot different from handing over lunch money to the bullies at school.

A giant in an ASU football jersey refused to give up his money. Billy watched carefully. Good idea. If everybody refuses, Gun Man won't get anywhere with the crowd. There's power in numbers. There were a lot of them and only one Gun Man. Maybe they could charge him.

Gun Man shot the giant in the knee. Blam! Even with the silencer muffling the sound, it seemed loud to Billy. The giant fell to the ground, screaming. The smell of the gunshot hung in the air. More wallets flew into the pillowcase. One woman threw in her entire purse.

A few people farther down the line began to pull out their cell phones to call the police. Gun Man pointed the gun at them. "You'll be next," he threatened. "And next time I'll aim for the head."

Marco began to crawl back into his sleeping bag, pulled his head in like a turtle.

"Marco," Billy cried out. "What are you doing? He'll shoot you."

"Don't say my name!" Marco wiggled deeper. "I know who he is. That's Nick. My sister's boyfriend. If he knows it's me, he'll shoot me anyway."

"Will he recognize you?"

"Don't know. He never paid much attention to me. But I know his name. I know where he lives," Marco whispered. "I need to call my dad. Hand me my phone." Marco's phone lay on the ground just outside his sleeping bag.

"No. Shut up or he'll hear you!" Billy whispered back.

Gun Man continued to move down the line, getting closer every moment. Billy reached into his pocket, clutching the money. His fingernails cut into his palms. If only he could think of something. Size obviously didn't help, since the giant was still on the ground, blood pouring from his leg and spilling out onto the sidewalk.

"Marco, come out. He'll get you."

Marco's eyes peered out from his sleeping bag. Gun Man was maybe twenty feet away. "We've got to run for it."

"We can't run! He'll shoot us!"

A few other people seemed to have a similar idea. The couple that Billy watched share the sleeping bag unzipped and scrambled into a run across the parking lot. Gun Man fired a few shots at them. A windshield on one of the cars shattered. The woman fell down. The man came back and helped her up and they ran behind an SUV. Billy didn't know if she got shot or just tripped. Either way, Gun Man shot at them when they ran.

"The cars," said Marco, now actively unzipping. "We'll run for the cars." He grabbed his phone as he stood up.

Billy wasn't certain what to do. All that babysitting, lawn mowing, and shoveling rock for Mr. Martin to raise the money for the system now damp from the sweat on his palm. The Orpheum Gen 3 had six-axis controllers. Gun Man was essentially stealing his new game system from him. The heat in Billy's chest swirled in a combination of anger and fear. He fought the urge to throw up.

Gun Man stepped up to the person next to Marco. Billy was desperate to distract Gun Man from looking too hard at Marco. He thought about stepping in front of Marco and handing over the money for both of them, but he couldn't get his body to do it. Gun Man stepped up to Marco. Gun Man's eyes were bloodshot and looked wild. He looked at Marco, shook his head as if to clear his mind, and looked again.

"Don't I know you?"

Marco's eyes stretched wide. "Me? No. I'm nobody."

Gun Man squinted. "You sure?"

Billy realized he had to try something to get the man's attention away from Marco. "Quick Draw!" he yelled.

Instinctively, he and Marco both reached for their phones at the same time, flipped them open, and snapped a picture of Gun Man. Gun Man blinked at the double flash. Billy charged him, hoping to knock him over. Unfortunately, Billy just bounced off Gun Man's chest, but the gun fell to the ground. Billy kicked the gun, and it skittered twenty feet across the parking lot.

The man chased after the gun, clutching the pillowcase. The Hummer that had dropped him off pulled around the corner of the lot. The tint on the windows kept Billy from seeing inside, but he heard a voice yell, "It's been six minutes. Get in."

Billy grabbed Marco's arm and half dragged him behind a red Suburban. Sirens sounded. Tires squealed on the pavement. The smell of rubber mixed with the gun smoke. Billy leaned out from behind the vehicle and snapped one more photo of the departing Hummer.

Three squad cars rolled into the parking lot from the other direction. As officers stepped out, the crowd approached them. Several people pointed at the departing Hummer. Others nodded toward Billy. Two of the officers rushed over to the wounded giant. Police radios blipped and squawked as the officers called for an ambulance. A squad car drove around the parking lot to try to find the couple from the sleeping bag. Billy and Marco crept out from behind the Suburban toward the officers.

One officer attempted to maintain control of the crowd by asking everyone to quiet down. When he asked if anyone had gotten a look at the man, Billy and Marco both raised their hands.

"We have photos." said Billy.

"And I know who he is!" Marco shouted.

The officer beckoned them forward. They both showed nearly the exact same shot of Gun Man. Marco told him Gun Man's name was Nick, explained about his sister, and described where Gun Man lived.

The officer nodded and Billy could tell that the officer was pleased. "You boys did a good job." Then he asked the crowd, "Did anyone see the vehicle?" A bunch of people called out that it had been a black Hummer.

Billy checked his camera. He had the back of the car. He showed the officer. The license plate was too small to read on the screen. The officer squinted at it and then asked if he could have the phone for a few minutes and make a call. Billy nodded. After pressing a bunch of buttons, the officer explained he had sent the photos to police headquarters. Then, looking around the crowd, he asked the boys where to find their parents. Billy knew the situation was too serious to lie.

"At home," his voice squeaked.

The officer looked hard at the boys, glanced at his watch and smiled. "Well, okay. Curfew ended over an hour ago, and I have no reason to believe you were here before then." Both boys said nothing. The officer asked for their contact information and they gave it to him. He suggested they let their parents know what happened. Both boys nodded in silence. Billy had known he would have to tell his parents where the game system came from, but now it would be a more complicated explanation.

An ambulance arrived, loaded up the giant as well as the man suffering from the kick in the chest. Sirens and lights blared as it drove away. The line reassembled around the area that the police had taped off to search the ground where Gun Man fired the gun at the giant.

After many questions and searching the area, only one police car remained for the rest of the morning. Some people from the line left, got into cars, and drove away. Billy and Marco rolled up their sleeping bags. Everyone remaining in the line gathered up their belongings. Billy figured they wanted to be ready for a quick escape in case anything else happened. He wished his heart would stop beating so fast.

The line had grown considerably shorter. Soon, several people farther up in the line began to offer Billy and Marco their spots in line. Before long, Billy and Marco found themselves at the front of the line. It seemed to Billy as though an eternity passed before another man who looked like he worked for Premium Electronics arrived. The crowd backed away cautiously.

The man walked over to the remaining police officers, talked quietly for a moment, and then went to the front of the store. He raised his hands to get the crowd's attention. "I understand there has been a disturbance in the parking lot," he announced. "The store was not affected, so we will open as scheduled." A cheer rang out when the man's keys worked in the door. "Please line up in an orderly fashion."

Billy shook his head. Orderly. Yeah, right. That man wasn't here a few hours ago to see all the action.

As the store manager approached the front door at 7:59, Billy and Marco both nodded at each other and said at the same time, "Quick draw!" and took pictures of each other about to enter into the store to purchase their Orpheum Gen 3's.

DEAD RECKONING
Gary Earl Ross

Don Prince's creased face glistened beneath the studio lights. Gloria, the make-up maven, applied more powder. Careful not to use her brush too close to the collar of his crisp ivory shirt, she worked quickly and efficiently, eliminating the mirrorlike glint of his prominent nose and masking the pouches beneath his watery blue eyes. Prince kept his eyes shut but his mouth open; he was used to talking through last minute make-up and would clam up only during the final few seconds, when Gloria sprayed his iron gray mane to hold it in place.

"So," he said to the middle-aged woman in an amber suit seated opposite him, "how is your involvement in *this* murder case different from all the others?"

Eyes closed as she permitted Gloria's assistant to powder the translucent skin of her face, Imelda Cross smiled faintly. "Oh, the images and impressions were much more intense than usual," she said. Her voice sounded like too much burnt coffee and too many cigarettes. "Much stronger—maybe because this case involved the unfortunate, and they have such sad auras to begin with."

"I like that," Prince said. "Gives us—" But Gloria pressed a finger to his lips and let loose with an aerosol can for three or four seconds, fanning away the mist afterward.

"One minute," the floor manager announced.

As Gloria and her assistant withdrew, Don Prince and Imelda Cross opened their eyes and looked at each other across the small oval table between them. "The unfortunate," Prince said. "I like that. Audience sympathy based on the old saying, *There, but for the grace of God, go I.*"

"Don't forget Detective Nash," Imelda said. "This is the first time I've brought along an actual police person so your viewers can get a glimpse of how I work with law enforcement."

"Doesn't hurt that she's young and pretty," Prince said, adding softly, "and black."

"Also recently divorced, if I detect you sniffing out your next ex-wife."

Prince laughed. "Or my widow. Her handshake tells me she's a tough one. She'd kill me for sure the first night. But she appeals to every major cable demographic."

The lights dimmed, leaving Prince and Imelda seated in shadow as a control room technician cued the signature news pulse music. "Now, live from New York," boomed the prerecorded announcement, "The Don Prince Intersection! Here's Don."

The pale blue set burst into light. Prince, in shirtsleeves and his trademark lavender tie with matching suspenders, stared straight into camera one, smiling his crooked smile, then began speaking in his deep television voice: "Good evening, ladies and gentlemen. Welcome. I'm Don Prince. Tonight we have a special show for you." The smile disappeared as he bit his lower lip briefly. "Some of you will recall news stories about a recent series of killings just up the road in White Plains. But some of you will not, because the victims were the least among us." He paused to assume a solemn expression. "The homeless, the mentally ill, those shunned by society. Who notices when such people are brutally murdered? Hardly anyone. It took three killings for police to see a pattern. It took a fourth before they had the good sense to contact my guest, and a fifth before the killer was brought to justice—just last week." He looked to his right, as camera one began to pull back. "Though it's been a while, tonight's guest is no stranger to this show. She's been with us many times before, taking calls and sharing the remarkable insights of her unique gift. Call her a medium, a psychic, a mystic—whatever. I'm just proud to call her my friend. Welcome, Imelda Cross."

Imelda nodded toward camera two, positioned so that to the viewer at home it seemed she was nodding at Prince. "Thank you, Don."

"So tell me, Imelda, what got you involved in the hunt for the White Plains killer?"

Imelda cocked her head, layered gray-blonde hair shifting only slightly, and tapped her temple with a long amber fingernail. "It was a caller to my help line," she said. "Her brother had gone missing from the men's shelter where he lived and she wondered if I might help locate him. I told her to talk about her brother, to describe their childhood together."

Prince smiled. "And for the sake of our first time viewers, why don't you explain why you asked for those details."

"Psychic connections can best be understood if they're pictured like floating threads," she said. "Little filaments of energy surround us constantly, overlapping each other, sending vibrations along countless paths. Only a true sensitive can feel them, but sometimes even the most gifted psychic needs help isolating a special thread. This woman had a connection to her brother, and I was trying to reach him through her." She took a deep breath. "All at once I was overwhelmed with darkness, red darkness, and I knew he had come to a bad end."

"How did your caller take the news?" Prince's voice had a practiced tone, as if he had been down this path with Imelda before—which, in fact, he had, many times.

"I didn't tell her right away, out of respect for her feelings. I promised her I would do my best to locate him and nudge him to call her."

"Nudge?"

"Sometimes a troubled mind is open to a redemptive suggestion. Though I already sensed the worst, I did not want to leave her without hope. Too often the truth is needlessly cruel."

"But the worst had already come to pass. Is that right?"

Imelda nodded sadly. "Yes." Then she spent the next several minutes describing how the man's body had been found hidden amid weeds in an overgrown lot near an abandoned factory. He had been dead about two weeks, smothered by someone wearing black leather gloves. Because the victim was just another vagrant, scant effort was put into investigating the crime and little note was taken of the single dollar in one of his pockets. A few weeks later another smothered body turned up, also with a dollar in a pocket. Then there was a third and a fourth. A reporter dubbed the killer *Dollar Bill*. "That's when I got involved," Imelda concluded.

"But you had already seen what was going on, correct?"

"After the first killing, I was attuned to the area, and I saw two more instances of red darkness, which I came to understand only after talking with a medical examiner." Imelda sat up straighter and leaned forward. "You see, when a person is strangled or smothered, tiny blood vessels burst in the eyes. What I was seeing—flashes of red fading to blackness—was the actual moment of death for these unfortunate creatures."

Prince looked at camera one and shuddered. "That, ladies and gentlemen, is creepy."

Imelda sat back. "My gift demands that I accept seeing the bad as well as the good."

Prince placed his elbow on the table and braced a fist under his chin. "Incredible, but that's not the end of it. Because of your help, the police were able to catch Dollar Bill."

"Well..."

"There's no need to be modest," Prince chuckled. "The good Lord saw fit to give you something most of us just don't have, and you put it to good use—bringing a killer to justice and saving lives. *Of one to whom much is given, much is required.* Isn't that how the saying goes?" He waved a hand dismissively. "I mean, you could simply use your talents to win the state lottery again and ag—"

"Heavens no!" Imelda looked horrified. "Such selfishness is...vulgar."

"Just teasing you, sweetheart," Prince said, reaching to pat her hand. "We all know you're the people's medium." From beneath the table he produced a blue file folder, which he laid on top and opened. "I have here clippings that report the capture of Dollar Bill and describe your role in the case. Care to tell us about it?"

"After her brother was found, my hotline caller called back to ask if he was at peace, and I assured her that he was. After the second and third murders occurred, she called again to ask if I could help find and punish the killer, so I went to White Plains." Imelda folded her hands on the tabletop. "Whenever I get involved in police work, I have to be very careful because of the doubters. This was no different. The chief of detectives—a man—told me flat out I was crazy. It was impossible, he said, that I could see the killer in my mind's eye."

"Sometimes men are such idiots!" Prince said.

Imelda laughed. "Present company excluded." Then she cleared her throat and continued. "After the last murder, I was introduced to a wonderful woman detective who listened to me. I described the man I saw and told her where he was likely to be found."

"What can you tell us about Dollar Bill?"

"He too was homeless, just like his victims, a mentally ill man named Ernie Schuyler, though I didn't know his name when I began to see him. He lived behind what was left of a burned out building, sleeping against the wall at night and wandering the streets for empty bottles and scraps of food by day. His aura was so strong it was evidence of a truly wretched existence." She shook her head. "Though he was a killer, I can't help feeling sorry for him."

"Why did he leave a dollar bill in their pockets?"

"It was simple, Don. He just didn't feel right about taking everything they had."

"Like the disc jockeys used to say when I was a youngster starting out in radio: *Be cool, be calm, and keep a dollar in your pocket.*" Prince held up a clipping. "Now, is this newspaper article correct? It says you *profiled* the killer, like an FBI agent."

Imelda lowered her eyes in a gesture of humility. "I wouldn't call it anything *that* fancy, just a vision."

"But you were right." He squinted at the clipping. "You described his appearance, his height, weight, hair, body type, clothes, even the corrugated fiberglass lean-to where he slept. The only thing you got wrong was his jacket. Yes, it was torn and filthy, as you said, but it was navy, not black. That's pretty close." He laid the clipping back in the folder and looked into camera one. "And pretty impressive."

Imelda shrugged.

"Let's take a couple calls and then we can get back to the Dollar Bill saga." Prince glanced up toward the booth, then down at the table, as if a telephone were there. "Hello, you're on the Don Prince Intersection with the amazing Imelda Cross."

A woman's gravelly voice crackled over the studio speakers. "Oh, Miss Cross, it's a real honor to talk to you."

Lips pursed, Imelda stared at the tabletop as if the caller's face were there. "Thank you, my dear."

"I have a question...about my late father."

"Was he a smoker?"

"Yes!" The woman sounded surprised and pleased at the same time. "He died last year, from a pulmonary embolism."

"I thought I saw some involvement of the heart," Imelda said, nodding. "What's your question?"

"The night before he died, we...we had words, and we said some things—"

"He forgives you, dear, even if you don't forgive him. But you do forgive him, don't you—for anything he might have said, for leaving you..."

"Yes..." The caller's breath caught.

"Your father is quite at peace and looks forward to the day he will see you again—but not too soon."

"Thank you, Miss Cross, thank you."

"You're most welcome."

The line clicked.

Don Prince looked at Imelda and said, "You just made that woman's day." Then he turned to camera one. "Go ahead, caller. You're on the air with Imelda Cross."

The studio speakers popped. "Miss Cross, hi. I'm Reggie from Detroit."

"Hello, Reggie," Imelda said. "How may I help you?"

"Oh, it's all good with me. Got a question for *you*, based on what you're saying about Dollar Bill. Ever thought about joining the FBI? I mean, with what you bring to the party—"

"You're very kind," Imelda said.

Prince smiled. "I've had the director on the show, and I'm sure he would be delighted to have someone of Miss Cross's stature...consulting on truly difficult cases. Thanks for the call, Reggie." When the caller was gone, Prince added, "I say consulting because to me you're too much of a lady to run around with body armor and a gun."

"Why, thank you."

Prince sat back and folded his hands across his abdomen. "But maybe I'm just too old-fashioned. My ex-wife told me that all the time. In fact, my *next* guest may prove it because *she* runs around with body armor and a gun, and she's every inch a lady." He looked to his left, with camera one swiveling to follow his line of sight as a stagehand slid a chair next to Imelda. "Ladies and gentlemen, meet White Plains homicide detective Monica Nash."

As camera one pulled back and Prince got to his feet, a shapely brown-skinned woman in a tailored burgundy pantsuit moved into camera range. Unsmiling, she walked toward the table, stepping over cables snaking along the floor, and shook Prince's hand. Then she sat in the empty chair beside Imelda, with whom she exchanged only a brief glance. Prince took his seat again and leaned forward on his elbows, offering Detective Nash a wide smile.

Monica Nash was in her mid-thirties, tall and fit, with straightened short hair, and engagingly wide brown eyes. She met Prince's leer without flinching and waited.

"Detective Nash—may I call you Monica?" Prince said.

"Of course," she said. Her calm, even voice was softer than her appearance would have suggested.

"Monica, it's truly a pleasure to have you on the show. Welcome."

"Thank you," Monica replied.

"Now, when did you get involved in the Dollar Bill case?"

"My partner Jim Starkey and I caught the third killing in the series; detectives from other precincts had worked the first two." Following Prince's barely perceptible nod, she shifted position slightly and gazed into camera two. "Because we were dealing with three different precincts, nobody saw a connection at first."

"Is it true," Prince said gravely, "that the victims' status as derelicts helped delay your seeing a pattern?"

Monica appeared to consider the question for a moment, then answered slowly. "It was not so much that they were derelicts as it was that there was no readily apparent physical evidence to connect the crimes. In fact, in all the scenes, it first looked as if the victims had died of natural causes."

"But then you noticed the petechiae, didn't you?" He shook his head and grinned into his camera. "Petechiae. Don't I sound sophisticated? So *CSI*. The petechiae are what Imelda mentioned earlier, the tiny blood vessels that burst in the eye." He looked at the detective. "If you'd care to explain, Monica."

Monica inhaled deeply. "Of course...Don. Actually, *petechiae* means *tiny dots*. When a person dies from having his airways cut off, there is an increase in pressure in the veins in his head. Capillaries rupture, leaving spots of blood the size of a pinpoint. These show up in many places but are especially noticeable in the eyes and eyelids."

"Did the medical examiner miss those dots in the first two victims?"

"Absolutely not. Sometimes the spots are so small you need a magnifying glass and a special light to see them." Monica smiled. "It's just that no one connected the dots right away."

Prince and Imelda both chuckled.

"I told you she was sharp," Imelda said.

"You're a natural," Prince said. "Maybe we can get you a show on *Court TV*." Then he made an effort to reassert the seriousness demanded by the topic. "So, these murders are taking place and the police are stumped and Imelda Cross comes to town and gives you the big break you've been looking for."

Still smiling, Monica patted Imelda's arm. "That's right. Miss Cross connected the dots. I knew at once there was something special about her. She just seemed to *know* things, and not just about the crimes. She knew about my divorce and Jim's bad back, and that our captain had once been shot in the line of duty."

Prince beamed. "That's our Imelda!"

"If not for her, we'd never have found Ernie Schuyler, aka Dollar Bill."

Imelda shrugged and offered a small, unassuming smile.

"And you made the arrest," Prince said.

"My partner and I took Mr. Schuyler into custody, yes." For a moment, Monica looked off in the distance, toward the back of the studio, as if in thought. "We caught up with him one morning, exactly where Miss Cross said he'd be, behind a burned out building in one of the old factory districts."

"Amazing." Then, feigning incredulity, Prince furrowed his brow. "Did he put up any kind of struggle? Any kind of resistance?"

Monica shook her head. "He was more than a little spaced out but completely cooperative. He even smiled and showed them to us when we asked him if he had leather gloves."

Prince was nodding, his acknowledgment of the floor manager's signal they were ready to cut to commercial. "Monica, you're to be commended for fine police work."

Monica leaned forward and locked eyes with him. "Would you like to hear more about Dollar Bill?"

"Perhaps, when we come back—"

"Maybe you'd like to meet him. He's here."

Imelda's mouth fell open, and Prince looked from her to Monica and back.

"Here?" he said, confused.

"In the back of the studio—" She pointed. "—with my partner, Jim Starkey."

"You brought a serial killer *here*, to my set?" Anger began to thicken his voice. "What the hell do you think—"

"Bring him down, Jim!" Monica called out. She turned back to Prince and Imelda. "With some of the company you keep on this show, I didn't think you'd mind." Rising, she looked toward the shadows at the back of the studio, as cameras one and two both spun to follow her line of sight.

"This is outrageous!" Prince stood and squinted toward the dark control booth. "Sam, go to commercial now and get security in here!"

"Can't, Don," a man's voice crackled over the speaker. "They got court papers."

"Then you're fired!" Prince snarled. "Directors are a buck a bushel."

Just then three men emerged from the distant shadows, two in front and one walking several paces behind. The man in the rear looked like a linebacker in a sports jacket too small and long outdated. The two in front were both middle-aged, balding, and clad in dark, off-the-rack suits. The shorter one was heavy and ruddy while the other was thin and sallow as a praying mantis perched on a dried daffodil. They crossed the entire studio, passing the floor manager and other astonished staff. The third man stopped beside camera two, and the two men in the lead went right to the set.

Monica and Prince were still standing, but Imelda, lower lip caught between her teeth, sank deeper into her chair.

"Don Prince," Monica said, "I'd like you to meet Ernie Schuyler."

The frail man stuck out his hand, which Prince shook hesitantly.

"What the hell is going on?" Prince demanded when he released the hand.

"A little reality TV," Monica said. "You see, Ernie Schuyler is no serial killer. He's just a mentally ill man who was homeless and off his meds, until we got him into the system and got him a psych work-up." She looked straight into camera one. "He's much better now. Ernie, can you tell us who gave you those leather gloves?"

"She's right there," he said in a reedy voice, pointing at Imelda Cross.

Imelda sprang to her feet. "That's a damned lie!"

"On the contrary," Monica said. "We can prove everything."

Imelda looked indignant. "Every *what*?"

Monica leaned toward her, the intensity of her gaze pushing Imelda back into her seat. "Every movement. Every misdirection. Every murder."

Now Don Prince's mouth fell open. "Are you saying Imelda Cross is...Dollar Bill?"

Eyes fixed on Imelda, Monica nodded. "Yes, we're here to arrest her for four murders, as well as obstruction of justice. That gentleman back there—" She pointed toward the big man in the ill-fitting sports jacket. "—is Detective Sergeant Wes Keller of the NYPD. Because we're out of our jurisdiction, he's been helping us investigate and he's here now to assist with the arrest and the transfer of custody. We planned to arrest her on this trip but then two days ago she called to invite me to join her on the Don Prince show. Incredible."

Monica Nash straightened to her full height and tugged her suit jacket down. "The first murder was exactly what it seemed, the probable robbery and subsequent smothering of a homeless man. Yes, the killer wore leather gloves. We found bits of leather in the victim's mouth, and he did have a single greasy dollar bill in his pocket, probably because the killer overlooked it. We haven't found this man—and it was a man, given the strength needed to dislocate the victim's jaw—because Imelda Cross threw off the investigation."

Amber nails tapping furiously, Imelda sniffed. "Why would I do such a thing?"

"Because your book sales are down, as are calls to your psychic help line and TV bookings like this one." Monica crossed her arms across her chest. "Guess high gas prices and a troubled economy, and all those websites that trash your powers, mean fewer people are willing to MasterCard $700 for a half hour of your time."

"I have all the money I need," Imelda said, waving a hand as if to dismiss everyone.

"We know. We have your financial records, and the bank-fresh singles you left in those dirty pockets. It's not money you crave, but attention." Monica began to pace back and forth, with camera one tracking her. "You needed something splashy to put your psychic 'gifts' back in the limelight. A real murder case, not the half dozen or so you claim, that no one's ever been able to document. You got the idea from the woman who called your help line. Once you learned the details of her brother's murder, you came up with a plan to make yourself catch a real serial killer. Then no one could deny your abilities."

"Are you implying I'm a fraud?"

"No," Monica said, stopping to look at her. "I'm saying it definitively. You *are* a fraud. You have no psychic abilities."

"But what about all the visions?" Don Prince interjected. "All the accurate predictions?"

Monica sighed. "If you track *all* her predictions, not just the bulls-eyes, you'll see she has a success rate of about six percent."

"Six percent?" Prince seemed unconvinced. "*Please*. Look at all the stuff she knew about you."

Monica held up her left hand. "It's almost gone, but the crease from my wedding ring is still visible." She jerked a thumb toward the stocky man beside Ernie Schuyler. "The back support attachment is plainly visible on Jim's desk chair in the squad room, and on the shelf behind his desk, our captain has a bravery commendation next to a crumpled bullet in a block of Lucite. If you think she's more than a good cold reader, ask her *where* the captain was shot." Monica fixed Imelda with her gaze. "Come on, Imelda. Try to remember the bullet. How badly damaged was it? Crushed enough to have hit bone? Or was there enough shape left to suggest a trajectory through muscle or soft tissue? And was that a limp the captain had, or did he hold his shoulder a little crooked?"

Imelda said nothing.

"Oh, yes." Monica snapped her fingers. "That caller earlier who mentioned her dad died of a pulmonary embolism? You said you saw heart trouble. Pulmonary means lungs."

"What's a cold reader?" Prince asked.

"Someone who processes his surroundings and uses what he sees to draw conclusions. A good cold reader can convince you he, or she, is a psychic based on information you've revealed unwittingly."

"So she's a fake. And she went to White Plains to kill people." Prince sat down.

Scowling now, Imelda said, "I never went to White Plains till I was invited."

Monica laughed. "EZ Pass records say you did. We checked them against the dates you gave your driver off." The detective shook her head slowly. "You came to our city and killed four poor people too weak to defend themselves, then insinuated yourself into the investigation so you could finger a fall guy. Crazy, living in a field—perfect. You gave him gloves like the ones you used to smother people. Gloves, by the way, with a different grade of leather from those in the first murder. Ernie's are French-made, available only at the Picard Style Shop in Manhattan, four blocks from your apartment. Solange says hello."

A few of the onlookers laughed.

"Then you profiled Ernie, getting everything right but the color of his jacket. Ah, but you were a little too clever with that one. Any serious student of crime knows the first true criminal profile was the work-up of New York's Mad Bomber from the 40s and 50s. When George Metesky was arrested, the only thing Dr. James Brussel got wrong was the color of the double-breasted suit he was wearing."

Opening her jacket to unhook a pair of handcuffs, she added, "And you didn't see this coming?"

NEITHER RARE NOR WELL DONE
Judy Starbuck

Murder is rarely well done. Read the paper any day. Someone snitches, the killer brags, or evidence is left at the scene. In the case of Matt Rich's death, it appeared to be an ordinary overdose. But I had seen his handwriting, and knew it wasn't so.

I'm Aimee Dionne. My friends Matt Rich, Lucy Wing and I team-taught a summer program for motivated middle school students at Sierra Vista Academy in Phoenix. We called our creative thinking unit *What's your Medium?,* and our goal was to get the students to think outside the box. Lucy served as our artist, Matt was our musician and I handled the writing.

We were confident that it would be a fun-packed six weeks. With daytime highs hitting 115 degrees, a school with a pool had no trouble enticing bright inner-city students. Our teaching assistants were known as Team Tran: three Vietnamese siblings who had themselves attended Sierra Vista for several summers. Ly worked with me, Sang with Matt, and the only daughter, Tien, with Lucy.

Since teens are always hungry, we used food as the central theme for our integrated unit. My class was called *Eat My Words*, Lucy's was *Devouring Art*, and Matt's was *Sing for Your Supper*.

Food was a central theme for Matt, too. The previous summer, he'd overheard some kids calling him the fat teacher, and he'd vowed, "I'm going to lose half my ass over the school year." He counted calories, exercised rigorously, and returned this summer fit and trim, and if I do say so myself, looked pretty good from behind.

Unfortunately, he had also become an evangelical fitness proponent who rode his bike back and forth to school even in the heat of June and July. Since he had "recovered" from his food addiction, he felt the need to share the good news with anyone who would listen. Lucy and I decided we liked him better fat.

Apparently someone else did, too.

On the fatal day, three weeks into the program, school began as usual at 8:15. Matt's silver mountain bike stood locked to the rack outside his classroom so I figured he was inside getting ready.

When the first bell rang, I took ten deep yoga breaths, then unlocked the door to welcome my students. The classrooms all opened to the outdoors, so competing smells of diesel exhaust from the buses leaving the parking lot, sweat from the boys with basketballs bouncing on the sidewalk, and the raccoon-eyed girls spraying a final gust of Aqua Net, greeted me as they entered. The final bell rang accompanied by the slap-slap-slap of the latecomers' flip-flops as they pounded the pavement.

After all the students had arrived, Sang came to my door and asked if I knew where Matt was. I shook my head. By 8:30, when attendance sheets had been checked and returned, Matt had still not arrived.

I was standing at the door watching for him, when the custodian, Jorge Hernandez, yelled down the hallway, "*Madre de Dios, Senor Rich esta muerto.*"

I told Sang to put in a call to the principal, while Lucy and I ran to the wailing custodian. Soon the principal, Mr. Magee, joined us at the scene. Turning the key, which the custodian had left in the lock, he pulled the faculty bathroom door open. We were hit by a sickening stench of human waste and death, cooked overnight in the desert heat. I covered my face with both hands to block the smell and sight, but snuck a glance through my fingers. Matt was in the same clothes he had worn yesterday, so whatever had happened must have occurred late in the afternoon or in the early evening when the campus was deserted.

Cold sweat ran down my back. Waves of white light blurred my vision. I tapped Lucy on the arm. "That's a syringe in his hand."

"I'm going to be sick," she said, and raced to another bathroom.

With shaky hands, Mr. Magee pressed 911 on his cell phone. He took a couple of steps back, but I could hear what he said.

"Overdose of some sort. That's right. The door was locked. History of substance abuse? I don't know. Okay, I'll check."

When he hung up, he told me to stay put in the steaming heat of the courtyard and took off toward the office. Jorge stumbled down the outside corridor mumbling a prayer. I was alone, just outside the small bathroom, with the door standing open. I could see Matt's body.

I didn't want to disturb the scene so I stayed still. Matt looked peaceful with no signs of fear or pain on his face. His gym bag containing Lycra biking clothes lay open on the floor next to him. There was a small orange insulated pouch on the countertop and an empty rubber-tipped vial in the sink. Next to it were some ground-up tan crumbs, kind of like parmesan cheese. Had he been eating something?

My eyes welled up and I stifled a sob. Matt had come to mean a lot to me over the years. We had worked compatibly, sharing a deep concern for our students and laughing a lot as we prepared our crazy musical skits and zany lessons. Mr. Magee thought Matt might have overdosed. I didn't believe it. More than that, I *knew* it couldn't be true, because I'd never seen any indicators of drug or alcohol abuse in his handwriting.

Lucy had roped me into taking Handwriting Analysis 101 at Phoenix College the previous winter. She said it would help us to better understand our students, but her real motive became apparent when she gave me a little red book titled, *Is He Write for You?* I guess she figured it's never too late for a thirty-seven-year-old.

If substance abuse had been Matt's problem, chances are his handwriting would have shown the telltale signs of irregular letter size and slant, as well as decreased legibility. Matt's script was consistently small, indicating concentration, and it stood upright, showing reason. If he had been overwrought with emotion, the slant would have leaned far to the left or right. Everything about Matt's writing indicated that he had a balanced personality with a slight tendency toward perfectionism. That made sense. In addition to being a musician, he was a scientist.

But I had noted other traits. He applied his letters with heavy pressure, indicating that he bore grudges and didn't easily forgive and forget. Also the loops in his "d"s were fat, showing sensitivity to criticism. I wondered if his years of being a tormented overweight kid had left him brimming with resentment.

I jumped when Mr. Magee's voice boomed over the intercom. "We are in lockdown procedure until further notice. Teachers, please make sure your doors are locked. I repeat. Teachers and students remain in your classrooms until you are instructed otherwise." I figured the lockdown didn't pertain to me, since Mr. Magee had instructed me to stay put.

Lucy reappeared, ashen-faced. "I heard Mr. Magee say he thought it was an overdose."

"Matt doing drugs?" I shook my head. "No way." Lucy sat down on a nearby bench. "You don't look so good, Luce. You'd better stay here with me for awhile. The Trans can handle the classes."

Lucy nodded, then took a deep breath. "Do you think Matt did something to himself?"

"I'll never believe that. He's been so upbeat about getting fit, and this has been our best summer ever. Until now." I shivered. "Besides, his handwriting didn't indicate depression. His "t" crossings were nearly at the top showing high goals and self-esteem, and his writing had an optimistic upstroke."

"Then you think someone else...? Someone here at school? But who?"

"I don't know." I shrugged. "I guess it could be anyone. I kind of doubt it was Jorge."

Lucy said, "He was too upset. Think of who had keys."

"Mr. Magee, of course. And the Trans since they clean the school. Yesterday I heard Matt complaining about Sang, said he was distracted and even fell asleep during class. Now that I think about it, Ly has been downbeat this summer. He looked exhausted today."

"Think of what the Trans have to do every day. They take care of their mother before and after school, work here with us during the school day, and clean the rooms after we all leave. They're probably just sleep-deprived."

I nodded. Their father had been shot to death in a robbery at the family jewelry store five years ago and their mother permanently disabled as a result of her wounds. The oldest brother, Vu, worked three jobs to keep the family together.

Mr. Magee had created jobs for the three younger Trans when he'd seen them wearing the same clothes every day and sneaking extra food to take home to their family. Sierra Vista Academy had become a second family to them. Still...

"Until someone proves to me this was an accident, I'm going to assume it was murder. I think we should start with the Tran family."

Lucy's narrow eyes opened wide. "You're right. And I know where we can begin. They each submitted a handwritten essay to get hired. But the papers are locked in Mr. Magee's office. We could ask him."

I looked at Jorge's key ring, dangling from the bathroom door. "I don't think we need to bother Mr. Magee."

When the police came, they told Lucy and me to join Mr. Magee in the administrative wing. As we walked away we saw the crime scene investigators arrive, carrying suitcases of equipment, while another officer strung the yellow tape securing a large area around the bathroom.

When we arrived at the conference room, Jorge sat on a chair staring into space, still mumbling prayers, and regularly making the sign of the cross. We waited until a burly, flat-topped officer, who introduced himself as Detective Norm, came to interview us. I went first. He asked about my relationship with the victim.

That question troubled me. The truth was that Matt remained a mystery to me, even after working with him for five years. I knew he taught chemistry at a different middle school during the year, but he had kept his personal life to himself. He never mentioned a family, a lover, or even a pet. Or anyone who might hold a grudge.

I told Detective Norm everything I knew, and that concluded the interview. He instructed me to wait until we'd been given the okay to go back to our rooms. When he was done, Lucy joined me.

It was early afternoon when Mr. Magee told us that grief counselors were with the students, and the medical examiner had completed his work and taken Matt's body. The counselors recommended that the program continue, and Mr. Magee asked us if we would be willing to stay on, saying, "It would be in the best interest of our students."

Lucy and I agreed that between us and the Trans, we could handle Matt's class. I felt relieved to know that school would continue, and wanted to be with people who had known Matt.

And figure out who did this to him.

While the counselors handled the students, Lucy and I reviewed the events of the summer, looking for anything that seemed unusual. All I could come up with were minor annoyances. Like the day I couldn't find the set of colored pens students used to illustrate their stories. Or when Lucy emptied all her drawers looking for the Ziploc bags she used to hold the students' collage materials. Then Matt's drumsticks disappeared. We had laughed and said that bad luck came in threes, so we were safe. But now...

When the last students had left for the day, Lucy and I scoured Matt's classroom for his lesson plans for the rest of the summer session. He kept his materials in Rubbermaid tubs with lessons organized in order. Since neither Lucy nor I were particularly musical, we pulled them all out trying to find something basic. Behind one of the tubs was a zipper bag. I opened it and found a syringe and several small bottles of a cloudy liquid kept cold with Kool-Paks. Next to it was a test kit and a stash of candy bars and oranges. "Matt had diabetes, Lucy." I set the bag on the counter.

She looked through the bag. "I bet that's why he needed to lose so much weight." Lucy wrinkled her brow. "Why wouldn't he tell us? He might have needed help sometime."

"Face it Luce, he never told us much of anything. Think of his secretive closed "o" loops. I wonder if he even told the nurse at school. Maybe he worried that he wouldn't get hired. I don't know." I raised my hands in exasperation.

Lucy came up with another possibility. "He could have accidentally given himself too much insulin."

I shook my head. "No way. He was super precise. Remember his left margins? They're big, so he was cautious and planned everything well."

Lucy nodded. "The autopsy will tell us."

A key turned in the door. Sang Tran bounded in, then stopped, looking at the drug apparatus laid out on the counter.

"Sorry, I didn't know you were in here." He backed toward the door, and said, "I'll clean later."

"Don't worry about it, Sang. We'll be working here for awhile. You can go home now."

Sang left, but a couple of minutes later, knocked and opened the door a crack. "Mrs. Wing, your husband says he's waiting."

"Okay, thanks." As the door closed, Lucy turned to me, "Aimee, don't do anything stupid."

I gave her an evil grin, but said nothing.

After she left, I walked around the room again, looking for something out of the ordinary. And there it was, on a table in the back of the room: tan granules spread across a sheet of notebook paper, just like the ones on the bathroom counter.

I put my nose down to detect a smell, then picked up a tiny particle to taste it. There was no smell, but it had a bitter taste. I suspected it could be some kind of poison, and ran to the sink to rinse any taste of it from my mouth, then folded the notebook paper around the granules and into a Ziploc bag, which I slipped into my pocket.

The parking lot was empty, so I grabbed my backpack and headed for the office. Jorge's keys got me into Mr. Magee's private supply closet that held the personnel files. The Trans' folder was easy to identify by its thickness. The kids had begun the program as students five years before.

Leaving the office, I went to the copier room, looking through the files as the machine warmed up. I had intended to copy handwriting samples of the three younger Trans, but was stopped by the signature of the oldest brother, Vu, who had filled out all the guardian forms. His angular stroke was written with heavy pressure, showing aggression and the need for power, with an extreme right slant that indicated he could go ballistic without warning. Maybe that was why those poor kids always looked so stressed.

I copied selected pages from the Trans' folder, then copied a few samples of Matt's handwriting. My palms grew sweaty as I stuffed the copies in my backpack and carried the originals back to the supply closet in Mr. Magee's office. I had kept my cool so far, but it was time to go.

As I opened the filing cabinet, the closet door snapped shut and the light flicked off.

Matt's killer could be right outside the door. My heart pounded. Where was my cell phone? Then I remembered it was in my backpack in the copier room. The door knob didn't move. No lock release on the knob. No way out.

But did I even want out? And who was out there?

My eyes adjusted slowly to the darkness. The air conditioning shut down automatically each day at five, so the temperature was stifling. Perspiration rolled off my forehead and stung my eyes.

The shelves were full of Mr. Magee's office supplies. Systematically I felt around from top to bottom, right to left, searching for a weapon. I found scissors, a hammer and screwdriver, and a six-pack of plastic bottles filled with some liquid.

After sticking my finger in one of the bottles, smelling it, and tasting a minute drop, I determined that the liquid was water. Hot and thirsty, I downed half a bottle, then poured the rest over my head and clothes. Through the door I heard my cell phone ring from the copier room. Two minutes later it rang again, then again. It had to be Lucy. Come on, Lucy, you know what I meant by that evil grin. Come on! When nothing happened I eventually sat down on a box, armed with scissors and hammer, leaned against a shelf and waited. And listened.

In a soggy stupor, I jerked my head at the sound of a key in the door and was instantly blinded as the lights flicked on. Squinting, I got to my feet with the scissors thrust forward in my right hand, and the hammer raised in my left. My vision began to clear and I could make out Lucy, Mr. Magee and a Phoenix PD officer staring back, open-mouthed, at me.

Lucy spoke first. "I knew something had happened to you. When you didn't answer your phone, I called Mr. Magee. We drove by your house and saw that no one was there, and got here as fast as we could. We saw your car still in the lot, so we called 911. After what happened to Matt, we automatically thought in terms of worst-case scenario."

Mr. Magee, hands on hips, looked at me with a scowl. "I assume you have some sort of explanation?"

Truth was generally the best answer, but I had broken a lot of rules, so I two-stepped around it. I admitted to taking Jorge's keys, but assured him that I planned to turn them in.

"Why were you in my office?"

"I heard you say you thought Matt had overdosed. I don't think so. He didn't make mistakes. I study handwriting analysis so I wanted to look at his writing again to see if I could learn anything else about him." I turned to the officer and pulled the paper packet with the acrid tan crumbs out of my pocket. "This was on a table in Matt's classroom. I thought it might be important."

The officer took the baggie and advised me, "Leave the detecting to us," while rolling his eyes.

"Gladly. And I hope you'll start by trying to find out who locked me in the closet."

Mr. Magee's face flushed. "We'll discuss this further in the morning. For your information, the door automatically locks when it shuts and the light goes out."

He hit on my last nerve. I straightened my spine and tried to look as dignified as possible, which under the circumstances, was not easy. "Mr. Magee, the door stood wide open while I was at the file cabinet. It didn't shut itself."

Mr. Magee gave me a look that could quell a thousand students. "I think you'd better go home, Ms. Dionne."

Lucy rode home with me so she could get the scoop and avoid the wrath of Mr. Magee. She fanned her face to remind me that I smelled a little ripe. We agreed to meet an hour before school at our favorite coffee shop to discuss the day ahead.

After a hot shower and four hours of sleep, I got myself to Jo's Java with high hopes that the fresh-out-of-the-oven sticky rolls and steaming coffee could revive me.

Lucy walked in five minutes later, headed right for the counter and ordered. "I'll take the strongest coffee you have." Then she plopped down across from me in the pink vinyl booth and spread out our lesson plans.

After we discussed how to incorporate Matt's coursework into our day, I pulled out the handwriting samples I had snagged last night. We took a few minutes to study them, and reached some conclusions.

Ly and Tien's script had a lot in common. Both showed light pressure and a downward slope. Their handwriting exhibited as much sadness as their demeanor had this summer. Their "m" and "n" strokes were retraced showing repression. Sang's writing, on the other hand, showed heavy pressure and his "o" strokes had lines crossed through them, indicating anger and deception. Sang's and Vu's writings had warning signs throughout.

I sat back against the booth and looked at Lucy. "What do you think?"

She held up Sang's essay. "This kid has changed. Look at his paper from last summer. The pressure was even and his writing sloped upward. He's turning into his older brother, and the other two are stressed to the max."

The Trans always arrived by 7:45, but 8:00 came and went without their appearance. We notified the office and Mr. Magee tried to contact their home. No answer. We asked him to keep trying and perhaps go by their house to check to see if they were safe. They had never been absent, or even late. That worried me, but Lucy and I had three classes of adolescents about to walk through our door, and they had to be our primary focus.

Noon finally arrived. Neither Lucy nor I were exactly sunny-side up after spending the morning with seventy-five students and no help. We found Mr. Magee waiting for us in the lunchroom and asked if he'd heard from the Trans. He gave us some unbelievable news. He had gone to their home and had found the blinds pulled. No one answered the door. When asked, the next-door neighbor said she didn't know where they had gone. She also said that their mother had died last winter.

I felt like I'd been sucker-punched. "What? She's dead and they didn't even tell us?" I stood and paced. "They sure disappeared fast. Could they be responsible for Matt's death?"

"Please sit down," said Mr. Magee. "I've contacted the police. They're investigating the Trans' disappearance. Your only job is in the classroom today."

He had a point. But that wasn't going to stop me. No way was I going to let this one go.

Just then Detective Norm came into the cafeteria and sat down next to us. He turned to Lucy and Mr. Magee, "Do you mind if I speak to Ms. Dionne?" The principal left the room, but Lucy went to the other end of the cafeteria and watched.

The detective spoke in a serious tone. "We examined the tan granules you found in Mr. Rich's classroom. They're cheese heroin."

"Cheese?"

"It's a starter drug for the middle school age group, made from crushed Tylenol PM and black-tar heroin. Addictive and cheap. It's sold in two-dollar bags. Do you know if Mr. Rich had been making it?" He paused. "And why didn't you turn it over to the police when you found it?"

My eyes narrowed and my response came out too sharp. "I found it right before I went to the office. No one was around. I planned to turn it in, but someone locked me in the closet. And, no, I don't know anything about it. I feel sure that Matt didn't either."

Detective Norm stood. "I'll be back to speak to you later." He left the cafeteria. I stared at his back until he was out of sight.

"What the heck?" Lucy said when she rushed back to ask me about it.

"Shh," I said, thinking hard, holding my hand up like a crossing guard. That was it. All the clues were in place. "I get it, Lucy. I totally get what happened to Matt."

When the last bus bounced out of the parking lot, I turned to Lucy, "Okay, we'd better get started. Come on."

Lucy looked puzzled, shrugged, then followed me to Matt's classroom. "What are we looking for?"

"I think the Trans made the cheese heroin in one of our classrooms. Probably Matt's."

She followed me into his room.

I stood in front of the sink and scanned the room from ceiling to floor. "Somewhere in here is a container filled with pills and heroin, along with the missing drumsticks, pens and Ziploc bags. So where would you hide them that no one would think to look?"

Lucy went to the other end of the room and looked at it from that angle. "Why do you think it's in here?"

"Because of the crumbs on the counter. I'll bet they crushed the pills here. Let's work out from this spot." I moved to the exact place where the granules had been and concentrated on what I needed to find. At the top of the cabinets on the west wall, nearly ceiling height, were board games stacked three high.

I pushed a wooden chair to the shelves and stood on it. Monopoly, Clue, and Life made up one stack. I pulled the Monopoly game off the top and flipped the lid. No houses, no Get out of Jail cards, just money. Real money. Ones, fives, tens and twenties, bound together with bands.

"Jackpot." I handed Lucy the box. "Call 911."

I rattled the Clue box. It sounded like a box of beans. But these beans turned out to be blue Tylenol PM tablets. I figured the game of Life held the heroin and decided to put everything back until the police arrived.

I got the boxes positioned in the same way, then said, "Let's get out of here until the police arrive. I have a feeling the Trans will be back to get this."

Lucy had just reached the 911 operator when the supply closet door swung open. She only was able to say, "Send help. Emergency," before she dropped the phone in alarm.

Silence.

"Lucy?" I turned to see Vu Tran holding a heavy black cloth over Lucy's mouth. She sent a terrified signal toward the closet with her eyes.

Ly and his sister, Tien were on the closet floor. Dark bruises tattooed Tien's arms. Ly's eyes were swollen to slits. Sang stood behind them with a baseball bat in his hand.

Vu said, "You'll both join your friend, Mr. Rich, very soon." He moved his hands to Lucy's throat and squeezed.

Lucy struggled to catch her breath in his grasp. Alarmed, I jumped off the chair, and lunged full force at Vu, knocking him off balance, loosening his grip on Lucy. She ducked and crawled behind a large wooden desk.

Tien screamed, "Leave them alone, Vu. They helped us. Get your nasty drugs. Go! Leave us all alone." She got up and ran to Lucy and crouched down beside her.

As Ly stepped forward, Sang raised his bat to swing at me. I ducked. The bat hit the cupboard with such force that Sang lost his footing. Ly rammed into him and threw Sang to the ground, pinning his arms to the floor.

Vu hurried to the cupboard where the insulin was stored and loaded the syringe. He held it up and began to move toward me. I couldn't worry about tampering with evidence at this point, and leaped back up on the chair. I jerked the top off the Monopoly box and sent a flurry of bills floating toward the floor. Next I grabbed the box of pills and added them to the cascading confetti, just as we heard the sound of sirens.

"Sang, grab the money. Out the back door," Vu yelled. Holding the syringe up, he backed out the door, right into the hands of the police.

Later Detective Norm said, "You can relax. We got a full confession from Vu Tran. He told us it was Sang who locked you in the principal's closet. Sang partnered with Vu in producing and selling the drugs. Together they murdered Mr. Rich when he caught them in the bathroom packaging them. He was there to give himself an injection. The Trans had taken care of their mother, who also had diabetes, so they knew how to administer a fatal insulin dose."

"What will happen to Ly and Tien?" I said.

"Relatives are coming to get them. The kids said to tell you all," he looked toward Mr. Magee, "that they appreciated everything you did, and will miss you."

Mr. Magee came over and faced Lucy and me. "I want to tell you it's rare to see teachers show such extreme dedication." He said, "Job well done," and shook our hands.

I said, "You can thank Handwriting 101."

This time Detective Norm didn't roll his eyes. Nor did he offer a handwriting sample.

MATTIE IN THE MIDDLE
Gigi Vernon

Late for her shift, Mattie rushed into the diner. At the squeak of the screen door everyone looked up. The joint was already full, every seat taken by the usual breakfast crowd of coal miners with their blackened fingernails and grubby overalls. When they saw it was her, they ducked for cover behind their newspapers.

The headline MURDER! had pushed the Depression and Pretty Boy Floyd to page two of *The Wheeling Gazette*. Grainy photos on the front page told the story. A Chevy coupe smashed against a tree. The victim, a young man, slumped and oozing black blood behind the wheel. Mattie's sister, suspected murderess, looking pretty and guilty as sin as the police hauled her away.

Mattie felt like she had been doused with icy water from the well. Stiff and numb, she could hardly make her arms and legs move. *Put it out of your mind!* she told herself.

A new girl, Lurana Morely from up the road, set down plates of steaming eggs and grits in front of customers. When Lurana caught sight of Mattie, she knocked a salt shaker over and busied herself wiping it up. Mattie headed into the kitchen.

Jem, the owner, stood at the grill, a corncob pipe in the corner of his mouth, grease splattering all around him.

"Sorry I'm late." Mattie tied an apron around her waist. "You hire a second girl?"

Jem took an egg in each hand, cracked them, dropped the yellow ooze onto the grill, and tossed the shells away. "You snooze, you lose, girl. That was the deal," he mumbled around his pipe, staring down at the bubbling eggs.

"You're firing me? I've always been reliable, and this is the first time I ain't been on time," she said, shaky with having to speak up for herself. "For Pete's sake, my only sister was arrested yesterday."

"A whole lot of hungry people expect to get a hot meal here."

"It's because of my sister, ain't it?" She leaned over so that he had to look at her. "I need this job. My Ma's sicker than ever."

He flipped the eggs, and ladled out dollops of slapjack batter onto the sizzling surface.

She tried again. "Heck, I'm an attraction." She flung a hand toward the tables, every seat full. "I'm good for business."

"Don't need that kind of business 'round here."

Her fingers clumsy, she untied the apron and hung it up. Embarrassment clouding her view, she made it out to the street, and banged into someone.

"Mattie Wilson!" a familiar voice exclaimed. "Just who I wanted to see. Let me snap your picture for the paper. Hold it!"

A camera was shoved in her face.

She ducked as it flashed.

"Goshdarnnit! Now what'd you have to do that for?"

Behind the contraption was a former schoolmate. "Luvie!"

"Don't call me Luvie," he said. "Nowadays I go by L.V. Heckathorn, official staff reporter for *The Valley Weekly*." His name might have changed, but he had the same boyish pudginess, long nose, and thick eyeglasses.

She batted the camera, an ugly, one-eyed frog of metal, away.

He began fiddling with it. "Do you know how much these things cost?" he complained.

She took off down Main Street. "Only Street" as her sister Araminda called it, which wasn't strictly true, but near enough.

Leesville, West Virginia, was the kind of town where everybody knew your business. In big cities like Roanoke or Youngstown or Hagerstown, Araminda had once told her, people didn't care to know every little thing about you. Here, townsfolk she'd known all her life stopped and gawked and whispered. Mrs. Petzold steered her two little girls away, like Mattie had the diphtheria, and jalopies slowed to get a look, like she was a dang animal in the circus.

Put it out of your mind. She pulled down her cloche hat, a hand-me down gift from Araminda, grateful that it hid her face, and skedaddled around the corner to the jailhouse.

"Official visiting hours ain't 'til four, missie," Sheriff Roberts said, as he pushed his bulk up from a chair behind the desk.

She avoided his big sorrowful eyes. He'd been one of her Daddy's best friends. Daddy must be turning over in his grave at this scandal. Her face felt hot and red as a tomato.

Luvie appeared in the doorway.

"You got plenty of pictures at the creek, son. Give it a rest, now," Sheriff Roberts said, closing the door. Luvie slunk away.

"Come on, Mattie, if you're coming." The sheriff shuffled down a hallway, keys and gun jingling on his belt. He showed her back to the two cells, and left her.

Araminda was stretched out on a striped mattress. She sat up when she saw Mattie. "I thought you worked the lunch counter today."

There wasn't no need to add to Araminda's worries. "I asked for a day off."

"How's Ma? Does she know?"

"She's holding up. I haven't told her anything. Doc give her some medicine for the pain. Makes her nice'n drowsy. He don't think she has much longer." She sniffed and blinked, then smiled. "They treating you all right in here?"

"Three squares a day." Araminda grinned. "Though I sure could use a smoke. Run by my room and bring 'em here next time you visit?"

"All right. Did he question you?" Mattie nodded in Sheriff Roberts' direction, reminding them both that the walls were thin.

"Sure enough. They're gonna be questioning you, too."

"They already did. What did you tell him?"

"Same as I told you and everyone else that cared to ask." Araminda rattled off her story. "This fine lookin' gent in a fancy suit comes into the barroom and sits at one of my tables. Me and him get to talking. After my shift, he gives me a ride to Ma's 'cause I'd promised to visit her. As we're going down the road, he tells me he's wanted in three counties for robbery and murder. He tells me he just robbed a bank in Wheeling, and he's laying low on account of him and his partner had a serious disagreement. I thought he was pulling my leg, hoping to get a kiss or something. Made me laugh so hard I just about busted something. He drops me off and I thank him and go inside. Next thing I hear he's shot dead and I'm a suspect. Simple as that."

Mattie nodded, and balled her fists in her dress. "You scared?"

"No, 'cause I'm innocent. Cousin Henry's gonna be my defense lawyer."

"How we gonna pay him?" Mattie asked nervously.

"He's doing it for free. 'Bonopro,' he called it. He says my case is circumstantial. They don't have no evidence to speak of. The Grand Jury'll acquit me, for sure."

"There's the witness," Mattie reminded in a whisper.

"So some busybody saw me get into the man's coupe. Sue me! That don't make it murder. Girls get in fellows' jalopies all the time. Saved me a long walk to Ma's."

"What about your busted lip and the bruise up side your head?"

"What about it? I tripped on a loose step on Ma's porch and fell. I told them my own sister was there when it happened." Araminda held her gaze for a long moment.

Mattie nodded hard, giving herself courage. "The sheriff or the lawyer know who the fellow was?"

"Nope. Lots of townsfolk saw him, but no one ever set eyes on him before. He wasn't carrying nothing with his name. And the shot that killed him sure made a mess of his face."

Mattie grimaced and swallowed. *Put it out of your mind!*

"The law is stuck trying to figure out who he was and I'm stuck here 'til they do," Araminda said.

"If they knew the fellow was a criminal, they might figure it was the partner that must've killed him. Then they'd have to let you go."

"All I know is they got nothing on me and I'm sitting mighty pretty." Araminda winked.

Mattie didn't see nothing to wink about. "They might hang you!"

"Don't fret. They gotta convict me first, and for that they need evidence and there ain't none. Sooner or later, I'm gonna be free and clear."

Even as little girls, Araminda had always been the brave one. And too smart for her own good.

From the jailhouse door, Mattie peeked out at the street. Luvie was gone, pestering some other hapless creature for a picture, no doubt. She hurried toward the train station.

The train tracks glinted in the sunshine like a pair of slithering black snakes. A train pulled slowly away from the station. She'd like to be on that train and leave this mess behind. Ride the rails to parts unknown, like Araminda had done before Ma took sick. If only they had the money. *Put it out of your mind.*

Behind the station was a dirt road lined with clapboard buildings that leaned toward the mountainside—a barroom, a pool hall, some coloreds' houses, and Araminda's boarding house.

Araminda's things—a carpet bag, two hat boxes, and a bundle—were set out on the porch of the boarding house. If it'd been up to her, Mattie would have quietly took them away, but Araminda would expect her to make a fuss. She entered the house, took a deep breath, and knocked on the landlady's door.

Skinny Mrs. Loomis answered in a dingy cotton dress and a hairnet. "It's about time. You here to pick up your sister's things?"

"You're kicking her out?"

"I don't care to have my premises searched by the law for a gun. This is a respectable place. Ain't no place for a murderer."

"She's not a killer."

"The sheriff's not in the habit of locking up innocent people, as far as I know."

"They made a mistake," Mattie said, her voice beginning to shake and her face heat up. She coughed and got hold of herself. "Fine. Araminda don't want to stay here no longer anyway, but she paid until the end of the month. You can give me the refund."

Mrs. Loomis wiped her hands on her dress. "The two of you've got some nerve."

On the way back to the jailhouse, an idea came to Mattie. She changed direction, head down to avoid curious eyes.

At the general store, all the ladies stared at her. The owner and postmaster, cheerful Mr. Hefner, didn't even greet her when she asked about mail. He just shook his head, his mouth twisted with disgust. There was no mail for them. Hardly ever was.

She turned her attention to the notice board by the door. The "wanted" posters were as thick as fleas on a stray dog, pinned up layers deep. She flipped through murderers, thieves, escaped convicts, and bank robbers. Underneath a poster of a man wanted for impersonating coppers, she found the fellow, wearing the same proud smirk he'd worn when she'd taken his supper order at Jem's. She tore the poster down and stuffed it in her pocket.

"Hey!" Mr. Hefner yelled at the sound of paper ripping.

Mattie hustled back to the jailhouse where sad, kindly Sheriff Roberts let her see Araminda again.

"I brought you clean unmentionables and another dress," Mattie announced.

"Looks like you brought near everything," Araminda said.

"Your landlady—"

"Mrs. Loomis always was a good soul." Araminda laughed. "Guess I'll be looking for a new room to live in when I get out of here, which is fine by me. Dig me out a smoke?"

"Sure."

Araminda lit up. "They didn't find nothing in my room to use against me."

"'Tweren't nothing to find," Mattie repeated. She tugged the wanted poster out of her pocket and handed it over. "I came upon this at the general store."

"That's him. Darryl Porter. Says here he robbed banks in Wheeling. I told them so!" Araminda grabbed Mattie's hand and squeezed it.

"I'll leave it with Sheriff Roberts on my way out."

"No! Show it to Cousin Henry first. He'll pass it on when he's good and ready."

"I wish we had the money for your bail. Then we could just up and leave."

Araminda dropped her hand, and her voice and face became hard. "Well, we don't. So forget about it."

Loaded down like a mule with Araminda's things, Mattie trudged to Cousin Henry's office.

"Mattie?"

She turned and was blinded by a flash. "Luvie!"

"I'm L.V. now!"

She dropped a bag and swatted blindly at him and his camera, like he was a sweat bee out to sting her.

"That's enough now, young man," someone else said. "I've got some private business of a confidential nature with this lady."

Mattie felt a hand grip her elbow to steady her. Her eyesight cleared and she saw Cousin Henry looking like a banker with white shirt and suit, slick hair, and shiny leather shoes.

"How about an interview, Mr. Burdage?" Another flash went off.

Ignoring Luvie, Cousin Henry gently tugged the heavy carpet bag out of her grasp. "I've been looking for you all morning, Miss Mattie. Might I offer you a ride home? My Ford's parked right here."

"Yes, sir. I'd be grateful."

Like a true gentleman, he opened the door for her, tucked her in, and stowed Araminda's bags and boxes.

"This'll give us a chance to talk," he said, starting the motor.

Mattie steeled herself, and forced her voice steady. "It's awful generous of you to help Araminda. Expecting no payment and all."

"My payment will be the satisfaction of knowing I've served the public by protecting an innocent woman. A service, I hope, that the public will remember come election time."

Outside of town, they turned onto the washboard of a country road, the pot holes and ridges bucking them, a tail of dust streaming out behind.

Cousin Henry shifted gears and slowed to a crawl. "If it comes to a trial, you'll be the chief witness for the defense. I'd like to hear your version of what happened that night."

"I already told the sheriff."

"Yes, I've reviewed your statement. I'd like to hear it from you, if you don't mind."

"Yes, sir. I was asleep that night. A car motor in front of the house woke me up. I lit a kerosene lamp, got the shotgun, and crept downstairs, not knowing who it could be in the middle of the night—"

"This is the shotgun the sheriff confiscated?" he interrupted.

"I explained the old thing is busted. The trigger is all rusted. It's just for show. Two women alone on a farm and all."

"Continue."

"I peek out and I see Araminda get out of a car. I can't see the driver. The car drives away and Araminda comes in." Mattie's face burned, like it was trying to melt away and leave her skull bare, but she stared straight ahead. "Araminda's wearing nice heels, like she always does. In the dark, she trips on the loose step on the porch and falls against a pail I use to fetch water from the well. I rush out to help her. Her lip was bleeding, ruining her dress. I get her inside. While I'm cleaning her up, she explains a fellow she met in town gave her a ride home. Then we went to bed." She finished, hoping he wouldn't notice her recital was memorized.

"So the victim went to the creek by himself after he dropped your sister off? Mighty suspicious. What would he be doing down at the creek?"

"I have no earthly idea, sir. Took a wrong turn, I reckon."

"Did Miss Araminda tell you he was a bank robber?"

"Yes, sir, but I didn't believe his boastful lies any more than she did."

He nodded, and Mattie hoped he was satisfied. She knew she'd told him exactly what she'd told the sheriff.

"But then I found this." Mattie showed him the crumpled poster.

He read between glances at the road. When he'd finished, he said, "Given time, the sheriff would have put two and two together himself, but this speeds up the process and proves your sister was telling the truth about one thing, at least."

"Will she be released?"

"No," he drew the word out, thinking, "but it does alter the case. I'm afraid it makes it worse. The prosecution will now have a strong, premeditated motive for Miss Araminda. Theft of stolen money. It'll mean the noose. My esteemed colleague, Mr. Pettley, will be able to argue that your sister lured Darryl Porter to a deserted spot in order to steal the loot. She managed to get hold of his gun and shoot him, causing him to wreck the vehicle and injuring her in the process. She then disposed of the gun, the blood-stained dress, and hid the money."

Feeling like the grits and coffee she'd had for breakfast might come back up, Mattie forced a laugh that came out more like a hiccup. "But that's crazy! That's not what happened! She's not a killer. She'd never plan to shoot someone. For Pete's sake, she can't even wring a chicken's neck. It must have been that man's partner that found him and done the shooting."

"I could counter that it was self-defense and Darryl Porter attacked her," he mused, "but without evidence, it'll just be her word, and what with Miss Araminda's reputation in town, her word won't count for much, I'm afraid."

A tear leaked down Mattie's face.

Cousin Henry handed her a fine linen handkerchief. "Now, now. Fortunately for Miss Araminda, a thorough search of her room at the boarding house, and your mother's house and land, didn't uncover the gun. Or any stolen bank money, for that matter."

Mattie blew her nose. "What would it take to get her released?"

"There's a lot of circumstantial evidence against her, but nothing concrete. Discovering this partner would certainly help her."

"Will the law search for the killer? A manhunt? Ain't that what they call it?"

"I don't know about a manhunt. But now they'll question witnesses involved in the bank robberies. With luck, someone will report having seen an accomplice."

An accomplice. Mattie chewed her lip.

Cousin Henry turned the car onto the gully of a track, and pulled up in front of the house.

The two-room farmhouse's porch sagged, and its tin roof was a sheet of rust. Chickens scrapped between the sheds, and the barn looked like it might collapse in the next breeze. The old outhouse was long overdue for a fill-in and a move. Since Pa's death, it was just her and Ma, and they couldn't keep the place up.

She climbed out. "Thank you. I can manage," she said, dismissing his offer to help with Araminda's things. Inside looked worse than ever, after the sheriff's search for the gun.

She checked on Ma, changed into overalls, and straightened up the place. Then she went out to hoe the vegetable garden in preparation for spring planting. They'd searched there too, digging up her potatoes, and shifting the manure pile.

Just a stone's throw away was the creek where their neighbor had come across the wreck and the corpse. When she and Araminda were girls, the creek had been one of their favorite places. They used to fish, and swim on hot days, and slide on the ice in winter. When they'd gotten older, Araminda used to take boys there for skinny dipping and necking. Never again.

Put it out of your mind. She kept her head and eyes down until the sound of voices drifted to her.

Through a screen of budding trees, she glimpsed three boys messing around in the creek. The Linden boys from the top of the hill. Those boys could stir up heaps of trouble. Hoe in hand, she started down the hill to run them off.

At her approach, the boys scampered through the woods.

The muddy banks of the creek were carved with deep ruts from the coupe and the tow truck, and churned by the footprints of the sheriff, the two volunteer deputies sworn in for the occasion, and curious neighbors. The big oak tree hanging over the swimming hole was gouged something terrible. Sickened, she eyed the mountainside on the far bank. Broken branches and trampled growth showed where the sheriff and his deputies had searched.

Put it out of your mind!

She started back to the house. If only an accomplice could be found. Maybe Luvie could help. She dropped the hoe, ran back to the house, scribbled a note for Ma, and changed back into her dress, hat, and town shoes.

The Valley Weekly newspaper office was above Mr. Hamilton's feed store. Inside, a radio blared, and yellowing newspapers were stacked everywhere—on the desk, shelves, filing cabinets, chairs, and in teetering waist-high piles on the floor.

Luvie was alone in the office, hunched over his typewriter, jabbing keys. At sight of her, he sprang out of his chair. "Look who it is!" Grinning, he tightened his loose necktie. "To what do I owe the pleasure of this visit?"

"What do I have to do to keep my picture out of the paper?"

"Well, now." He scrunched up his face with thought. "How about a little smooch?" He puckered his lips.

She pecked him on the cheek. "Aren't you even going to offer me a seat?"

He got over his disappointment at the kiss, cleared a chair of newspapers, and set it before her. "How about an exclusive interview? How's it feel to have a sister accused of murder? Have you visited her? How's her spirit in the face of the noose? Does she have any words for our readers?"

"I'm not supposed to talk to anyone about the case."

"Come on, be a sweetheart. This story could make my career. It could be my ticket out of this old, dying, hillbilly town."

"Luvie—"

"L.V.," he corrected. "Then what are you here for?"

"You've known me and Araminda since we were knee-high," she began uncertainly.

He pulled up a chair across from her, and put a hand on her knee.

She pushed it away. "Help me save Araminda, and both of us will give you exclusives afterwards."

"Both of you!" He whistled.

"That fellow was a bank robber. Him and his partner had a falling out. His partner must have been the one that done the murder, but they don't believe Araminda. They think she's making the whole thing up to save herself."

"So the victim was a bank robber? With a partner? That's good." He pulled a pencil from behind his ear, licked it, and jotted on a notepad.

She nodded. "Could be you'd find a picture of the bank robber on a wanted poster."

"What else can you tell me?"

"I'm not telling you nothing, you understand?"

"Sure."

She continued. "Could be a wanted poster would tell you that he robbed banks in Wheeling."

"You don't say?" He fussed over the papers on his desk until he found the phone. He picked up the receiver. "Louise, get me *The Wheeling Gazette*. Elton 5498 is the number."

The operator connected Luvie. "Tom Hallstead?" he asked the other end. "A colleague of mine," he said to her while he waited. Tom's voice came through as a buzzing gnat. Luvie fired off some questions, then settled down to listen, the phone pinched between shoulder and ear, while he scribbled.

Luvie hung up. "Now we're getting somewheres! Got some dates and page numbers for articles and photos on the robberies." He unbuttoned the top button of his shirt and loosened his tie. "Let's take a look."

It wasn't exactly what she had in mind. But she didn't have any better ideas. "Where'd all these papers come from? Why do you keep 'em?" she asked.

"I'm a newspaperman, girl! I gotta keep informed of world events. Train brings 'em every morning from all over—New York, Cleveland, Washington, D.C."

They found the issues of *The Wheeling Gazette* and settled down to read.

Most of the stories were accompanied by the photo from the wanted poster. Chilled, Mattie read about the coppers killed by Darryl Porter. No mention of a partner or accomplice. Dusty and disheartened, she went on to an issue just a few days old with a different photograph—a getaway with a blurry figure of a man cutting across street traffic toward a parked Chevy coupe.

Was that a face, the face of an accomplice, behind the wheel? She stood up, knees shaking, hardly daring to breathe. "Looka here, L.V.!"

Mattie and Araminda threaded their way through the train until they found an unoccupied car. The train crawled out of the station as they stowed their belongings in the bins above the seats.

"Look!" Araminda exclaimed, pointing out the window at their farmhouse.

Mattie pressed her nose to the glass. The farmhouse slid around a bend as the train strained up the mountain.

"You gonna miss the old place?" Araminda asked.

"I'll miss Ma, may she rest in peace, but not Leesville. And not the scandal. I'm awful relieved to leave that ruckus behind. Wish we could have given Ma a decent funeral, though." Mattie wondered whether it had dawned on Araminda that the scandal had tipped sickly Ma into an early grave.

"Wouldn't be a good idea to go flashing around money all the sudden. Once we get fixed someplace, we'll order a real fancy tombstone for her and Daddy."

They settled back in their seats.

Araminda reached for a crumpled copy of *The Valley Weekly* left behind. The headline read MANHUNT! Underneath was the photo of Darryl Porter fleeing the bank next to a photo of a man with a broken nose and jutting chin who'd been identified as Darryl Porter's accomplice.

"You're sure the partner is dead? That Darryl really killed him before he got to town?" Mattie whispered, though there was no one to hear.

Araminda lowered her voice, too. "Darryl was a real bad man, a killer, but he wasn't no liar. Dang lucky for us, too. Just look at his accomplice. Sooner shoot you than look at you. What a pair!" She laughed harshly.

"What happens when the law finds the partner's corpse and figures out he was already dead when Darryl Porter was killed? Will they come after us?"

"We'll be long gone and outta state, thanks to you. It pays to have a reliable sister watching your back." She patted the purse full of stolen cash sitting on her lap. "You're a cool-headed one all right."

"No more than you are," Mattie said, avoiding her sister's eyes.

"What are you going to do with your half?" Araminda asked.

"I don't really deserve half."

"Sure you do, partner. Couldn't have done it without you."

"Don't call me that." Mattie swallowed. *Put it out of your mind.* "The gun isn't in there too, is it?"

"Don't fret. It might come in handy."

"We agreed to leave it," Mattie grumbled. "It *was* an accident? You didn't mean to shoot Darryl Porter?"

"How can you ask that again? I told you. My plan was to get him stupid drunk and take his money. But he caught me and tried to kill me. No one would have believed it was self-defense. If you hadn't helped me push the coupe away from the house down to the creek, they would have hanged me for sure. And it was your idea to hide the gun and the loot in that stinky old outhouse, where the sheriff and his boys didn't bother to dig too deep."

"Let's not talk about it. Not ever again."

Mattie stared out at the fields and mountains flowing by. *Put it behind you.*

HEIDEGGER'S CAT
Warren Bull

What do you say to a man whose son just died? How do you explain that, even if his son was your college roommate, you hardly knew him? Some university housing flunky had thought it would be a good joke to have Charles, who'd traveled extensively in Africa and Europe, room with me, a kid who had rarely been out of the ghetto. When Mr. Adeleye called and said he wanted to meet with Charles's friend, Tweener, and me, I couldn't think of a way to refuse. I told him I didn't know how to contact Tweener, but he said he'd take care of that. When he said he wanted to meet us at a place where his son spent a lot of time, I immediately thought of Heidegger's Cat. I blurted that out before I stopped to think. He said he would meet us there the next morning at nine.

The bar was in the ghetto just beyond the university. It was a popular place, especially with white students who got a kick out of venturing into dangerous territory. I'd only been there at night when it served cheap beer, burgers and fries, but I'd heard rumors that during the day the menu included drugs, sex, and guns. In the daylight the decaying bar and surrounding neighborhood looked like a war zone. Considering that the Brims and the Rolling 50s both wanted this turf, I suppose it was. My battered Chevy blended in with the cars in the neighborhood.

I saw Tweener sitting at a sloping table, talking on a cell phone. He switched it off and put it on the table when I joined him. Mike Morris—Tweener—was tall and lean, with lighter skin than mine. As a sophomore and a junior, he started for the basketball team as an undersized power forward, where he made up for his lack of size with determination, timing and smarts. In his senior year, he was replaced by a taller, stronger player. Although he made several attempts at professional basketball in the United States and Europe, he found that he was too short and not explosive enough to be a forward. His quickness and outside shooting didn't reach the incredible levels required of a guard. Stuck in a body between what was needed for either position, he became known as Tweener.

Tweener gave me a hard look. "Man, this is one bad idea."

"Then why are you here?" I asked.

He shook his head. "Staying away would be even worse. What do you know about this dude, Robert?"

"Mr. Adeleye? He's on the staff of the Nigerian embassy, a secretary or attaché or something like that."

Tweener glared at me. "Chucky said his dad was head of security."

"Okay. He's head of security. What difference does that make?"

"Man, do you ever get that head of yours out of your books? The man knows about weapons and interrogation, probably about torture, too. He's going to ask us about Chucky. What we have to do is keep our cool. Be respectful and tell him nothing."

"There's not much I can tell him."

"That's it. Stick to that."

A group of ebony-skinned men wearing mirrored sunglasses pushed through the door. Two by two they walked through the bar, looking into every corner and inspecting every customer. Two of them stopped by our table and stood without speaking. The other customers were hustled out and told to stay away. Two took the barkeeper through an open door into the kitchen and closed the door behind them. I suspected that there were other men outside surrounding the building.

One of the men standing by our table pulled out a cell phone and spoke into it in a language I didn't understand. Then Adeleye entered. He was a massive, heavily muscled man. His skin was so black that it seemed to have a blue tint to it. His tailored suit cost more than the combined value of everything I owned.

He spoke in a deep, angry voice, "Gentlemen, thank you for coming."

I said, "I'm very sorry for your loss, sir."

Adeleye stared at me. "Can you even imagine what the death of my son is like for me?"

"No, sir," I said, "I cannot."

Adeleye turned toward Tweener. "Can you?"

Tweener shook his head and looked down.

"At least you do not pretend," Adeleye said.. "That is something. Not much, but something. Charles was the one son I had who might have been able to step into my shoes some day. The others are either mindless thugs or too soft to survive. He was my only hope that our family would be able to thrive in the world community that Nigeria is finally entering. Now my hopes are dead."

He sat down at the table.

"I am both a man of the modern world and a man of tradition. In my traditional culture, when a young man of promise dies, we hold an inquiry into the cause. People accused of contributing to his death are given a chance to prove their innocence. That is why the two of you are here. Robert, you were his roommate. Tweener, you were his friend. I ask you why did he die? I know he overdosed on heroin. That caused his death. My question is why did you allow him to die?"

"Is this a trial?" I asked.

Adeleye glared at me. "The trial may come later. We will follow the customs of my country here. If it comes to a trial, it will not be like any trial you have ever seen. I understand that in English one meaning for the word trial is ordeal. That is what you might face."

Tweener said, "You can't do this. You could get in big trouble."

Adeleye shook his head. "I can do it. I have diplomatic immunity. My men are embassy staff. Speak to me or I will draw my own conclusions. Then it will go hard for you. Robert, how did you help my son Charles?"

"I tried to be a friend to your son. At first he was interested in classes and studying. Then he started hanging out with a fast crowd all night, sleeping through classes and not doing assignments. When I found out he was using drugs, I warned him. I warned you, too."

Adeleye looked at Tweener. "Besides supplying him with drugs, how did you help Charles?"

Tweener sneered at me and said, "I don't know what Robert told you about me, but keep in mind that he's what we call an Oreo. He's black on the outside, but inside he's lily-white.

Chucky got bored studying all the time. He wanted to be a playa'. I introduced him to some tight girls and straight brothers. Maybe I shared some weed with him once or twice. I never touched coke, meth or heroin with him. Chucky got into that on his own."

Adeleye turned to me. "What do you say about that?"

I answered, "I don't know. I stay away from that crowd. I've got to keep my grades up to keep my scholarship or I go back to the hood. I want to qualify for funding for med school later on. Tweener tried to play his way out of the hood. He made it. I'm trying to study my way out."

I paused. "I do agree with him in one way: Charles decided to take drugs on his own. Nobody forced them on him. He caused his own death."

Adeleye glowered at both of us. "Charles paid for his mistakes with his life. He has been punished. But there are others who share in the blame and they must be punished too. You offer nothing but excuses. I am not surprised. You are like your ancestors—weak. They were slaves in Africa because they were weak. That's why my ancestors sold your ancestors to white men to be their slaves here. Robert, you let Charles down. Tweener, you introduced him to the people who sold him drugs. That's why I hold you both responsible for my son's death."

"We didn't give him drugs," Tweener insisted. "Other people are guilty of that."

Adeleye said, "I know. I will find them, too. I will find everyone involved in my son's death. The guilty will be punished. I promise that. I will start with the two of you."

He reached into his suit coat. Tweener flinched and I blinked. Adeleye brought out his closed fist. When he opened his fist, half a dozen dark brown kidney-shaped beans fell on the table.

"Calabar beans. They come from the doomsday plant. We call them 'esere peas.' In my country, if a man accused of murder wants to prove that he is innocent in the way our ancestors followed, he will publicly swallow one or two beans, believing that he will live and that will demonstrate his innocence. I once saw four men divide a bean to decide which one of them would end up with a worthless woman. They all died in agony. The woman left with another man who later wished he had died too."

I stared at the beans on the table.

"You can swallow a bean or I can have my men force one into your mouth and hold your jaws shut," Adeleye said. "It does not matter to me which way you take them."

Tweener shoved the table at Adeleye and jumped to his feet. Adeleye's men tripped him, drove him to the ground and wrenched him over onto his back. Two men knelt on his arms, while two others immobilized his legs. A fifth man pinched Tweener's nostrils closed. When Tweener opened his mouth to breath, the man dropped a bean into it.

Adeleye said, "If you spit it out, I will have you killed very slowly, very painfully. Three of my men used to work for Idi Amin."

Tweener started to cry, keeping his mouth closed.

Adeleye looked at me. I picked up a bean, took a breath, put the bean into my mouth and swallowed it immediately. The taste was as bitter as sin. Almost immediately my mouth filled with saliva. I began to gag. My heart pounded. My face got hot. I stood up and ran to the bathroom. On the squalid floor in front of a toilet, I knelt with my sides heaving and tears streaming down my face. Finally I vomited the entire contents of my stomach. I thought I would die right there with the smell of human excrement in my nostrils, but slowly my heaving lessened. I don't know how long I stayed on the grimy floor, happy just to be alive.

I had to think.

I had never heard of Calabar beans but I thought about their effects. They had to contain toxic alkaloids. I had not chewed the bean. Vomiting got it out of my system. That was consistent with its use as an ordeal. Some who undergo the test live; others die. There was a harsh traditional African wisdom to the process. An innocent person, wishing to prove innocence, would swallow and purge. A guilty person, fearing to show guilt, would hesitate and then have trouble swallowing with a dry mouth. Probably, the longer the bean remained inside the body, the more toxins would be released.

Adeleye had plans to track down the pushers who had sold drugs to Charles. He wanted to add African killings to the home-grown drive bys and our slow self-inflicted genocide through drugs and violence. Although I ached for Adeleye's loss, and I, myself, had fantasized about cleaning out the "business" men and women whose drugs and lifestyles poison young Blacks, I knew the "collateral damage" from the conflict would introduce new horrors to the community already drenched in violence and despair.

When I could, I stood up. Gingerly I walked out of the bathroom and back into the bar.

Tweener was dying near the front door. From his contorted position, I knew he was out of his mind, feeling pain beyond misery. I didn't like the man. He'd been quick to taunt and belittle me. He bought into the sports delusion that destroys so many young black men. He thought sports would make him a millionaire and a star; that he'd be set for life after a few years in the pros. When that didn't happen, he settled for being a minor celebrity, and pusher of light-weight drugs. On the other hand, he was smart, and persistent. He had hung on until he earned a university degree. Once the sports fantasy finally died, he might have wised up and made something of his life. He deserved a chance anyway. I felt anger start to build within me about another brother's wasted life.

Adeleye and his men sat around tables and watched Tweener's life drain away. They nodded to me and I joined them. I did not think Tweener should die surrounded only by strangers.

I remembered. In the fourth grade the word came down to me. Only girls study hard. Don't be too white. If I'd had Tweener's physical skills, I might have looked to sports to earn respect. I might have become one more body in the pipeline of young brothers served up in sports arenas as gladiators to entertain the man. Most sports encourage brothers to maim and cripple each other while the crowd cheers them on. I didn't have those skills so I endured taunts, name-calling and occasional ass whippings, but I studied hard. I graduated valedictorian, which led to more scorn.

My low SAT scores puzzled me until I actually got to college. Then I found out how badly educated I really was. My most advanced high school classes did not mention Christopher Marlowe or quantum physics. I had to have tutors and to audit hard classes before taking them for credit. My first year grades were so low that I nearly lost my scholarship. I knew that if I failed it would confirm other students' prejudices about my entire race. I survived, like I survived in Heidegger's Cat. And I learned one thing that the Asian kids seem to know at birth. I might not have the background to compete or the highest intelligence, but I could outwork and out-study any son of a bitch on the planet.

Almost as if he could hear me thinking about him, Adeleye said, "I did not expect to see you again. According to our traditions, you have been tested and found innocent."

He still sounded angry.

"Thank you," I said.

I looked at the men sitting around and began to speak. "Let me talk to all of you. Mr. Adeleye accused me of complicity in his son's death, due to my failure to look out for Charles. I was tested and found innocent. Now I make the same accusation. I ask for the same trial."

I looked at Adeleye.

"One man deserted your son in an unfamiliar culture that kills young black men every day without regret. When notified of difficulties, that man said he was too busy to respond. He did nothing and Charles died. Of all the people in the world, that man had the greatest capacity to help. He did nothing except to blame others for his failure to act."

I paused.

"He did nothing to save his own son." I focused my eyes on Adeleye. "I accuse you."

He shook his head. I picked up a stray Calabar bean from the table.

"You say you are a man of tradition. You say that in your culture when two men disagree they may duel to see which one is lying and which is telling the truth."

I took out my pocketknife and cut the bean in half. I picked up one half, put it in my mouth and swallowed it.

"I say you are responsible."

Adeleye shook his head again. "Don't think you can come in here like one of your American cowboys and challenge me to a gun fight. You have no rights here. You cannot tell me what to do."

When I headed toward the bathroom, Adeleye was staring at the piece of Calabar bean in front of him and sweating. The men were staring at him and leaning toward him.

Hunched over in pain, holding my sides, I staggered out of the bathroom half an hour later. The place was as empty as a tomb.

* * *

A few days later, a friend and I were reading different sections of the paper in the student union when he let out a whistle.

"Listen to this," he said. "You remember that they found Tweener's body lying on the sidewalk and suspected he died from a drug overdose? Well they did an autopsy and determined that he died from alkaloid poisoning. They're not sure if he died by accident, suicide or murder. How strange."

"At least they can't say we're all junkies."

My friend said, "You're finally sounding and looking like your old self. Even you can over-do studying, you know. For a while I thought you had mono. Did you find anything interesting in your section of the paper?"

I said, "I see here that the Nigerian ambassador has appointed a new head of embassy security."

"Is that interesting?" my friend asked.

"It is to me."

HOCUS-POCUS ON FRIDAY THE 13TH
Kris Neri

Friday the 13th—a date when disasters pile up like cars in fog-bound freeway crashes. If I've learned anything from experience, it's that anything can happen on that cursed day. And this was the worst of the 13th's. Also, most likely, my last. A terrorist's bomb—in my hands!—was about to blow us all to Smithereens, wherever the hell that was. Just because I'd insisted Friday the 13th wasn't any unluckier than any other date, and, yeah, because I claimed I chatted with the dead. Colossal whoppers even for me.

But the story didn't begin at that charity ball, dedicated to the naïve proposition of bringing peace to the Middle East, where I anxiously waited with four hundred of the rich and oblivious to visit the Hereafter in tiny bits.

It began days earlier at the FBI, with the world's most annoying goddess.

Before I march through Heaven's Gate, I should introduce myself. I'm Samantha Brennan, fake medium, scam psychic, and bogus spiritual advisor to the stars here in Los Angeles. When I'm lucky. Truth is, I wasn't doing well financially. Hard to figure when you consider all the creativity I bring to my clients' readings. Don't tell me I'd do better if I actually could commune with the Great Beyond. Trust me—all mediums are fakes. No matter how yakky they were in life, the dead aren't big on chitchat.

So, naturally, when the goddess dangled the promise of pay before my chubby little nose, I came running. When I showed up for our meeting, she pushed up the sleeve of her boxy gray suit, stared at her watch, then glared at me with her big, blue eyes. "You're late, Samantha."

You might think that since she had that divinity-thing going, while I was the earth-bound mortal, that she'd be wearing a frothy gown and I the dorky duds. But it was actually the reverse.

"Ever consider wearing a watch?" she demanded.

Nope. Who would take me seriously? Shouldn't a psychic *know* the time?

She tapped her sensible shoe against the floor of the Los Angeles field office of the FBI. Awfully earth-bound of her, I know, but Annabelle Haggerty is as much flesh-and-blood as you and me. And she isn't anything like either of us. She's a direct descendant of the ancient Celtic goddess, Findabar. When Haggerty kicks it, she won't die like we will, she'll be "called home," as she puts it, to *Tir na n'Og*, the "land of the young," in the Celtic language, where she'll live for eternity.

While Haggerty droned on about the value of punctuality, I poofed up the skirt of the hot pink organdy gown I wore. To say our tastes differed was the understatement of the millennium. Of course, stodgy dress was required in her job. While she truly was a Celtic goddess, Annabelle Haggerty was also a Special Agent of the FBI.

"Samantha, the Bureau wants you to renew your association with Dodi Drake."

You remember Dodi, the widow of Manfred Drake, the vice president a few administrations back. A man so inflexible that, in a poll taken during his lone term, the majority of Americans chose him as the politician most likely to be hiding a broom up his ass.

"Happy to, only Mrs. Drake warned me never to find myself in her line of vision again."

Anger caused Haggerty to pinch her full lips together. "Because you're so unreliable. Why don't you consider being less of a flake?"

That was like asking a duck to sing opera. He might stand center stage and throw his whole heart into it, but it wasn't going to sound too good.

"Leave Mrs. Drake to me, Samantha. I'll see that she asks you for a reading."

Given her secretive smile, I knew Haggerty planned to use her special powers, making that a red-letter day. As a goddess she does have powers, which she's mostly too stingy to use. I know,

I've begged for the Lotto numbers loads of times. I suspect, it's that she likes functioning as the ordinary mortal she wishes she were. Crazy, huh?

She went on to tell me about the charity ball Mrs. Drake was chairing to raise bucks for some ill-fated drive for peace in the Middle East. Only now, because it had been scheduled for Friday the 13ᵗʰ, Dodi was thinking about postponing it, even if it was less than a week away. The Bureau wanted me to assure her it was safe to go ahead with it.

"Is it? Safe, I mean?" I asked.

Haggerty laughed, a sparkling sound that all the gods share. "Not at all. The international chatter says a terrorist plans to blow up the ballroom and everyone in it. We want to catch him in the act."

"Why not cancel it?"

"Because our intelligence might not be as good next time."

I gulped uneasily. "And if you don't catch him?"

Haggerty snapped her fingers. "Then the L.A. glitterati will go up in a puff of smoke."

Funny. She said that like it was a bad thing.

That's how I ended up back in Dodi's high-powered world.

Surely the most conventional of political wives, Dodi hadn't changed much since the old man bought country real estate. She still wore those dowdy knit suits, and still softened her nasty zingers with correct, even vapid, smiles.

She looked at me now over the half-glasses perched on her long nose. "Lovely to see you, Madame Samantha. I'm glad you're not holding that..." She cleared her throat. "...unpleasantness against me."

If that was how she described a restraining order.

She finally clued me in to the date dilemma and worked herself into a dither about it.

I drew myself up and said, with as much dignity as someone in the jester suit I wore today could, "That's amateur spirituality, Mrs. Drake. There's absolutely no validity to it."

I could barely keep from laughing. Validity? At one time I never swallowed any of that woo-woo crap, even if it was the way I made my totally inadequate income. I regarded supernatural concerns as the province of the terminally trusting, and karma, just a nightclub in West Hollywood. But since I met Haggerty, I'd seen too much I couldn't explain.

My spiritual superiority didn't win Mrs. Drake over. She insisted I consult her late hubby on the matter. Even if I wasn't sure what to believe any more, the one truth I clung to was that the dead don't communicate. It's the primary characteristic that separates them from the living. Everything mediums do is purely hocus-pocus. But I was nothing if not accommodating, when a paycheck was involved.

Because the rubes expect a good show, I faked a trance, then said, "Manfred Drake, your former plane cries out to you." And I put the matter to him.

People think my job is easy, just a matter of telling my clients what they want to hear. But that's the rub—how should I know what they want? Not psychic, remember? But what makes a good fake medium is the ability to observe. I opened my eyes a smidge and spotted a photo of the old fart. Straining, I read the inscription, "To Snooks, from her Man." Gag me.

I swayed on the couch beside Dodi and said in a dreamy voice, "Manfred says, 'Snooks, don't worry about the date. Have your party.'"

Dodi gasped. "Snooks? Why he hasn't called me that since before his first mistress. He had a few, you know."

More like a few thousand. But that detail did the trick, convincing Dodi to go ahead with the ball.

"Uh...that other matter we used to discuss, Madame Samantha. Does Manfred still feel the same way?"

Well, Dodi had made one tiny change in her otherwise conventional life. Since the old man kicked it, she'd taken up with a succession of boy-toys, each less suitable than the one before him.

"He's still livid, Mrs. Drake. Absolutely writhing in anger."

Dodi sighed with satisfaction.

I'd never admit it to Haggerty, but that was why Mrs. Drake decided she didn't need my services. Even before I started stalking her. Whenever she asked me how her husband felt about her latest protégé, I assumed she wanted to believe he was okay with it. How was I to know she only took up with them to show

Manfred she could have her flings, too? It's like they all expected me to read their minds.

As if on cue, Dodi's latest diversion strutted into the room behind one of her Secret Service agents. The handsome young black man cocked his hip and sneered at the departing agent. Everything about him—from his shaved head, to his black leather clothing, to the dark shades he wore, which couldn't have been easy to see through indoors—screamed of cool contempt. A nasty shiny scar that cut across one cheek took him out of the ranks of drop-dead gorgeous and put him firmly in the bad boy category.

"Madame Samantha, this is my...friend...Antifreeze, a rising hip-hop star," Dodi said in a simpering tone.

Even if I couldn't actually hear Mr. Drake, I knew what he had to think about this one.

"Yo, bitch," Antifreeze said matter-of-factly. Was that greeting meant for Dodi or me?

Her, I guessed, since she flushed, like poetry had just turned her little head.

To my surprise, though it wasn't as easy to detect on his mocha-colored skin, he flushed, as well. Why would a bad boy act ashamed for the kind of street remark you'd expect him to make?

That question puzzled me even after I returned to my car, a classic, if well-oxidized, 1966 Mustang convertible. I sat behind the wheel, clutching the big black purse I always carry, trying to make sense of it. Why would a guy, who dubbed himself "Antifreeze," blush for calling a woman something that, while nasty in most circles, seemed pretty tame by hip-hop standards? While rummaging through my bag, I came across a Post-it pad on which some words were scratched. "Check out the bad boy," the Post-it read.

Did I write that? I must have. Who else would write a note on my pad?

I raced to the Bureau and found Haggerty in her claustrophobic little office. I blurted out the gist of my session with Dodi and warned her about Antifreeze. To my surprise, she ignored my advice about Mr. Freeze, and focused instead on the outcome of my pseudo-message from Mandrake.

"Well done, Samantha," she said, with a tip of her sleek auburn head.

Much as I like praise—a rare enough occurrence from her—I didn't think she appreciated my real discovery.

"Oh, we know all about Antifreeze," Haggerty said with a flip of her delicate fingers. "Real name—Eddie Eagan, a man with a record clear back to the cradle. But the last time he came out of prison, he went off on some spiritual retreat, and it seems to have changed him. He hasn't gotten in trouble in the last few years."

While Haggerty went to report my success to her boss, I pawed through my purse in search of some candy. Dodi always scheduled my readings for late morning, yet she never invited me to lunch. Rude. Then again, how much off-the-clock time did I want to spend with her and 'Freeze? I came across that Post-it pad again. This time it read, "Check the Social Security records."

Wow, I was sure getting good ideas. I just wished I could remember when I wrote them.

When Haggerty returned, I asked her to look up his Social Security account.

With a sigh, she said, "Samantha, you keep Dodi set on that date, and let us worry about Mr. Eagan."

"But you're not," I wailed.

"Because he's not a threat. The hip-hop wannabe is more interested in getting a record contract than blowing up a roomful of people who can help him get ahead."

Although that made sense, I couldn't give up on that note. After more cajoling, she finally tapped some keys on her desktop computer to call up Eddie Eagan's Social Security account.

"Cons usually get civilian jobs while they're on parole," Haggerty said. "We see contributions for some time, before they fall off the honesty wagon."

As she predicted, that pattern had been consistent in Eddie's case. Until the last time he came out of the hoosegow. No Social Security contributions in over three years.

Haggerty flexed one of her slim shoulders. "So? Maybe Dodi keeps him. She might be generous."

"She's never been generous with me."

Haggerty's gaze narrowed. "Samantha, this concern isn't like you. Do you know something you're not telling me?"

I held out my open palms to show how little I knew about anything, a sad fact I've largely come to accept.

"You're not seeing some kind of a vision, are you? I've always said that you might have genuine—"

"Not that again." Haggerty thought I might have real woo-woo abilities. But she was wrong. I am so lacking in prescient powers that, if I were about to be hit on the head by a two-by-four, my premonition of pain wouldn't kick in until the headache wore off. And that's the way I like it. I want life to be a total surprise. "Nope, I'm a complete sham."

"Sometimes we need to accept our true natures."

The pot calling the kettle *noir*.

"Why can't you leave the security concerns to the Bureau?"

"Because Dodi insists that I attend the ball, too," I blurted.

Haggerty smiled knowingly. "That's our girl."

Okay, so I have a highly developed sense of self-preservation.

"This is a state-of-the-art operation," she assured me. There would be a total lockdown of the ballroom wing of the hotel. Between the times set in the security computer, nobody would get in or out. "And we'll shut down cell phone service to it." They even had some electronic explosives detector, so even the smallest amount would be discovered. "You see? It's totally under control."

Easy enough for her to say. The security room was probably as fortified as a bunker.

I tried to let it go, I really did. But worry sat on my fat chest with all the weight of a piano. The next day, I saw *another* note on my purse Post-it. "Follow the bad boy," it read.

When was I writing all this? But hey, it was a good idea. I staked out Dodi's condo, having taken the precaution of bringing lots of chocolate bars in case Antifreeze kept me waiting. Since I went through them with lightning speed, fortunately, he didn't.

Carrying an over-the-shoulder duffle, he dropped in on his benefactor late morning, stayed for a few minutes, then left. I noticed the pimp-stride vanished once he moved beyond the range of Dodi's windows. He walked like a normal person then. Actually, with the mincing little steps that replaced that strut, he walked like a nerd. He caught a bus at the corner. Bad boys take the bus? I tucked the Mustang behind it and followed.

The bus deposited him at a gas station mini-mart. Antifreeze-Eddie, with his cheek scar glistening in the sunlight, jumped out and went straight to the men's room. Ten minutes later, *someone* came out, still carrying the duffle. But it sure didn't look like ol' Freeze. This guy wore dorky clothes and a wig. And the scar was gone!

When he walked away, I tailed him on foot. All the way to a library, where he went through the employees' entrance. A library? I finally found the chameleon, working behind the reference desk.

I told him we had to talk, and the eyes I hadn't been able to see behind those shades at Dodi's place widened to the size of dinner plates.

We went to a coffee shop around the corner.

"Look," I said, leaning across the Formica table, "I know who you are, Eddie."

"No, you don't. I'm not Eddie—that's my cousin. My real name is Daniel Stewart." He shrugged. "If you want a career in rap, you don't achieve it with a degree in library science. Eddie's record is what I need."

"And he doesn't mind you using his identity?"

Kind eyes stared off. I understood now why he kept them covered in his bad boy role. "He might not know. Eddie got religion during his last stay in prison, and he's become involved with some spiritual group. My aunt knows I'm using his name. She didn't mind, at first. I help her sell the beaded purses she makes, and she appreciates that."

"Beaded purses?"

His face brightened. "Really great ones. I'm having her make an evening bag for Dodi."

A guy that into purses had no business in hip-hop.

"But lately, Auntie acts uncomfortable around me. Maybe she's not as okay with my using Eddie's identity as I thought."

I noticed the absence of the scar. "But the scar? How do you...?"

Daniel pulled from his pocket a white piece of cardboard, covered with a number of shiny strips. "A makeup artist makes them for me. Scars to go."

Hmmm. Maybe I could get her to produce something that would make me look thin. "So, you work at the library and for your aunt?"

"I need the money. Starting my career has proven to be awfully expensive."

"Dodi doesn't give you—"

He shook his bewigged head. "Not a dime."

"Do you two...?" I wiggled my eyebrows suggestively.

It took a moment until he caught my drift and screwed up his face. "No! She just wants people to think so."

She wanted a dead guy to think so. But it was good to know I wasn't the only fraud.

The poor slob reeked of sincerity, and that was gonna hurt him in the music world. Hell, it surprised me it hadn't hurt him in the library. This isn't a town that values honesty, making it a perfect spot for me. But just to be sure I was reading him right—since despite Haggerty's claims, I have absolutely no spiritual abilities—I dashed back to the Bureau and told her about Daniel-Eddie's double life, and asked her to check Daniel Stewart's Social Security records.

With an annoyed grimace, she did. "Actually, Daniel has two jobs."

"Yeah, I told you—he works for his aunt."

Haggerty shook her head. "That one must be off the books. His other FICA-paying job is as a waiter at the hotel where the charity ball will be held."

I shrieked, "And that doesn't bother you?"

Haggerty shrugged. "Maybe that's where he and Dodi met. How many occasions do a vice presidential widow and a rap artist-librarian have to get together?"

I'd felt so sure about Daniel, but people fool me all the time. *Really* not psychic. I began to fear that he had just played me like a fiddle.

The days leading up to the ball passed in a blur. I kept reassuring Dodi about the date. And I needed a fitting for the gown I'd be wearing—a rainbow-printed fifties prom gown that I found at the vintage store. Sadly, it had to be let out. I also followed Daniel. But apart from his library job and visiting Dodi, his only stop was at some house in South Central, where he picked up an object wrapped in tissue paper. The beaded purse, I guessed.

I didn't arrive at the ball till the last minute. The valet parking lot beside the ballroom was already filled with loads of high-priced tin when my wreck joined the mix. Dodi glowed when she told me how grateful she was to Manfred for encouraging her to go ahead with things.

Yeah, the man was a prince. Dodi wore a soft lavender dress that fell in smooth lines over her slim body. I didn't see any beaded purse yet; Daniel must have been even later than I was.

I found Haggerty and her fellow fibbies in a security command center off the ballroom.

"Nice getup, Gidget," she said. "Does that gown glow in the dark?"

Okay, so maybe the rainbow stripes crossing my gown were a bit bright. The way I saw it, I could either be a better fake medium, or I could dress the part. My gigantic black purse also struck an odd note.

"Did you catch him yet?" I demanded. "Did your explosives sniffer turn up anything?"

Haggerty shook her head. "There's no explosive device here yet. But the international chatter still indicates there will be." She looked at her watch. "Better be soon, too. There won't be a way in or out shortly."

Great. One of the other agents buzzed someone in. A waiter entered carrying a tray of dinners for the Bureau folks. Since he was a black man with a shaved head, at first glance I thought he was Daniel. But a closer look showed him to be an older man, with a cynical demeanor. Now *this* guy could make it in rap.

I followed him out through the security room door, which clicked shut behind us. "Hey," I said. "Bring me a tequila, willya?"

"Get it yourself," he said with a sneer.

Whoa! Snotty. You could tell his tip was guaranteed tonight. Instead of turning toward the ballroom, he went through the outside door. I could have told him that door was about to seal shut, but I figured the staff had to know. Served him right if he got locked out. I stared after him, as he sauntered across the parking lot. Off in the distance, something shimmered on his face. But by then, I really needed that tequila, and I went back to the ballroom in search of a more congenial server.

Instead, I ran into Dodi. She showed me the lavender-and-cream bag Daniel had given her. I had to admit the beading was good. But the bag, when she handed it to me for a closer look, proved to be unexpectedly heavy.

"What's in here, Mrs. Drake? Your entire Secret Service detail?"

"It can't be any heavier than yours, Madame Samantha." Her gray eyes narrowed on my shoulder suitcase. "Perhaps instead of my paying you for readings, we can exchange services. You can communicate with Manfred for me, and I can teach you something about..." her thin lips curved in disapproval "...style."

And after that, maybe she could teach me to suck eggs. When I opened her purse, I found it remarkably small, compared to its outside dimensions. Not much in it, apart from an electronic keycard to the security center, something Haggerty didn't offer me. I palmed it, partly so I had access to Haggerty, but mostly to pay Dodi back for dissing her medium.

I found my assigned spot at a rear table, seated beside a skinny man in a baggy rented tux. Obviously, the loser table.

When Daniel came by, I told him what a nice job his aunt had done with the purse, without mentioning how heavy she made it, or how little space she left inside.

"My aunt really seemed nervous when I picked it up. I think she's about to tell me I can't use Eddie's identity anymore."

"Yeah, that's a shame. Where can I get some tequila around here?"

Daniel shrugged. "Why ask me?"

Because when he wasn't being a gigolo for a certain former Second Lady, he worked there. But if he didn't want to admit it, I wasn't going to press him. Besides, I saw the wait staff carrying trays of champagne flutes. Close enough. I was thrilled to see the waiter who smart-mouthed me wasn't among them. Maybe he really did get locked out—wouldn't that have been funny?

Time inched by, and the fibbies still didn't swarm over any suspects. What were they waiting for? After wolfing down a rubber chicken special, I used Dodi's keycard to let myself into the security room. When the door clicked shut behind me, I stared in disbelief. With half-eaten meals before them, all the Bureau people had keeled over. Dead? No! I fell to my knees beside Haggerty. I would never tell her, but I almost cried with relief when I realized she, like all of them, was just drugged.

Holy shit! The waiter must have knocked them out with tainted food. I thought about the fact that he had reminded me of Daniel. That wasn't simply because they were both black men with shaved heads. There had been a resemblance.

Outside the security room, I hurled myself at the outer ballroom doors, but they were sealed shut. I stopped some cute guy in designer eveningwear and demanded his cell phone, which my own finances didn't permit.

"Cell phones don't work here, sweet cheeks," he said with a smile that produced unexpected dimples.

Sweet cheeks? If I survived this night, I'd look him up.

Daniel happened by just then. "Daniel!" I shouted.

"Antifreeze," he muttered through clenched teeth.

"Whatever. The truth, now—do you work here as a waiter?"

He frowned. "When would I? The library, my aunt's purses, Dodi and my music career—that eats up all my time."

But someone on that job was using his Social Security number. Was it such a stretch to think that while he co-opted his cousin's identity, that Eddie had claimed his? I remembered the way the waiter's cheek had shimmered, like a real scar might. Eddie, the waiter? The terrorist?

And it all came down to me? Me, the most unreliable flake in the universe.

I stumbled back to my table and pawed through my big black purse for something that would help. Help how? To stop an explosion? *Get real, Samantha.* To my surprise, someone had written "Purse" on the Post-it pad.

Who the hell was writing those notes?

I ignored it. With four hundred-plus lives on the line—and most especially, mine—who cared about some notes.

A man's voice suddenly said, "The purse, you idiot. Get the purse."

I poked my index finger into the arm of the geek beside me. "Okay, my bag might be big. But you have no right to call me an idiot."

He turned my way. "I beg your pardon."

"You can beg all you want, pal, but I—"

It hit me then: the voice I heard—it wasn't his. And it wasn't outside, but *inside* my head. "Manfred?" I asked.

The geek beside me started to say, "No, my name is—"

"Not you, dweeb!" I shouted.

"Of course," the voice in my head said. "Am I not the one you called out for? But you are a hard person to reach, my girl. Do you know how difficult it is for us to speak?"

Didn't know, didn't want to know.

"The purse, you fool. It's the purse."

I got it! Finally, I knew which purse the old fart in the Great Beyond meant. Wouldn't Daniel's aunt have become a tad skittish if she helped her terrorist son build a bomb into Dodi's purse?

Dodi stepped up to the podium on the stage at the front of the ballroom. The beaded evening bag hung from a slender strap over her shoulder. Without giving it a thought, I lifted my skirt and galloped toward the stage like I was scoring a touchdown. Dodi's welcome speech sputtered to a halt, as she watched my approach. On the stage, I tried to yank the beaded purse from her shoulder, but she held onto it.

"I knew I shouldn't have removed the restraining order," she shouted, increasing her hold.

"Gimme the purse, Mrs. Drake, or I'll tell everyone what you *don't* do with Antifreeze." The audience members must have thought that was something kinky that had to do with solvents.

But my threat worked. Once she relinquished it, I grabbed the purse and dashed backstage. But what was I thinking? There were no doors that would open. With that vile thing clutched in my hand, I ran back and forth helplessly. We were goners, all of us! Me first!

Then I spotted a window, and a folding chair. I hurled the chair through the glass. Once the window broke, I threw the purse with all my might.

One one-thousand, two one-thousand... The explosion knocked me on my fanny and caused a ballroom full of people to scream frantically. Good thing they didn't know all their high-priced cars had just been reduced to metal toothpicks.

I tracked down the cute guy and asked to borrow his cell phone again. With the window open, so to speak, the phone worked, and I summoned Haggerty's boss. He used the hotel's security computer to override the locked doors, and took over.

After testing the drugged food, the case came together. The FBI picked up Eddie at his mom's home. Eventually, they proved the "spiritual retreat" everyone mentioned, was really a terrorist training camp.

Weeks later, I chided Haggerty for her failing. "If you weren't so bent on seeming totally human, you'd have sensed the food was tainted. What's the point of having special powers if you won't use 'em?"

She acknowledged that truth with a solemn nod. "And what about you, Samantha? I've maintained you had spiritual abilities, and you do. You communicated with the dead, after all."

"I'll admit it if you will, Haggerty."

But I wouldn't really.

All I was willing to admit was that anything can happen on Friday the 13th.

Even some mighty real hocus-pocus.

TEXAS TOAST
Suzanne Flaig

"Helluva party," Buck Johnson mumbled as he staggered across the dining room of his spacious Texas mansion. "Bring me another one of them Jack Daniels, Dollie Mae," he hollered to his son Jeb's fiancée. Standing at the open sliding glass doors, he stared out at the huge patio that extended past the fountain sparkling with red, green and blue spotlights, into the darkness at the far end. There, a large brick barbecue pit and a bar flanked the pool. *All mine*, he thought. *I built this whole spread on my own, from nothin'.*

Dollie Mae sashayed up alongside him, handing him his drink. She backed off, but not fast enough. Buck grabbed the drink with his left hand, wrapping his right arm behind her while reaching up and squeezing her breast. She jerked back, and the old man cackled, then took a hefty slug from the glass. He stumbled out onto the patio. Although the July night was hot, he felt cold and clammy, dizzy and weak. Buck weaved and careened past the fountain into the darkness.

The fires still burned in the barbecue pit, where earlier that evening, the cooks had grilled steaks to order for his 83rd birthday bash: Buck preferred his steak medium rare. He swayed slightly and blinked his eyes. The scene blurred. He felt that tingling sensation in his fingers again. Maybe he should lay off the booze, like Doc Bennett told him to. *No way*, he thought. *I'd rather die than give up booze or broads.* Buck shook his head and the view came back into focus.

Shivering, he turned back toward the warmth of the still glowing barbeque pit. I'll just sit down for a minute, he thought, perching on the brick ledge and watching a loose brick tumble over the edge into the hot coals. *What's that foul odor?* He glanced around, causing his head to spin. Disoriented, he tried to stand, dislodging another brick from his precarious seat.

As his sight dimmed, he saw a familiar figure approach. "Dizzy... Help me..." he muttered. "That smell... So strong... What..."

Buck's liquor glass shattered as he fell backwards into the barbeque pit.

After twenty-five years on the force, Harry Thornton thought he'd seen it all. But the sight and smell of Buck Johnson's char-broiled body overwhelmed him. Harry pulled a handkerchief out of his back pocket and covered his nose. He coughed. The stench hung thick in the air.

While the medical examiner kneeled over the body, Harry surveyed the scene. He stared at the black soot marks in front of the barbecue pit, and the shattered glass. A few bricks lay scattered near the mouth of the pit, next to a charred towel. A green garden hose stretched across the patio like a lazy snake, and pools of water darkened the flagstones around its path.

"You okay, Harry?" the ME asked as he stood up and motioned for the EMTs to load the body into the waiting ambulance. "It looks like he sat on the edge, the loose bricks collapsed under him, and he fell back into the hot coals. Seems somebody tried to douse the fire with the hose, and smother the flames with a towel. Hell of an accident."

"Accident. Yeah. That's certainly what it looks like." Harry coughed again. "God. That smell. It's disgusting."

"You're around dead bodies enough, you get used to all kinds of smells," the ME said, strolling toward his car. "Next time, try sticking some Vicks up your nostrils."

Harry rolled his eyes. "The witnesses are waiting in the den." He turned toward the house. "Let me know what you find out at autopsy."

He was still coughing when he entered the den, where a statuesque brunette stood center stage. Lorraine Johnson, Buck's wife. "I'm Detective Thornton," Harry said, flashing his badge. "I know this is very difficult for all of you, but I've got to ask you some questions."

"Let me get you something to drink for that cough, Detective Thornton." Lorraine smiled graciously, and glided out of the room before he could respond.

Harry took out his notebook and turned toward the middle-aged cowboy slouched on a brown leather settee by the window. "You must be Jeb Johnson, Buck's son."

"Yessuh," the man replied. He wrapped his arm around a voluptuous redhead, whose face would have looked as gorgeous as her body, had her makeup not been smudged and her eyes red and swollen from crying. "This is my fiancée, Dollie Mae Adams," Jeb said. She seemed more upset than the recently widowed Mrs. Johnson.

Then Jeb motioned toward the couple sitting by the fireplace. "My father's partner in the cattle business, George Patterson, and his wife, Martha." The man nodded, the woman glared.

Just then Lorraine returned with a glass of water. "Thank you, ma'am," Harry said, trying not to stare at her exposed cleavage. He forced his eyes upward, noting that the beaded blue strapless gown matched the metallic blue of her eyes.

The aroma of cigars and leather, mingled with the floral scent of Lorraine's perfume, replaced the acrid odor of burnt flesh. Harry's coughing subsided.

He took a closer look at his surroundings. Sturdy furniture covered in dark brown leather, large mahogany desk, stone fireplace flanked by matching armchairs, and of course a well-stocked bar. The only adornment on the desk, Harry noted, was an ornate leather desk blotter and matching cigar humidor. No stray papers, family photos, or indications of business dealings. Although shelves lined the walls, there were no books on them.

Lorraine got right to the point. "Why did you ask us all to wait here, Detective Thornton? Why are the police even involved? My husband's death was an accident."

"So it seems," Harry answered. "But a very unusual accident, wouldn't you agree? It's just standard procedure to investigate uncommon deaths. Especially when it involves one of the most esteemed members of our community." *And the most wealthy*, he added silently.

Harry turned back toward the group assembled in the den. "Now can someone tell me what happened here tonight?"

They all started talking at once.

"It was at the end of…"

"Buck just went outside…"

"It was horrible…"

"He was really drunk…"

"We heard him screaming…"

"Hold it!" Harry shouted, raising his hand like a traffic cop. "We'll have to do this one at a time. Mrs. Johnson, you go first. Tell me everything you know about the events leading up to your husband's death."

Lorraine's deep blue eyes bored into Harry's. "Well, Buck had been drinking pretty heavily, like usual, but he was fine. The man can hold his liquor. He was standing by the patio doors the last time I spoke to him. I had gone into the foyer to say goodnight to our guests when I heard this horrendous screaming. It came from out back, so I ran to the patio. At first, I couldn't see much—the lights were shining on the fountain, blocking the view beyond it, but the sound and smell…"

She hesitated, her nose wrinkled in distaste. "I heard Jeb yelling for the hose. George unraveled the garden hose, here at the side of the house, but it didn't reach far enough. By that time, Buck had stopped screaming. There was nothing we could do. I came back and called 911."

Five long years, Lorraine thought. *That's how long I've put up with that old geezer. That's how long I've been waiting to inherit all this. And finally Buck's gone. The result of another one of his drunken stupors. How perfect. But if I want to collect, this cop has got to believe that it was all an unfortunate accident.*

Lorraine was a cool customer, alright, Harry noted. Her husband burned alive, right before her eyes, and yet here she stands, cool and calm, reciting her statement like a detached observer. Not a hair out of place. No signs of distress marring that exquisite face. He stared at her. She didn't flinch.

"What did you say to him?" Harry finally asked.

"I beg your pardon?"

"You said you spoke to your husband right before he went outside."

"Oh," she said. "I don't remember."

"Did he seem confused? Slurred speech? Anything out of the ordinary?" Harry asked.

Martha Patterson snorted. "Slurred speech, but nothing out of the ordinary. He was drunker 'n a skunk!"

Lorraine shot Martha a withering look. Harry raised an eyebrow and turned to Martha, who looked like she was just chomping at the bit to get in her two cents' worth. "Mrs. Patterson, is there something you want to say?"

"Well, if you ask me," she spat out, "he didn't know what he was doing. Buck was so damn drunk he couldn't walk straight, let alone think straight. He stumbled past us with hardly a thank you! He probably mistook that barbeque pit for his bed. I'm just surprised he didn't pull Little Miss Dollie Mae in with him, the way he was pawing all over her."

At that, Dollie Mae let out a wail and sprang toward Martha like a hungry jungle cat. Harry quickly stepped between them and held the redhead at bay. Lorraine didn't move, but if looks could kill there'd have been two more dead bodies on the premises.

After separating the women, Harry turned to Jeb. He studied the man lounging on the leather settee. Jeb had the air of those spoiled brats born to money, who think the world owes them everything. Harry said, "Mrs. Johnson told us that when she heard the screams, she ran to the patio and you were already there."

"Yessuh, I was," Jeb drawled.

"Did you see anyone else out there?"

"Besides Daddy, you mean?" He paused, as though thinking. "Naw."

"What about before you went outside?"

Jeb glanced at Martha, then tightened his grip on Dollie Mae's shoulder. "I was sittin' in the corner, talkin' to Dollie Mae here." He gave her an affectionate look, then continued. "She got up to go to the powder room, so I moseyed on over to the patio. I'd seen Daddy go out. By the time I got outside, I couldn't see him anymore, so I started toward the fountain, when I heard a thump and a scream. I ran past it and saw Daddy on fire, rollin' around like a calf that just got roped. He was screamin' like crazy, and I yelled for the hose, but it was too far away." He shrugged. "I just couldn't get to him in time. He got quiet, layin' there, charbroiled medium rare, cooked just like his steak."

Jeb smirked, thinking about what he could buy with all the money he'd inherit. *Dollie Mae and me can live high on the hog now. And with a sexy stepmother like Lorraine, a man could have the best of both worlds. Daddy had certainly become a problem I had to do something about. The old man had enough money to take a bath in thousand dollar bills, and yet he kept me on a measly allowance. I won't have to worry about that, anymore. He can't take it with him, can he?*

Harry turned his attention to Dollie Mae. She avoided Harry's gaze, squeezing a used tissue. Why did she seem to care more about the old man's death than his family did? Grief showed in her eyes. Or was it fear? Or guilt?

"Do you have anything to add, Miss Adams?"

Dollie Mae looked at the carpet. "No."

"Where were you when Mr. Johnson started screaming?"

She looked over at Jeb. "I guess I was in the powder room."

"What did you do when you heard what was happening?" *This is like pulling teeth*, Harry thought.

"Um, I came out to see what was going on. Everybody was on the patio, like they said."

"Did you do anything to help?"

"No. It was all over by then."

Dollie Mae bit her lower lip, thinking about the events of the evening. *I'd been plying Buck with Jack Daniels all night; that was my job, according to Jeb. What did he think I was, a common barmaid? Catering to the old man was a bitch, but Jeb promised that if I played along, the payoff would be worth it. I'm not so sure about that any more. I never expected things to end this way. Jeb was supposed to be running interference, but he kept disappearing. He told the cop we were together just before Buck's accident. But I know that wasn't the truth.*

Next, Harry questioned George Patterson. "You're Mr. Johnson's business partner?"

The little man hooked his thumbs into his suspenders and said, "Yeah. Buck and I've been in the cattle business together for over forty years. Good friends as well as business partners. Martha's sister, Livvy, was Buck's first wife and Jeb's mama. She died young, God bless her soul. So you could say we're more like family."

"You tried to put out the fire with the garden hose?" Harry asked.

"Sure did," George answered. "Wasn't long enough to reach, but I tried. Damn shame."

Yeah, Buck and me go back a long way, George thought. *Too long. I couldn't wait for the old bastard to kick off. Now that Buck is gone, my financial troubles are over. I would have preferred to be at the racetrack tonight, but Martha wouldn't let me skip this shindig. Glad I didn't. I wouldn't've wanted to miss these fireworks.*

Harry nodded, then turned back to Martha. "Did you see or hear anything more than what you've already told me, Mrs. Patterson?"

Martha Patterson, silver hair teased and lacquered into an impressive beehive, forced a smile, while her glacier-blue eyes sharpened into icicles. "Up until Buck's horrible accident, it was a lovely party," she said. "Lorraine organized it with her usual efficiency."

About as lovely as a drunken orgy can get, Martha thought. *I can pretend to like the bitch, but she's only a young hussy after Buck's money. The money that rightly belongs to my sister Livvy's boy. Well, I made sure Buck knew all about Lorraine's true colors. Jeb deserves that inheritance. And he'll take care of George and me, just like I took care of him.*

The next morning, Harry returned to the ranch. The maid answered the door and ushered him into the den. Lorraine stormed in. "What's the meaning of this?"

Jeb strode into the room right behind his stepmother. "Why are you bothering Lorraine now? We're in mourning. We have a funeral to prepare."

"I'd like to speak to your stepmother alone, Mr. Johnson," Harry calmly answered. "But don't go far. When we're through, I have a few more questions for you, too."

Jeb scowled, then stomped out of the room.

Harry turned his attention to Lorraine, who stood facing him, arms crossed, eyes burning with hatred.

So, the unflappable Mrs. Johnson really can show some emotion.

Lorraine was dressed in black, but her strange idea of mourning attire caught Harry's attention. She complemented her skin-tight black velvet jeans with a black silk western shirt embellished with rhinestones and fringe. A black patent leather belt and black high-heeled cowgirl boots set off the ensemble. Harry's heartbeat tripled.

"Mrs. Johnson," he said, taking a deep breath. "Please let me explain. Can we sit down?"

Lorraine composed herself, but remained distant. "Of course. Where are my manners?" She led him to the leather sofa.

"Ma'am, I'm sure you understand that in cases like this, an autopsy is standard procedure. Certain tests must be performed, for example, to find out whether alcohol was a factor—"

"A factor!" she interrupted. "Of course, it was a factor! We all told you that!"

"Yes, ma'am, you did, but I'm afraid we need the physical evidence to corroborate your statements. The coroner has to run a series of tests on your husband's body, because of the unusual nature of his accident."

Lorraine was still in a snit. "I will contact my lawyer about this shoddy treatment," she declared.

"I'm sorry, Mrs. Johnson, but I need to ask you a few more questions now."

"I already told you everything last night."

"Yes, ma'am, but that was just a preliminary investigation. You were all very upset." *Yeah, right. About as upset as a bunch of vultures can get,* he thought. "Now we need to get your official statement, if you don't mind going over it once again."

"Of course I mind, Detective, but I guess I have no choice, do I?"

"No, ma'am, you don't," Harry said, "and the sooner we start, the sooner it will be over."

"The autopsy report's in," Harry told the Captain. "Buck Johnson died from the burns he suffered when he fell into the barbeque pit. Of course, his blood alcohol level jumped off the charts, too."

"Are you saying Buck's death was an accident, after all?"

"Wait, there's more," Harry said. "The ME also found arsenic in his system. It wasn't the cause of death, but it could have been if the old man hadn't fallen into the barbecue pit first. Plus, we found chisel marks on the bricks of the barbeque pit. It looks like they were deliberately loosened. And remember that towel that we found near the body? It was saturated with lighter fluid."

"So someone caused Buck's accident. Any idea who?"

"Not yet, Captain. But it looks like whoever it was, wanted to be sure the job got done."

"Okay. Who wanted him dead?"

"All of them," Harry snorted. "Everyone who was there had a motive. Money tops the list—they all needed it, for one reason or another. Buck's wife, Lorraine, expects to inherit a bundle. She likes to spend it on clothes, jewelry, you name it. She also spent Buck's money on a herd of her own, and I don't mean cattle. Her young lovers include her stepson, Jeb, by the way. If Buck found out about that, he'd probably cut off the money, or file for divorce."

"Would she kill to get her hands on that money?" the Captain asked.

"Are you kidding?" Harry said. "Young, beautiful wife and old, rich husband? It's a classic."

"Any real evidence?"

"We did find a bottle of arsenic in Lorraine's bedroom, but no prints and she claims she was framed. It's possible. Anybody could have planted that bottle to throw suspicion on her."

"True. Our first suspect is always the spouse. What about Buck's son? He expects to inherit, too, doesn't he?"

"He sure does," Harry said. "Another big spender. Word has it that his jet-set habits caused Buck to warn Jeb that he'd cut him out of the will if he didn't settle down. Both Jeb and Dollie Mae had reason to stop that from happening."

"What was Dollie Mae's motive, other than hoping to marry into money?"

"Isn't that a good enough motive?"

The Captain laced his hands behind his head and propped his boots on the desk. "Greed is always a believable motive, Harry. But we need solid evidence, not guesswork."

"She and Jeb could have been in it together," Harry pointed out. "Dollie Mae had the best opportunity to tamper with Buck's drinks. Buck had his own private decanter of Jack Daniels. According to the bartender, Dollie Mae was delivering his drinks to him all night, except for once, near the end of the party, when Lorraine ordered a glass of whiskey for her husband."

"Who else benefits from Buck's death?" the Captain asked.

"The business partner, George Patterson. He's been embezzling from the company for years. His gambling debts got out of hand, and he became desperate for more money. There's a chance Buck found out and confronted him, but we have no proof. And get this: Before he went into business with Buck, George Patterson worked as a brickmason. Remember those loose bricks from the barbecue pit? We're pretty sure someone deliberately loosened them."

Harry continued, "And then there's George's wife, Martha. Her sister, Livvy, was Jeb's mother. She died when he was just a young boy. Martha hates Buck, but apparently dotes on Jeb. Some say she'd do anything for that boy."

"What's the chance that all those things you mentioned—the loose bricks, the towel, even the arsenic—are merely coincidences, and Buck's death was simply an unfortunate accident?"

"You know I don't believe in coincidences, Captain."

Harry attended the reading of Buck's will a week later. "What a bunch of cold-blooded moneygrubbers," he told the uniforms who were stationed outside. "Cover every exit. All the suspects have been pointing fingers at each other. I'm expecting some excitement inside, and one or more of these characters might try to bolt. Let's see if we can catch us a murderer."

Harry walked in and stood at the back of the room. When the lawyer read the will, all hell broke loose. Buck had left everything he owned to charity.

Dollie Mae started screaming at Jeb. "You couldn't wait for the old man to die. And you weren't with me when your father went outside, like you told the police." Then she laughed hysterically and said, "You killed him, didn't you? And it was all for nothing."

Lorraine turned a sickly shade of white. "No, no... That can't be," she moaned, turning to Jeb for support.

Martha moved in, pulling Jeb to her side. "Poor boy, you deserved all of it. That's why I told Buck about Lorraine's infidelity."

"You bitch!" Lorraine yelled. "You meddling old witch!"

"Don't talk to my wife that way," George exclaimed. "Besides, I heard that the police found a bottle of arsenic in your room. You weren't just cheating on Buck, you were poisoning him, too."

Lorraine screamed, "I was not! I don't know how that poison got in my room."

"I do," Dollie Mae said. "I saw Martha sneaking into your room with a bottle on the night of the party, when I went upstairs to the bathroom."

In the silence that followed, they all turned accusing glares toward Martha.

"That little golddigger's lying." She turned to her husband. "You believe me, don't you, George?"

George paused, then said, "Martha, you told me on the way home from the party that you had solved all our problems. What did you mean?"

"I.. I... Nothing," she stuttered.

"She did it!" Lorraine yelled. "She killed Buck and tried to blame it on me."

"No...that's not how it happened," Martha said.

Harry moved forward. "Exactly what did happen, Mrs. Patterson? Did you murder Buck Johnson?"

George said, "Don't say any more, Martha. I'm going to call our lawyer."

Harry pressed on. "You thought that if Buck were dead, he wouldn't discover that your husband had embezzled money from the business. Isn't that right?"

"You've said enough, Martha," George interrupted.

Jeb said, "Aunt Martha, is that true? I thought I saw you outside right before I heard Daddy scream, but I didn't want to say anything..."

Harry moved in. "You have the right to remain silent..."

"Ungrateful wretches! All of you!" she screamed. "Sure, I wanted that old man dead, ever since my sister Livvy died. You all wanted him dead, too. You just didn't have the stomach to do anything about it."

When Harry cuffed her, she admitted everything. "I laced his bourbon with arsenic, then hid the bottle of poison in *her* room." She pointed at Lorraine. "Figured it was only fair. She took Livvy's place, after all."

Lorraine turned to Harry. "I told you I didn't have anything to do with the arsenic," she gloated.

Martha flashed an evil grin, then continued. "I loosened the bricks on the barbecue pit, too. Told Buck that Dollie Mae wanted to meet him out by the barbecue. Hah! Couldn't resist that, could he? Then I followed him. He was so woozy that it was real easy to push him over." She started laughing. "I soaked that towel in lighter fluid, too. And threw it on top of him to fan the flames. Woo-hoo! What a sight!" She smirked. "I hid behind the fountain until everyone came running out, then pretended to help."

"Why'd you do it, Aunt Martha?" Jeb asked.

"I did it for you. Livvy wanted *you* to have that money. Buck drove her to an early grave, and all he's done since is deprive you of what's rightly yours. Now it turns out that even in death, he cheated all of us."

Martha raised her chin in a haughty gesture. "That old geezer deserved to be turned into a slab of Texas Toast."

ROSE
John Randall Williams

Rose's hip stabbed her at seven. She stretched her legs under the quilt, finding a position her pelvis liked, and then she waited for her bladder to wake up and force her out of bed. In her mind she clicked through her schedule for another Monday: KRON news until nine, then *New York Crime Scene* on cable 53, then over to cable 56 for its fraternal sibling, *Miami Forensics*, followed by the Judges: Ray Brown, and Jody. During lunch she'd watch KTVU news, and then another *New York Crime Scene* on cable 25. In the evening, she switched over to *Las Vegas Crime Scene* and then, after her nap, the five o'clock KRON news followed by two of the national news broadcasts: ABC and CBS. Rose loved Dan Rather; was heartsick for a week after his retirement. Then dinner and Tuesday's prime time reality shows beginning with *Police Call*, over to channel five and *Real Life Forensics*, followed by *Challenge of Fear*, which she watched about half of, with sideways glances at the disgusting parts. Her day would end with the eleven o'clock news on KRON, creating a neat KRON symmetry, the channel already set to start the next day.

Rose milked her single cup of Earl Grey tea and settled into the overstuffed easy chair facing her twenty year old Zenith, a gift from Lenny for her 59th birthday. Rose didn't like going out, what with all the murders and muggings and drug traffickers and rapists, and just plain crazy folks infesting San Francisco. She knew how bad the world had gotten; she saw it every day on TV.

At noon a standoff on the peninsula dominated the news. Some deranged man held his poor family hostage and the police were negotiating, trying to save him and his wife and child from the hunting rifle he brandished from a window. Rose sank deeper into her chair. She bit into half a tuna fish sandwich, enraptured by the events unfolding on screen, comforted that this violence existed in two dimensions. She could turn it off, but she knew she wouldn't. Better to be scared by the news than to suffer the deathly silence of loneliness.

She went to get a glass of milk and discovered that she was out. "Darn," Rose swore to herself. That meant a trip to the Syrian. If she left now, she would be back in time for the beginning of *New York Crime Scene*. Rose liked the big, bold Inspector Joe Spangle with his outrageous Texas accent, so out of place in Manhattan. He reminded her of her late husband Lenny, though he looked nothing like him. Lenny had been short and quiet. But like Lenny, Inspector Joe Spangle was a man you could trust to find the answers. Where Lenny, an engineer for the National Traffic Safety Board, had meticulously reconstructed the chaos of an accident scene, Inspector Joe would do the same for a crime scene. Sometimes, it almost felt as if she watched Lenny puzzling out the details on her TV.

Rose put her light blue jacket on over the blue velour one-piece jogging outfit Lenny had bought her many years ago. She slipped her white all-sports onto her feet without touching the Velcro tabs. She stood in front of the mirror beside the front door and patted her naturally gray hair, cut short for practicality, and for the nth time, as Lenny would say, considered the strictness of her choices. But she had no choices. Lenny and his slimy broker, Bob Cusher, had made all her choices in the crash of 1987.

Rose grabbed her everyday purse, really the only one she ever used, and carefully made her way down the flight of stairs to her building's security door. She checked the entry through the glass; looking left, then right, then left, and then right again, as she always did, making sure no predator skulked in the corner shadows. Then she opened the big door slowly, so if someone did lunge she could slam it shut by letting go. At the wrought iron gate Rose recommenced her right- and left-looking, while twisting the handle, pushing the gate and stepping out onto the sidewalk.

Suddenly, the rude young man from the fifth floor barged through the gate on her heels. He wore ear plugs, sunglasses, a stocking cap, blue jeans, and a black shirt. He ran by without a nod of courtesy for an old woman. Rude! On the street Rose kept her head up and her eyes moving, possessing her space just like Inspector Joe suggested, telling the murderers and muggers and rapists that she was aware, alert and ready with the mace can gripped, pale- knuckled, inside her jacket pocket: no easy pickings here, you murderers and muggers and rapists. She gave a wide berth to a urine-soaked homeless person, its sexual persuasion smothered by multiple shirts and sweaters and pants, each worn through to the next and black with filth. It pushed a shopping cart brimming with greasy paper and empty milk cartons, clanging with black garbage bags of bottles and cans. Rose watched it pass with her best right eye.

The Syrian at the counter smiled and said his usual hi. He reeked of the alien spices he ate. Rose counted her change carefully, grabbed her quart of milk and said a stern thank you, with no kindness, mind you, don't give him any ideas. Show no weakness, that was the key. On the trip back up the street the homeless man was gone, but a couple of young black men in dirty blue jeans and black T-shirts were arguing, yelling at that rude young man from the fifth floor, right in the middle of the sidewalk. Rose did not approve of the young man, or his mother, a drunk that Rose had seen three times stumbling up the stairs, clutching her bottle like it could hold her up. Rose carefully stepped off the curb. Her heart beat in her ears as she walked a perfect half-ellipse around the knot of young men.

She pulled her keys out before she reached her brown brick building. A quick left, right, left, looking for trouble inside and out, as recommended, before opening the gate. Inside the entry she relaxed a little. Rose climbed the two steps to the security door and inserted her key. Something dark attracted her attention. It sat on the entry's black and white tile floor in a triangle of shadow in the corner on her left, below the wall of tin mailboxes. She backed her key out and bent down to see. A gun. "My God," she blasphemed quietly. It was a hand gun of some sort, maybe a .38, the same gun shown on all those crime scene shows. Rose's father had owned guns. Lenny hadn't touched one until the day he died.

Rose bent down and picked up the gun. It was too dangerous to leave lying around. It was heavier than she'd anticipated. When she heard someone clumping down the stairs inside, she quickly dropped the gun into her jacket pocket. The weight pulled her jacket down on that side. One of the kids from the new family on the third floor jumped down the last steps and held the door for her. Rose said, "Thanks," with a measure of meanness for the correct effect, and then she scuttled through, trying not to make eye contact with the young man, lest he see an opportunity. She hurried up the stairs, unlocked her door, stepped inside her apartment, and then locked, bolted and chained the door again.

Rose placed the milk and her handbag on the kitchen counter and pulled the gun from her jacket pocket, hefting it in her hand, admiring the weight, the precise manufacture, how one piece fit another with hair-thin accuracy. It was silvery, with a dark brown, deeply cross-hatched handle. The gun represented the mathematics of matter and space turned to a simple purpose, something Lenny probably would have appreciated if his own relationship with a firearm had lasted longer than the time it took to blow his brains out. She laid it on the table beside her TV chair.

Rose put the milk away after pouring herself a small glass and drinking it. She washed the glass out and put it in the strainer. During the rest of that day, and into the night, Rose gazed at the gun more than she did her TV. In the middle of *Real Life Forensics* she picked it up again and carefully turned the cylinder, listening to the clean clicks as each chamber came in line with the barrel. She opened the chamber and was surprised to find it loaded. She turned the cylinder some more, counting six brass and steel bullets. Their ends looked like tiny Muni tokens without the SF cutouts. When Rose went to bed she took the gun with her, laying it on her bedside table, pointing it toward her bedroom door. Its single eye kept guard as she slept.

The next morning Rose felt restless during the KRON news, so she concocted an appetite for poached eggs and put on her light blue jacket, carefully placing the gun in one pocket. She exited through the security door without looking left or right and did the same with the security gate. She turned toward the Syrian's store, but a crash startled her, stopped her. The rude young man from the fifth floor had caught the gate and swung the wrought iron back hard, smashing it against the cage.

"Young man!" she yelled, grasping the gun inside her pocket, laying her finger gently over the trigger, envisioning *Crime Scene* and all the after-facts, condensed to two dimensions, wrapped up in an hour: self defense, old woman is a hero. She caught his attention despite the earplugs. He scraped off his headset along with his stocking cap, revealing a wild flash of blond hair. "What?" he said, grimacing as if she'd hurt him.

"Young man," she repeated, not sure what she'd started. "Young man, you shouldn't bang the gate like that. You could wreck it," she said, catching up with herself, but unable to think of a better word than 'wreck'. Lenny would have known the warp and weft to a degree of centimeters. Her grip on the gun tightened.

The rude young man from the fifth floor smiled. "Oh, hey," he said, his cheeks dimpling and flushing at the same time. "I'm sorry."

Rose felt relief wash through her. She let go of the trigger as if it were hot. He was a handsome, man-sized child. He shuffled from one foot to the next, expending all that energy like it was free and forever.

"Sorry, I mean, I didn't mean to startle you," he said, laughing.

Rose appreciated that he described the matter better than she had. He had startled her, made her grab the gun. She didn't give a whit about the gate.

"I get so distracted, listening to the tracks." He grinned and spread his arms. With a rather graceful swing of one hand he pointed a finger at his belt and a little box clipped there. "I produce videos, you know," and he bent at the knees, pointing both fingers to either side of Rose's head. "And these tracks just blow me away, like, I'm composing videos in my head, you know? It's…it's…you know, it's like wild, you know?"

Rose nodded at the young man from the fifth floor. Actually, she did know. Lenny used to talk about his math like that, trying to think of words that didn't exist. "Yes," she said, admitting her connection. "Yes, I do know. My name is Rose." She held out her trigger hand.

The young man from the fifth floor took her hand and tugged it gently. He pushed a bang off his forehead. "Glad. My tag's Kyle. Nice-to-meetcha."

"Nice to meet you, Kyle." Nothing given away, nothing risked, that was the key. But Rose could afford a smile. She had the gun. Kyle nodded and restored the cap and the earplugs in one fluid motion that ended as a wave goodbye. His gawky legs propelled him quickly around the corner.

She started toward the Syrian's store. She watched the new homeless person making the rounds of their block. His/her bags of cans and bottles seemed to register the same level of clanking as yesterday, as if he/she hadn't turned anything in for cash, maybe never turned anything in, keeping the black bags as a savings account against the storm. As if living in filth was not a rainy day, everyday. Rose touched her gun, running a finger along the barrel, across the hammer, down the spine of the grip. She looked up into a cloudless sky wedged between the brick fronts and anchored cornices of the Tenderloin.

Rose discovered that the Syrian lived in back of the store. He was the only one watching the store, so he couldn't enjoy the beautiful day except to stand or sit on his cement stoop. Yes, going to the bathroom did entail a certain risk. He laughed and smiled and bowed to her as she exited with a half dozen eggs. She didn't even complain about the outrageous price.

Was it the gun? she thought. Did it allow her to look at the world again? To see the sky and everything below it in terms wider than her fears. The weight in her jacket pocket felt like an invisible shield. Young people being loud and brash passed her by and she didn't alter her trajectory at all. She walked around the block, observing her neighbors. She'd forgotten how much she enjoyed watching people.

The next day Rose skipped her morning TV altogether and caught a bus to the Mechanics Library on the edge of San Francisco's Financial District. She took the gun. She hadn't been downtown since Lenny died, but managed to find her way around just as well as twenty years ago. Rose used the library's computerized card catalog to locate a good book on handgun safety. She spent the morning in the airy reading hall on the second floor, sitting at one of the soaring windows, enjoying the warm sunshine, periodically looking up from her book to watch the pedestrians on Market Street. The gun book said that handguns should be cleaned regularly whether or not they were used. Rose had no idea how long it had been since her gun's last cleaning.

That night she watched the news without cringing at the images of murder and mayhem. The next morning, Rose took the bus downtown again, this time passing the Mechanics Library. She exited at Post and Montgomery, following Montgomery a block to Market. One of the historical F Line trains rolled past, its steel wheels screaming so loud everyone on the street winced. She crossed Market and walked up the slight hill between Montgomery and Kearny to the Boulangerie Café. Rose used to join Lenny and his friends there for lunch. She'd been a little surprised it was still in business after twenty years.

She picked up a meager breakfast of Earl Grey tea and a bran muffin and sat outside, watching people. Two young Asian men in leather jackets brought their coffees to the next table, glancing at her in a way that once would have had her ducking her eyes and clutching her mace. But now she didn't mind, she stared back. The weight in her jacket pocket rested comfortably against her thigh. "Enjoying the weather, gentlemen?" she called to them as the tall one looked at her again. "Uh, yeah," he said. "Too nice for class." His partner ignored them both and stood, joining the pedestrian flow down Market. "Enjoy your day," she said to the tall one as he jogged to catch up with his companion.

The next morning, after cleaning her tea cup, Rose sat in front of the TV without turning it on. She cleaned the gun thoroughly with a chamois and some household oil. She dressed in her best dark pants suit. In her day she'd been the daring one to wear a pants suit, now all the women wore them. Rose emptied her everyday purse onto the kitchen counter. From the pile she pulled a few dollars and some bus tokens, and put them in her jacket pocket. She pulled on her best white gloves and put the gun in the purse. She took the bus downtown. At the Boulangerie Café, she picked up a cup of Earl Grey, and took the same seat on the patio beside Market Street. Everything was perfect. The morning was clear and cool. The sidewalks were jammed with nine-to-fivers clutching Starbucks cups. She waited for one of the F Line trains to trundle forward from the intersection at Kearny. Its wheels ground the rails, sounding like a giant baby's scream. Rose cradled her purse with her left hand. She put her right hand inside her purse and stood. She turned to face the table next to her.

"Bob Cusher?" she asked the man sitting there sipping coffee and reading *The Wall Street Journal*. She had to be sure. She'd seen him take the same seat, at about the same time the last two days.

"What?" he said, squinting, wincing at the sound of the train.

Rose braced herself and pulled the trigger three times fast, watching calmly as the slugs bloomed like red roses on Bob's white shirt front. The impacts threw him backward. Rose took a deep breath, clutched her purse to her waist and strolled into the flow of pedestrians. Behind her someone screamed. Rose kept walking, slowly removing the white gloves and dropping them into her purse. She walked all the way to the Embarcadero. The sirens of at least five police cruisers were tearing toward the Boulangerie Café. Rose crossed Embarcadero at the light and turned right, walking three blocks to the pedestrian pier next to the Waterfront Restaurant. A couple of young men were fishing in the bay at the end of the pier. Rose walked almost to the end. She leaned over the railing and, making sure no one was looking, dropped her purse with the gun and the gloves into the bay. The little black bag made a small splash and sank immediately.

Rose filled her lungs with moist bay air and tried to relax. She remembered that horrible look on Lenny's face when all the margin calls started coming in. She remembered him swearing at Bob Cusher for talking him into buying stock on margin. And then she imagined Inspector Joe Spangle going over her crime scene. There'd be witnesses, lots of them, but the shooting happened so fast their descriptions would be all over the map. That's how Inspector Joe would have described it. The forensic evidence would be there, fragments from her purse, the bullets, stray hair, all the millions of bits of potential evidence found in a public place, but without a suspect to measure them against, they'd merely point to a blank. Rose had an association with Bob Cusher, through Lenny, one that could be checked if the police bothered to contact every widow of every client he'd had in the last twenty years. She doubted they would. It was, she hoped, the perfect murder—quick, in a public place, seemingly random, with the murder weapon permanently disposed of. Rose walked back up to Market Street and caught the 5 Hayes as it turned off Front. With luck she could still make it home in time for the afternoon episode of *New York Crime Scene*.

A FAVOR FOR THE MAYOR
Howard B. Carron

I always closed my restaurant, The Cove, on Monday, shopped for supplies, and tried to enjoy a day when I didn't have to contend with any customers.

On one weekly trip to Manila for supplies, I hit the usual snarled traffic on the two-lane road. When I pulled out to pass, I saw a small shady spot on the left by a roadside stand. Cautiously I headed towards the stand. Suddenly the road disappeared, and the car dropped down about six inches. The crunching sound, accompanied by a tremendous engine roar, alerted me to the unhappy conclusion that I had probably damaged the exhaust system. Immediately, four youngsters surrounded me, three of whom were carrying concrete blocks and the fourth a six-foot length of two-inch pipe. These kids had taken advantage of an unfinished roadway construction job and applied their creative talents to make a few pesos from unsuspecting motorists. Sighing with frustration, I prepared to bargain and get my car back on the road. After some hurried negotiations, we agreed upon a price. The boys lifted the front end of the car slowly with the pipe, expertly placing the concrete blocks and sliding the car back on the road, bringing the car and pavement even.

I reentered the creeping stream of traffic to Manila amidst the good-natured smiles of the other drivers and the whoops and hollers of my recent mechanics. Now, in addition to a screaming transmission on my beat-up, ten-year-old, 1958 Isuzu, the sounds of a battered exhaust system announced my arrival. One bright spot in this whole day came with a message that my "new" car was ready for pick up. I say "new" because it had been built from scratch, a copy of the 1941 Lincoln Continental Convertible on the frame and running gear of a late model Toyota. I had always coveted that car. In fact, once I'd come close with my 1937 Lincoln Zephyr three-window coupe with its twelve-cylinder engine and mechanical brakes. Since parts for it were almost impossible to get, and the body had suffered greatly from the local humidity, I had decided to upgrade to my dream car. I picked up the car and drove it back to the restaurant, where I had some prep to do for the next day.

After about an hour in the kitchen, I couldn't resist going outside to look again at my beauty. Cream-colored leather upholstery and a deep forest green lacquer paint job just glowed in the dusky evening light. Just then, Paco pulled up in his 1968 Firebird. No one could mistake the car, white with blue trim and a huge Firebird painted on the hood. For the usually undemonstrative and basically conventional Lt. Francisco "Paco" Aurora, his wheels provided a peek into an earlier persona.

"Paco, what brings you here tonight?"

"Well, Burt, Mayor Yukuo Ochida has a rather serious matter he wanted to discuss and asked me to bring you along."

I've known Paco for a long time. He never does anything without a serious reason, so I just turned off the lights and locked up my restaurant. We drove to the outskirts of Angeles City, passing on the way the Coconut Vinegar plant that the mayor's family owned, and approached a large dwelling, something between a Japanese temple and a traditional Filipino home. It was perched along the edge of a large rice paddy that was home to countless green frogs whose song filled the night.

Mrs. Ochida welcomed us at the entranceway and handed us pairs of house slippers, an integral part of the Mayor's Japanese upbringing, and led us to the study. A gracious hostess, she brought Paco a glass of Johnny Walker Red and a bottle of San Miguel Import for me.

Mayor Ochida wore a casual *Barong Tagalog*, a traditional shirt worn outside the trousers.

"Permit me to apologize for taking up your time, Mr. Cohen, but a rather unusual matter has come to my attention. Perhaps Lt. Aurora will explain."

Paco nodded and placed his glass on an end table.

"We seem to be having a rash of unexplained robberies involving individual victims. During the last several nights, some rather important businessmen have been robbed of large sums of cash after business dinners in your area."

I poured a couple of inches of my San Miguel into a chilled glass, making sure the foam was only about a half inch. "That seems like a routine police matter to me."

Mayor Ochida laughed politely. "Stealing in my city is never routine, Mr. Cohen. This matter is all the more confusing because we know the exact whereabouts of the victims on the night they were robbed, yet we are unable to determine the method or the persons responsible."

Paco swirled the ice in his glass of scotch. "It is a matter of pride. The very fact that these robberies happened in my jurisdiction casts a shadow of shame on everyone involved—the restaurants and clubs that cater to the constant business gatherings, as well as on the people who are being victimized. It means that everyone who might have useful information is reluctant to talk for fear of adding to an already shameful situation."

I turned to the Mayor. "Mr. Ochida, what is it that you and Lt. Aurora want me to do?"

The mayor stood up behind his desk. "Mr. Cohen, as a respected businessman and restaurateur here, it would not be unusual for you to invite employees or associates out for an evening. Lt. Aurora, of course, would accompany you as a guest."

"What you're trying to say is, I'd make good bait."

Paco placed his glass on the table and straightened his jacket. "Lure, Burt, would be the more precise word."

The slightly hazy morning sky, filled with high-drifting particles of volcanic ash, reminded me that Mayon Volcano had recently awakened from a 15-year slumber. Despite the ashy air, I washed and waxed the car, then went inside the restaurant and shared breakfast with Ted L'Orange. Ted is a Manila journalist who writes a weekly column called "Over a Glass of Irish Mist," and a regular morning customer. I discussed Paco's plan for me to host parties until we gained some insight into the rash of robberies. He volunteered to join us, quickly promising that it would not appear in his column.

That night, I went to four popular, high end nightclubs with Paco and Ted. Casual questioning of the ever-present hostesses revealed nothing beyond expressions of regret. At each stop, I made a show of a healthy bankroll, but no one seemed to be paying undue attention. Paco finally suggested that we call it quits for the night. "It may be that we will have a better chance to acquire information on some other occasion."

I laughed. "You mean to tell me police investigation depends on chance?"

"To some extent," Paco said slowly, "many matters in life are chance events—such as driving one's car on a non-existent road."

In the morning, I was setting the menu specials for the day and sharing some coffee with Ted, when Lt. Aurora walked in and took a seat at our table. "We have a serious new development, Burt."

"What happened?"

"Murder." He pulled a notebook from his jacket and opened it.

"The man was Reuben Ortega, owner of a store that rents videos and also makes copies for selected customers." Paco put the notebook away and looked at me and Ted.

"It is very bad. Ortega was stabbed, and his body thrown in the river near the Tropicana Bar and Grill, only a few meters from the entrance to his residence."

"Why would anyone want to kill him, Paco?" Ted asked.

"I believe that Ortega was robbed and then killed because he could identify the person responsible."

Ted frowned. "*Hindi, maganda!* Not good!"

"No good at all," Paco agreed. "The newspapers have already been critical of the robberies, and the slaying is certain to produce increased pressure for a solution." Paco looked at Ted pointedly.

"Not my type of news," Ted said, "but I certainly understand the concerns."

"So what do you plan to do now?" I asked.

Paco adjusted his belt, smoothed his jacket and said, "Tonight, if you and Ted do not mind, I would like for you to be more conspicuous in your display of wealth."

After meeting Paco at The Cove, we took a cab and stopped first at the Restaurant Salvatore, located upstairs from a nightclub that changes ownership or name every few months. Roughly opposite the Clarkton pick-up service on Fields Avenue, Salvatore's is owned by Jun and Annabelle Plantillas. They serve fairly good pizza and a few Italian specialties, which are surprisingly authentic. Their Spaghetti Fra Diavolo is based on a sauce I taught Jun how to make. At any rate, as I finished off the last mouthful of osso buco, which I suspect was made from carabao, a man sitting to my right turned and grinned, speaking in tormented English. "Pretty good 'Eye-talian' food, eh."

"Actually," I replied in Tagalog, "considering the animal who supplied the shanks, it is quite good."

He smiled apologetically. "I guess you live here in Philippines a long time. You must be retired military or maybe you have business?"

"I'm in the food business. Tonight I'm just relaxing with some friends." I nodded at Ted and Paco. The chances of my getting information on the robberies and murder from this fellow seemed pretty slim, but I enjoyed the attempt.

"*Talaga?* Is that a fact?" The man cleared his throat, and then continued. "Maybe I can be of service." He removed a somewhat worn business card from his wallet and handed it to me. "I work for the Emerald City Driving Services. If you wish, I can arrange to pick you and your party up later." He leered. "Even take you to some interesting places. Or just take you home."

I examined the card and turned to my companions. Leaning closer, I asked, "Why don't we make the Cotton Club our last stop? Is it okay with you if Marcello picks us up there? That way we don't have to wait for a cab if it's a busy night."

"*Sige,*" Paco said. "That suits me fine."

I handed de Castro one of my own cards. "Yeah, why not? If your fee isn't too high, you might as well take us to the Cotton Club on Don Juico." The figure he named, while slightly higher than cab rates, was reasonable. I paid the check and Marcello went to get his car.

Paco took some garlic-roasted peanuts from the half coconut receptacle in the center of the table. "Your idea of ferreting out some information is interesting, Burt, but I don't think there's much chance that it's the right one."

"Why not?" I insisted. "Who's the last person a man usually sees before he returns home from a night of business socializing?"

Ted looked up from his snack of cheese lumpia. "Since no one who drinks responsibly would drive, it would be a friend or a hired driver."

Paco looked unconvinced. "And how many seriously dishonest taxi drivers or disreputable driving services do you know about?"

Ted grinned sheepishly. "None, Paco. Nevertheless, when we go out for an evening, someone must take us home."

Paco looked across the room, watching the five young women dressed in red jackets, white blouses and black slacks as they arranged glassware and made other preparations for the crush of customers who would start crowding in after nine o'clock.

"Assuming a criminal inclination in some aberrant taxi operator, how does the unfortunate passenger manage to lose his money without being aware of the crime?"

"I don't know about you, Paco," I said, "but if I make the rounds after a long day at the restaurant, I usually manage to sleep all the way back."

Paco pushed his chair away from the table and stood up. "To humor you, I will return to headquarters and reexamine the names of the places the victims frequented and leave instructions for my men to check the records of the taxi companies they used. That, I assume, will satisfy you."

"Leave nothing to chance, Paco. That's my motto."

Paco stared down at me for a moment. "Very well. I will meet you and Ted at the Cotton Club."

The feeling of a minor triumph remained until I remembered that Paco had our expense money with him.

Lt. Aurora handed the police sergeant a list of names and ordered him to start calling the taxi companies. Nothing else could be done until morning. Well, maybe...

Frowning, Paco clasped his hands behind his back and began pacing the office. Emerald City, the name of the driving service, rang a distant bell of memory. Paco glanced at his watch. Ample time remained for him to get to the Cotton Club. He walked to the Communications Room, pulled up a stool, and typed out an information request to all of the major stations on the teletype link.

Thirty minutes later, the machine commenced a staccato reply. Paco leaned over the machine, his expression anxious, then ripped the completed message from the teletype and read it again. According to the records, one of the major criminal organizations based in Manila—Yakuza and Chinese Triad gangs—controlled Emerald City Services. Tucked away among their suspected activities in gambling, drugs and prostitution, a seemingly legitimate string of driving services in Manila, Cebu, Subic Bay and now Angeles City thrived.

Chewing his lip nervously, Paco tapped out another data request. This time, the replies took less time; there were no arrest records for a Marcello de Castro, but the police in each of the major cities where Emerald City Services operated a driving service reported a number of unsolved robberies, all at night.

The pieces were falling into a pattern. If the Triad enlisted men without prior arrests, they could undertake the driving service robberies periodically without drawing suspicion. But would a man like Marcello de Castro kill? Yes, if one of his victims were sufficiently alert to catch him in the act, threatening to spoil another source of illicit income.

Paco's thoughts flashed onto Burt and Ted. There might, then, be a very real element of danger if Marcello picked them up. Paco dialed the number for the Cotton Club and waited for an answer.

Ted's eyes widened as we entered the Cotton Club. "*Mahal, Naman,*" he whispered. "It's going to be expensive."

His reasoning wasn't hard to follow. The hostesses were all young, beautiful and dressed in flowing evening gowns. The star attraction, Regina, was one of the diva singers of the Philippines. The piano player rambled through a slow New Orleans jazz number while the rest of the band members assembled their instruments and made ready for the opening show. The long, U-shaped bar was elaborately hand carved, and the chairs surrounding the tables were upholstered in rich, red velvet that glowed softly under massive chandeliers. We were still gawking when one of the hostesses walked up to us, smiling.

"You've got to be Burt Cohen, the legendary chef of The Cove." She rewarded my look with a tinkling laugh. "My name is Lea. Lea del Rosario, and in case you can't figure it out, I'm not a native. San Diego's home."

I returned her smile. "Okay, Lea, so what are you doing here?"

She led us to a table in a quiet corner of the club, and then went on: "My family has relatives in San Fernando, and one of them manages the club. When I visit every few years, the job helps meet expenses and it keeps me in touch with the local scene."

I liked her. "How'd you know my name?"

"Lt. Aurora called and left a message. He wants you to call him at his office." Hmm, so much for being legendary!

After we each ordered a scotch and water, I borrowed the phone at the bar. Paco's line was busy. I waited a few minutes and tried again. Still no luck, so I rejoined Ted at the table. Lea del Rosario sat down with us, and we began swapping stories about life in the States. Several drinks later, and after a wonderful performance by Regina, I remembered Paco and went to the phone. This time there was no answer. When I went back to our table, Marcello stood there.

"I'm ready to drive you home, whenever you wish."

"You ready to go, Ted?"

"Yes, I am a little tired."

"*Sige*, Marcello, we're all yours."

Ted closed his eyes as Marcello started the cab, and, after a few moments, I did the same. My plan was to fake sleep and see whether Marcello would try anything suspicious. However, soothed by the familiar sounds of the entertainment district—the cries of vendors selling hot roasted peanuts from pushcarts, the shouted advertisements of barkers stationed in front of garish nightclubs, the roars of tricycles as they revved their engines waiting for their fares outside of bars and restaurants, to say nothing of the multiple glasses of scotch—I let myself doze off with thoughts of sharing the Jacuzzi I recently installed at home with my lovely wife, Maria. I didn't awaken until I heard the sound of my metal gate being dragged open.

Ted was no longer seated next to me. "Did you take my friend home first?"

Marcello got out, opened the door, and leaned in. The light of the nearly-full moon framed his figure.

"*Opo,* Mr. Cohen. Yes sir, he is home now, and so are you."

Still groggy from my nap, I stumbled into the house.

Lt. Aurora's voice was tight with emotion. "I am so sorry, Burt. It is my fault that this happened." Marcello had been lying, for Ted had never arrived home, and now he was being held for ransom.

Paco declined an offer of coffee from Maria, pressing his hands flat against the kitchen table. "If I had not delayed so long at my office, I could have returned to the club before you and Ted left with de Castro, and our friend would not be a prisoner."

I took Maria's hand. "And if we'd used our common sense, we would have waited. It's more my fault than yours, Paco, because if I hadn't been asleep, Marcello wouldn't have tried to take Ted." I felt sick. "Probably he had to hurt him to do it without tipping me off."

"From the way you've been moving and your thickened speech, I think you either had too much to drink or were drugged, or both," Paco said.

Maria squeezed my hand. "No one is at fault, Burt. Everything that went wrong was a matter of chance."

Chance! I was getting tired of the word. "Yeah, maybe." I tapped the note that had arrived hours ago by messenger. "Do we pay the ransom to Marcello and let him go free, or do you take your men and go after him?"

Paco shook his head slowly. "Burt, the note is explicit. Marcello threatened to kill Ted if you do not go to meet him as instructed, by yourself." He fished a bent cigarette from a pack in his shirt pocket. "It is what de Castro has not written that causes me anxiety."

"Like what?"

"Even if you pay, Burt, there is no guarantee that Marcello will not kill Ted, and try to kill you."

The amount de Castro wanted was large—he had taken time to check me out. "We've got the money from the bank. I'd give anything we have to get Ted back unharmed."

"Fortunately," Paco said, "we may have a slight advantage."

I couldn't think of what it might be; after two days of anxious waiting, it seemed to me that Marcello de Castro held all the high cards.

"I believe that de Castro assumes you will pay without going to the police. It may be in his thoughts that your restaurant would be damaged by the scandal that would erupt if harm befell Ted, and he is willing to take this risk. If he succeeds, he will rise dramatically in the Triad organization."

"I can follow that, but my question is still the same: what the hell do we do?"

"Do, Burt?" Paco stood up and gave Maria a hug. "We will take the money to the place specified by de Castro, which is not far from here. We must try to take him by surprise with a minimum of support. After that, we can only do our best."

Lt. Aurora drove slowly over the unlit back road behind Balibago, and then stopped at a clearing by the foot of a small hill, cutting the lights and engine.

Moonlight, diffused by a thin layer of clouds formed by the ever-present heavy humidity, revealed little more than a dirt pathway surrounded by firethorn trees. "You said this was a museum, Paco?"

Paco drew his non-issue revolver, a .44 Magnum, and checked the ammunition. "Actually, it is an unfinished building, part temple, dedicated to the Kamikaze pilots who lived here and flew out of Clark Air Base. A bombing raid damaged it badly during World War II and its completion has been hampered by the memories of the atrocities committed by the Japanese troops stationed at Cabanatuan."

I couldn't think of anything else to delay the inevitable. "Okay, I'm going to get started." I took a flashlight from the seat, picked up a large brown envelope crammed with pesos, opened my door, and got out quietly.

"Remember," Paco said softly, "I will not be far behind."

The wind blew sharply, and I sensed the rain coming in behind it. The top of Mount Arayat, brooding behind the temple, lay shrouded in darkness. I turned on the flashlight and started up the path.

Charred plank steps led to the entrance. As I turned the flashlight in an arc, I could also see that many of the supporting beams were splintered and fire-blackened. Cautiously, I made my way up the planks and stood at the gaping entrance. A long, dazzling display of lightning to the south revealed Marcello's leering face in the doorway.

"Inside," he ordered, "and move very slowly." I complied, directing the cone of light toward the floor. De Castro moved closer, waving the gun at me. "Now give me the money, *Pare.*"

I held out the envelope. "Where's Ted L'Orange? You promised to let him go once you got your money."

De Castro reached out and grabbed the envelope with his left hand. "I will now take you to your compadre, and both of you will depart together, to your graves."

I heard a rumble of thunder beyond the mountain, and then the crack of Paco's voice. "Do not move, de Castro, or you are dead!"

Marcello fired two quick shots toward the entrance, then turned and ran as I dropped to the floor. As I lay in darkness, the broken flashlight somewhere on the floor, I heard a whisper nearby. "Burt, Burt, are you all right?"

"Yeah, no damage." I got up, heart thudding, and felt Paco's hand on my arm. "He's in here somewhere, Paco."

Outside, a driving rain began, slapping hard against the roof. "I'm going after him, Burt. Please remain where you are."

From the occasional flickers of lightning, I could see Paco moving toward one of the corridors branching away from the large, empty chamber we were in. Nothing could keep me glued to a safe spot while Paco put himself in danger. Almost total darkness surrounded me as I groped my way along the walls toward the interior of the temple. Then, almost too quickly to register on my mind, I heard a strange, high pitched twitter, followed almost instantly by a series of flashes and sharp explosions.

Paco's voice, a few meters ahead of me, spoke calmly. "It's safe now, Burt." A small flame spouted into existence. Paco, cigarette lighter in one hand, knelt by Marcello de Castro.

"Is he dead?"

Paco searched for a pulse in de Castro's throat. "No, but he will cause us no more problems. Now we must hurry. I am very concerned about Ted."

We left de Castro bleeding on the floor and started our search. It ended in an alcove toward the rear of the museum. Ted sat there, propped motionless in a corner, hands and feet tied, a gag in his mouth. I held the cigarette lighter, and, for a second time that night, Paco felt for a pulse.

"Paco?" I asked. "How bad is he?"

In the unsteady yellowish light, Paco seemed to be a thousand years old. "We must hurry to the hospital, Burt."

I wasn't in the mood to enjoy even the luxury of the Mayor's well-appointed van as we sped southward in the fading afternoon light. Each of us was wrapped up in his own thoughts. Our destination this day was a mystery: Paco had kept it a secret from everyone.

As we passed Tagaytay, Ted unconsciously touched the white bandages binding his head and addressed Paco.

"Excuse me, Paco, but would you mind explaining how you managed to stop de Castro so effectively when you could not see him?"

Paco, who turned to face us, smiled. "First, join me in some of Mayor Ochida's excellent scotch. I seem to be developing a thirst. Besides, I have an interesting tidbit of information for you. It seems that the hostess who served you at the Cotton Club was a cousin of de Castro, and did, in fact, doctor your drinks."

Paco produced a bottle of Johnny Walker, glasses and ice.

"Here's to Ted's fortunate recovery, and to the end of a most unpleasant situation." Fortunate was the right word, I thought. Ted's hairline skull fracture and concussion could have been a lot worse.

Ted wiped his mouth with a napkin. "I'm still curious about how you were able to shoot de Castro in the dark."

Paco rummaged through his jacket pockets until he found a pack of cigarettes. "The place where de Castro took you after, ah, rapping your head so rudely, started out as a smaller version of the Chion-in Temple in Kyoto. However, as I told Burt, the community interrupted it because of their aversion to things Japanese. Luckily for all of us, the interior was completed and escaped most of the fire damage."

Ted was smiling broadly in apparent appreciation of the information, but I was in a fog.

"Interesting, Paco, but so what?"

Paco smiled at me tolerantly.

"In the feudal days of Japan history, Burt, temples were sometimes robbed of their treasures, so a famous architect designed floor boards that make a sound like the bush warbler when someone walks over them." He emptied his glass and paused while Ted refilled it. "As you may guess, this sound alerted the guardian priests and thwarted theft."

"So you simply fired in the direction of the bird song and chanced to hit de Castro."

Paco answered solemnly. "As I have said so often in the recent past, much of life is a matter of chance, and much of success is knowing how to make the most of it."

His answer did nothing to lighten my foul mood. "What about Emerald City Services, that Marcello de Castro worked for? Is it chance that lets them get away with this while others in their employ continue to do the same thing?"

"Not so much chance," Paco said, "as the necessity for slow, legal procedure in a civilized land. Sooner or later, they will make another mistake and we'll have them."

ART CAN BE MURDER
Carole Sojka

"So, anyway," Tony said to the woman, "the idea of the piece was that the artist, this guy Roger Welken, would tunnel out of a sealed space under the gallery. It was a metaphor, he said, 'artistic striving for freedom.'" Tony and the woman stood side by side in front of one of the pieces in the current show at the Corbett Galleries.

The crowd swirled around them, women in jewels and designer dresses, men in suits or casual wear, mixed with those wearing paint-splattered jeans or tights topped with sweatshirts or stretched-out sweaters, some of the women in leg warmers with high heels or ratty sneakers.

The woman turned to him now, looking into his face. She attracted attention—very black hair, pale skin, wearing black eyeliner that made her dark eyes sink back into her face like glowing coals. She was tall and very slender, dressed all in black.

She kept glancing around the gallery, like she was looking for someone—maybe a well-known artist or critic, anyone else worth talking to. Corbett Galleries was one of the most important in New York. Lots of top name artists. This was a big show, at least that's what *The New York Times* had said. The paintings on the gallery walls were huge and riotously colored but decorative, like Rorschach figures in fiesta colors, the brightness draining them of any seriousness they might have assumed in black and white.

He wondered what she was doing here. Probably an artist—or a groupie. "What brings you out tonight?"

Her eyes swung away from him, and he knew he'd made a mistake. Bringing things into the present would lose her. She was a looker, too. But she was watching out for somebody else.

"Nothing special," she answered. "I thought I'd meet somebody here, but I don't see him."

"Who?"

"Eddie Mars. He said he'd like to see my stuff." It looked like it made her happy just to say that Eddie Mars was interested in her work.

"Yeah. He says that."

"What do you mean?" She sounded angry.

"Means he wants to get into your pants."

"And he isn't interested in my art?"

"That's about it."

"That's bullshit."

"That's just Eddie."

"Okay, so tell me about Roger Welken. Where did you fit in?" she asked. She turned toward him and maneuvered herself so she could watch the front door. "I'm Karen, by the way."

"I'm Tony," he said, sticking out his hand. "I worked in that gallery at the time." He saw Karen glance around again and knew he would lose her if he didn't say something interesting. "You remember it, don't you? The guy died."

Her eyes swung quickly back to him. "He died? I don't remember that. Must have been a while ago. I bet I wasn't even living in New York then."

"Yeah. Ten years ago, I'll bet." Ten years exactly, he thought. He knew he had her attention now.

"What made you bring it up?" she asked.

"It was just on my mind. Gave the artist his fifteen minutes of fame, didn't it? Even though he died."

"So, you worked there?" she asked.

"I was the gallery assistant, jack of all trades, helped set up the shows, clean up. Good lookers staffed the gallery during the day, but I did the heavy lifting."

"How did this Roger Welken—I vaguely remember him now—come up with the idea?"

"Performance art wasn't as big then as it had been in the 70's, but it was still around and could be sensational. That was his medium. He said his body was his canvas. He'd cut himself, had somebody shoot him with a bow and arrow, came close to getting electrocuted in one performance. But here, he took a real chance."

"More than getting shot?"

"The shooter was a friend, not just anybody. The tunnel idea wasn't as controlled. "

"Why? Weren't there enough safeguards?"

"He thought there were plenty. But he was sealed off for a long time. That was the problem with the medium."

"What was the problem?"

"It had never been done before. Anything could happen."

"Yes, I see." She stopped looking around and asked him, "How long was he down there? What about food and water? What about bodily waste? He couldn't come up and use the toilet, right?"

"Yeah, that was a problem. I was the one who sealed him in—reporters and TV were there to see it. The whole project was set up with closed circuit television, so everyone could see what he was doing. It was very popular—on the news every night. 'Artist digging for freedom,' that kind of thing. With shots of him digging in this closed space."

"Tell me more about this Roger Welken."

"What do you want to know?"

"How'd he manage the physical stuff?"

"He took a lot of water down with him, and some food—trail mix, dried fruit, that kind of thing. He fasted before he went down, to minimize solid waste, but he needed lots of water."

"Then he had to pee, right? All that liquid. I can't help thinking about that. Nobody ever explains."

"He had a portable toilet with chemicals in it. The kind of thing they have in recreational vehicles. There was a little alcove in the room where the toilet was out of camera range. He needed to dig through several layers to get himself out, and he didn't know how long it would take."

"How long did it take?" Her eyes wandered the room again, even while she was talking to him, and Tony wondered what it would take to really get her attention.

Just then, the door of the gallery opened, and Eddie Mars, dressed in black, dark hair falling into his face, sauntered in.

"Excuse me," Karen said. "There's Eddie. I'll be back."

Sure, he thought. Sure you will.

She ran over to Eddie Mars, calling to him, "Eddie, I was afraid you weren't coming. I've been here for hours."

Mars pushed her away, not roughly, but as though he wasn't sure who she was. "Yeah," he said, "good to see you, too."

Eddie headed into the gallery, surrounded on all sides by women—all young, all beautiful. He acted like he didn't notice.

Tony's thoughts returned to Roger Welken and his tunnel to freedom.

He'd hated Roger from the first time they'd met and the arrogant asshole had looked at his sculpture. It wasn't there for anyone to look at; it was just stored there. He hadn't asked Welken's opinion.

"Whose garbage is this?" Roger had asked Kevin, the guy who managed the gallery. "Are you showing this shit? It's kindergarten-level. Makes me want to puke."

Kevin had looked embarrassed. "It's Tony's work," he'd said. "He's storing it here."

"Who the hell is Tony? Certainly lowers the value of my work if this is the kind of no-talent stuff you're going to show."

"Tony's right over here," Kevin said quietly. "Keep your voice down."

"What the hell do I care? It's garbage—plain and simple." Roger Welken had walked out of the gallery, and Kevin, meek and scared of losing him, had followed. Tony had been left alone in the gallery, his face burning as though he'd been slapped.

Tony looked at his work, trying to see it with a critic's eye. He'd put so much into it. He still thought it looked good, despite what Roger Welken said. He locked up and walked to his apartment. He wanted to hit Welken, beat him to a pulp. Nobody had asked his opinion. That night Tony dreamed of murder.

Kevin talked to Tony when he came into the gallery the next morning. "I don't know whether you heard Roger Welken yesterday evening." He looked uncomfortable, as though he'd rather not have this conversation.

Tony decided to play dumb. "No. I didn't."

"Well, he wanted to know whose sculpture yours was—what you have stored here."

"So?"

"So, he didn't like it much. Said I had to get it out of here."

"And you said?"

"I said I would." Kevin looked embarrassed but determined.

"I thought you were gonna give me a show. That's why it's here."

"Well, maybe. But not 'til after Welken's performance. He's a big deal. He's gonna bring us a lot of attention." Kevin looked over Tony's shoulder, reluctant to meet his eyes.

"Not us—you and the gallery."

"Yeah, I guess. So when can you move your work out?"

"You want me out of here?"

"Not you. Just your stuff. I need you to stay and help with Welken's performance. It's going to be a bitch to set up."

"I'll think about it."

But in the end he did stay. He moved his work into storage and organized everything for the performance. He never got his show, but he knew he'd have his revenge. He would find a way to kill Roger Welken.

Tony glanced around the Corbett Galleries, then strolled to the refreshment table and replenished his plastic glass from a bottle of cheap wine. No matter how much the artist charged for his work and no matter how large the gallery's percentage, the wine was always cheap. He took a couple of crackers from a tray, wandered over to another group and listened to them analyzing the paintings on display.

"Beyond enigmatic," said a woman whose long blond hair hid the scars from her face lifts.

"Inert," pronounced a middle-aged man in a well-cut suit. "Too ingratiating."

"I found them excessively cute," said a young woman in overalls and a long-sleeved tee shirt. "Very disappointing."

"I don't think cute, exactly," said a thirtyish man with gelled hair sticking up in lethal-looking spikes. "But I can't parse the symbolism."

At a pause in the general criticism, Tony asked if anyone had seen the recent show of performance art, a revisiting of process.

"Oh, no," said the blond. "Too seventies. Historic."

"Way before my time," said the woman in overalls. She took the arm of the spiky-haired man, and said, "Come on, Shawn. I wanna see Loranne before she leaves." She pulled him away.

"I saw it," said the prosperous-looking man. "Hard to tell anything about that early work, what with the only records being poor quality video and photos. Once the people who were there are dead, that'll be the end of it."

"I guess," said Tony. "Do you remember the one where the artist died trying to get out of a sealed space under a gallery?"

"Sort of. How long ago was that?"

"It wasn't as old as the pieces in that show. Maybe ten years ago."

"Ancient history. Why're you bringing it up?"

"I was there, worked at the gallery. I've been thinking about it."

"Stupid stunt. How long was he down there? A week or so, wasn't it?"

The blond asked, "That was in New York?"

"Eight days. We had him on closed circuit television, watching him all the time."

"Darling," the man said to the blond. "You weren't into art. You were still married at that time." Then he asked Tony, "So what happened? He died, right?"

"He died the last night. Heart attack. Looked pretty painful, but he was dead before anyone could get to him."

"Interesting, but still a stupid stunt." The man touched the blond's arm just as a woman in a clingy black dress walked over to the group. She wore diamonds in her ears and around her neck and wrists, and when she moved, the stones flashed in the bright overhead lights.

"Where have you been, sweetheart?" she asked. "Who have you been talking to?"

He kissed the woman quickly on the cheek and said to Tony, "I'm sorry, I don't know your name."

"Tony Gagosian," said Tony, extending his hand. "And you are?"

"I'm Matthew Marks," the man said. "This is my wife, Bettina. And this is Angelique." He gestured to the blond woman who smiled and said nothing.

"What do you do?" Tony asked Marks.

"I'm the CEO at Tinnatral."

"What does Tinnatral do?"

"Electronics. Software. Right now we're beta testing a tablet computer with Wi-Fi and Bluetooth connections, integrated webcam and Wi-Fi VoIP capabilities. It's going to be the up-to-the minute way to get programs like computer-based phone systems to the mobile masses." He looked smug; the others looked stunned.

Finally Bettina took a breath and said, "We must be going, darling," and grabbed Matthew's arm. Although she had shaken Tony's hand and smiled at him, she had not looked at Angelique.

After they left, Tony turned to Angelique and asked, "She doesn't like you or something?"

"I'm sleeping with her husband," said the blond and yawned. "Why do you keep telling this story? I've seen you before, and you always tell the same story."

"No reason. It's just on my mind."

She bade him goodnight and headed toward the cloakroom. He looked around for another group. Maybe there was someone else he could talk to. Everyone seemed to be ready to leave. He spotted Karen trailing along behind Eddie Mars with three or four other women. Like a harem.

He stopped at the Brite Spot on the way home and greeted Frank behind the bar. He ordered a tequila shooter, then another and a third. He felt nothing. He'd like to get so wasted he wouldn't dream, but that never seemed to happen.

Once he'd tried to tell Frank the story of his perfect murder, but Frank didn't know anything about art and thought the whole thing was a big joke. Besides, bartenders were like priests, weren't they? Couldn't tell anyone.

The whole thing had gone so well. He had wanted to see if he could do it—a performance within a performance. Nicotine—extracted from cigarettes, distilled with ether into an eluate. He'd painted the liquid on one of the walls. He didn't want to kill him too soon. It was pretty toxic stuff, but he wasn't sure how it would work. If Welken died and he'd caused it, he'd be famous. If it didn't work, nothing lost.

He paid his tab and walked the two blocks home. The city seemed quiet tonight. He climbed the stairs to his apartment, sober but slightly out of breath when he reached the top. In ten years, he thought, he'd have to find an apartment in a building with an elevator. Ten years. That was how long Roger Welken had been dead. That was how long he'd been a murderer. And it hadn't even made him famous.

A WORLD MORE REAL
Rachelle N. Yeaman

It's funny, 'cause I came out west looking for adventure. I mean, I knew all the covered wagons were bolted down out front of restaurants and casinos now, and all the wild Indians had become Native Americans. I knew it was computer companies flocking to Phoenix along with tourists and snowbirds. And I knew that the Lost Dutchman's Gold was just a tall tale told because people need tall tales about the places they live. But hey, it's the Wild West, right? Big Sky Country, with mountains and jumping cactus and killer sunsets. Well, we don't tell the tourists that the sunsets are half pollution, that that gorgeous orange band on the horizon is backlit smog. Of course, the fierceness of a proper monsoon can't be beat, with the towering thunderheads marching over the desert behind the fresh smells of wet dirt and creosote.

But that's as much mystery as is left. The adventure's dried up, the folk tales have been paved over. There's still some magic left if you're one of those Sedona crystal-gazers who goes searching for vortexes, but otherwise it's business as usual. Traffic's still a bitch, and the supermarket still runs out of my favorite creamer. And even though I've got honest-to-God tumbleweeds rolling down my street when the wind's right, it ain't no Wild, Wild West anymore. Finding one of those big damn scorpions in the medicine cabinet is the breadth of the adventure in the twenty-first century, and I'd just started figuring, well, the world's a small place now.

And then I watched a man get killed. He wasn't five feet away, under the yellow glow of a sulfur streetlamp. I remember every second of it, replay it over and over, hundreds of times in the two weeks since. I was just walking; why waste the gas to drive six blocks? And I'd hardly left the bar, it was maybe four storefronts behind me. I heard shuffling footsteps and then a surprised grunt that never got to become a shout. Before I could turn around, the bum's neck was sliced open, right along the artery, with a plain, wood-handled knife, and blood arced high and dark. The killer had his back to me; I could only make out his dark silhouette, so much shorter than his victim, with dark hair. But over his shoulder, I saw the wide, glassy eyes of the wild-bearded man while the murderer bent his head to drink from the gushing wound. The victim was some crackpot Nam vet still in his army coat who was known to hang around a trailer park west of us during winter. Except he was in town two months early this year and muttering more than ever. People took to calling him Minnesota George, but no one knew why, 'cause his real name turned out to be Norman Alexander Maroni. In his last living minutes, I watched him gasp and struggle, stabbing the air with a six-inch blade, and I swear he hit his mark more than once, but the silhouette clung to him without noticing, mouth on his neck as though in the most intimate embrace. George's knife arm dropped; his eyes rolled back with the fading of his adrenaline, the vulgar slurping of his life. I don't know how long it took. I don't know how long I stood and gaped and felt my whole body contract. Heroic impulse nothing. I didn't understand—don't understand—how my night at the bar, still a bit light in the head, laughing with the guys, lamenting the Suns for another season, had got to this incomprehensible moment, how I couldn't even figure out what was happening in front of me, how I was all alone with it and no guidance, no preparation. And George's eyes just got dimmer, his head tilted further back, his knees folded more. He gasped a few more times, leaning further into his murderer, using him more for support while his limbs jerked with little, desperate spasms. His arms fell completely, the knife clattering on the pavement. His head lolled back at an obscene angle, and the drinking didn't stop. The coroner said there was hardly any blood left at all in the end. When the silhouette stopped, pulling back like a man just coming out from between a smooth, tight pair of thighs, George collapsed like curtains off a rod.

I told police that the murderer ran down the alley between Cal's bookshop and the bank, and I never saw his face. And I didn't, really. Except that when he took a step back from the corpse, I was sure he was about to turn on me next and that I should have started running hours ago. But he vanished instead. A shrink'd just say that I'd lost my mind by that point, that I was seeing things, but I swear to God and heaven and Elvis fuckin' Presley that his whole body drifted toward the alley; his feet had come off the ground like the hand of God or Satan had picked him up, and he got fuzzy around the edges, like he was just a bad photograph in the real world. Then he was gone, vaporized like in some damn TV show with spaceships and laser guns. I heard running footsteps in the alley, and a car came along, and I was still staring at the black shadow on the bank's stucco wall when Jeremy Ramirez took me by the shoulders and told me to snap out of it, and what the hell happened?

I didn't know what to tell him because all I could think was that a ghost had killed this man, and I knew that that didn't make sense. Something between my brain and my tongue had disconnected; I couldn't get the rush of thoughts to turn into any words at all until I found myself back in the bar, with Elvis playing on the juke box and everyone crowded around. Jo dropped a shot of her best whiskey in front of me. The cigarette smoke and the feel of the pressboard bar top under my fingers brought me back to reality, like I had just come out of a movie. I wanted to remind myself it was all fiction, and this was real. Except that really, I felt like I was drifting back into the movie, and the dark and the ghost and the body were trying to push through the door.

"He just killed him," I told the half circle of eager faces. I started to hear police sirens in the distance, and somehow that prompted me to down the whiskey. The heat rose from my chest and my throat into my brain, and the fog started to break up. I could feel my limbs again, weak and trembling, but there and attached and mine. I realized that everyone'd been real nice about not mentioning my wet crotch, and I told them what had happened. Then I told the police, and Jeremy talked about finding me just staring, and not a drop of blood on me, and no one could believe that I hadn't seen the face, or that I hadn't been attacked. But what the hell else could I say? I never mentioned how I saw the murderer disappear, and police concluded it was some sort of ritual killing. Maybe by one of the cults they heard met sometimes out in the middle of the desert under a full moon and whatever.

Two weeks, and nothing got clearer. My boss gave me a couple days off work and I spent ages on Google, combing through black-and-red websites about blood drinking and shape shifting. More bullshit about vampires and ghosts and the chubracabra than

I ever wanted to know existed. I read tales of horror written by spotty teenagers that needed a night, or hell, an hour, with something larger and curvier than their own hands. I found people that thought they were werewolves, that thought they were Vlad the Impaler reincarnated, that wrote insane porn about the Blood Countess, who I guess killed and tortured hundreds of peasant girls before anyone noticed. If I saw one more flaming skull, one more pixilated coffin, one more blood-dripping homepage title, I was going to hunt down the little halfwit webmasters myself and give them a real good demonstration of reality, just like the one old George got.

I still got sympathetic glances at the bar, and Jo still forgot to ring up my last beer most nights, but it was old news to everyone else. The murder was becoming old news to me, too. Things like that happened. My time on the Internet proved how sick a lot of people are, and in Tucson, people get shot and stabbed and beaten all the time. That was a fact of life that I understood. It's just the way things are. Except that men going blurry and disappearing is not the way things are. But I was working real hard to get myself to believe that I was insane, that my brain snapped, and that's all there was to it. So I couldn't trust my own mind, so what? That's better than not trusting the world, than not trusting that what's real is real is real, and that it's got to be that way, always, because folktales are just folktales because people like stories, and there's no room any place to defy everything science ever said. But the bar was good because it was real, and the cracks in the fake leather on the stools were real, and the scratched-up beer mugs were real. And Jenny Hastings was really real when she explained to everyone why she'd have to quit her job again and find something new, like she seemed to every six months, and how much more money her work was worth, except she never came out on top with any new employer. Old Ivan was real. He sold antiques from all over the world, real old stuff like in museums, and he always came in with his big white Stetson and bolo tie and faded jeans like he'd been out on some ranch instead of negotiating prices with men in Beijing and South Africa and Quebec. And he liked to tell us stories, old legends and ghost stories he learned when he traveled all over. He sat where the bar met the wall in the middle of the room and drank his beer and told us all about African spooks and Native American spirits and everything.

Except that last night, while I was staring into the foam at the bottom of my mug and not really noticing much around me, like the way that no one really sat next to me anymore, Old Ivan took the stool to my right and waved to Jo, who set a fresh beer in front of each of us.

"What's this for?" I asked, touching it and finding the glass perfectly solid and cold. I should have been able to put my faith in the solid, cold glass.

"You just look like you need it," he answered, fingers tapping the bar top lightly. He had some vague accent from someplace, Europe I guess, 'cause he's so white. His vowels weren't quite right, and his voice was smoother somehow than any American's. "I'm just a bit concerned, Sean. It's like you're getting further and further away from us each day."

Me and Ivan had never been real close, so I looked at him sideways. But he was only looking at me like he wanted to know what I thought about all the construction on the I-10 and not like he was being critical or rude or anything. It was some kind of relief to have someone notice and care that I wasn't myself. I sipped some beer to be grateful and shrugged at the rows of liquor bottles behind the bar.

"I'm just not over it. I guess I should be, maybe. Everyone else thinks so."

"No one can watch that sort of thing and really be the same."

I nodded because I was pretty sure I'd heard Dr. Phil, or some other chump, say the same thing before. I'd always thought I was a bit tougher than most, at least in the head. I never let things get to me.

I saw him look at me in the mirror behind the bottles. "All right," he said. "You don't want vague consolation. You had the shit scared out of you, and now you don't know how to deal with it."

"Something like that," I consented with another gulp of beer. It was dark and strong, probably one of the imports that Jo kept for Ivan.

"You saw something happen that you can't fit into your perception of how the world is meant to work."

I looked at him sidelong again, but he didn't continue, or even look like he wanted me to answer. I wanted to tell him that he didn't know the half of it. I wanted to laugh and tell him the truth, tell him how I was unhinged, and had stayed unhinged, and still can't tell the difference between real and fake, between thoughts in my own head and what's in the world around me. I smirked into my beer because it was just ridiculous now. There was a Bon Jovi song on, and somehow that just made it funnier. God, I was cracked.

And then I looked at him properly, still kind of smiling, and I said, like a joke, "Hey, you know all sorts of stories an' shit. What do the mountain tribes of Timbuktu say about people up and vanishing? Like you've got your eyes on them the whole time, and they just sort of float like they ain't real anymore and fade away into the night—only it's no magic show."

Ivan took a patient sip from his mug. "There are all sorts of stories about different powers that people can have. I suppose the most common one is ghosts. But then there are uncountable legends about different spirits and gods and demons taking human form, and many of those are said to come and go from this world at will. Most any folkloric creature you can think of has some mythology about disappearing, or moving with inhuman speed, or becoming invisible, from angels to vampires."

"Vampires?" I asked sharply, without really meaning to. I hadn't been listening much, but that word had soaked up so much meaning, or more confusion than anything, like static, that it shocked my head at the slightest mention.

"Sure." He stared at me, and I stared back at him, feeling like he was trying to figure me out, like maybe I'd given too much away and he could guess the rest. "But you know, myths and folktales tend to be fluid. Common characteristics of an evil spirit and how to get rid of it can vary almost village to village, if you dig far enough down. And there are different stories of humans turning into animals in most any culture; werewolves are but one western example. In Japan—"

"You know," I said, because I really didn't care about Japan, "I really thought he was going to kill me. I mean, why do you go up to a guy and drink his blood and not even slash the witness standing five feet away?" I had asked my brother this, and a couple guys at work, and the woman in an Oro Valley diner who usually served my coffee and sometimes chatted with me. No one had an answer. Mostly they just told me to count my lucky stars or thank God because maybe He was trying to tell me something. But I thought it was more likely the other guy was trying to get to me, 'cause God didn't speak through psychotic cultists, not even the ones on the Christian channel. "And why does a guy drink anyone's blood, anyway?" It came out strained, like there was something in my throat that I had to push past to speak. "Sick."

I thought about drinking some beer, but my hands were shaking. I had a hard, tense lump lodged in my stomach, holding all of my nerves so tight that everything kept shaking. "Damn it."

Ivan touched my shoulder, and I remembered the bar and the music and the people and the thick haze of cigarette smoke and how that was all reality, how there was an outside world, and I shouldn't be so caught in my own head.

"You need some fresh air," Ivan said.

I got up and let him guide me because my head was spinning, and all the people I knew became fragmented and blurry. A loud laugh cut into the chorus of that Bare Naked Ladies song about it all having been done before, and I couldn't quite reconcile the interruption with the song. My brain was lagging and missed the connects and disconnects in the middle. Usually I had a good laugh while the world swayed and everything seemed somehow more surprising, but tonight the alcohol just made the edges between my thoughts and everything else fuzzy. I could hardly tell one from the other, even when Ivan led me out the back door and into the old parking lot.

But the door closed on the bar, and everything got quiet and dark. We went to his pickup and sat on the tailgate, and I had to hold on to keep upright. There were too many lights to see the band of the Milky Way, but I could see the silhouette of the Catalina Mountains by the way they blocked out the stars in one mass of perfect black.

The parking lot gave me less to think about, and the dry breeze soothed my head.

"Can I ask you something?" Ivan said.

I shrugged and nearly lost my balance half way through, so I just said "Sure" instead.

"You were standing that close to the murder, but you never ran away. You never did anything about it, either. Why just wait and watch?"

I'd wondered about that a thousand times already, and the answer always came back simple and empty. "S'all I could do. S'like my legs got disconnected from my brain. I couldn't feel anything, just stare, like I was a ghost or something, not really there but still able to see and hear. And I think...I think maybe it broke something in my head." I made a point of not looking at Ivan. "There're things...images in my head that I remember, but they don't make sense."

Ivan stayed quiet for a bit, and maybe that's why I had told him in the first place, because he wasn't dismissing it or calling me crazy or giving me empty sympathy and a greeting card "It'll all be okay in the end."

"I doubt anything broke," Ivan finally said. "I'm an old man, Sean. I've traveled the world. I've seen things...well, no one really believes in what I've seen. When they do, they're usually crackpots or more than a little desperate, at least around here. In the 'civilized' countries. It's easy to keep your eyes closed here."

"You don't even know what I've seen. What I think I've seen. I must've just...I don't know, lost a minute or two or something. Watched too many scary movies, played too many video games, drank too much beer and caffeine, ate too many cheeseburgers—something."

"If you truly were insane, you wouldn't be this upset."

"So what then?" I demanded, swinging my head around to look him in the eye. My vision swam, and I started to pitch forward, but I clenched down on the tailgate and stayed on. "Either I'm insane, or...or the whole *world* is. Either I saw something that didn't happen, or it did happen, and then what? And then it's *real*? People really do up and vanish? I don't think I can believe that. I won't believe that. I'm screwed either way."

"You don't really believe that." He said it like he knew it, not like that's how he wanted it to be. Not like he was talking down to me. I wish he'd been talking down to me. I could have told him he was wrong then.

"Doesn't matter." I slid down off the tailgate, still holding on to keep steady. "I'm going home."

"Just a moment. Do you remember the stories I told about Romanian vampires, about *Strigoi*?"

I nodded, more because I had read volumes of vampire mythology than because I really remembered his stories. "You trying to tell me you think some Romanian sicko with two souls showed up in Tucson and sent his doppelgänger out to feed? You are crazy, if you believe that."

With a little concentration, I started a mostly straight line across the parking lot. I hadn't even got past the mirror of his truck when Ivan called, "Old Minnesota George had a knife out."

I stopped, but kept staring at the trailers on the other side of the street. "Yeah, well, didn't do him any good, did it?"

"How did he get it out so quickly, I wonder?"

"He pulled it out when he was attacked."

"His neck was slit before he knew what hit him."

I turned around, looking up at Ivan, who stood in the bed of his truck, leaning on the top of the cab and watching me. There was a connection to make. I had all the pieces and a feeling like being sick that I knew something that I hadn't known a moment ago, and that it was a horrible thing to know. But I couldn't think of what it was. I took a couple steps back from Ivan, not liking his big, white hat all of a sudden, like it was hiding something in plain sight, like it wasn't supposed to be there on that white head, like it was the daytime suit and tie of a superhero's arch enemy.

"What's it matter? Didn't help him. He's still dead."

"Old Minnesota George was coming toward you with the knife drawn. He might have killed you."

"Is that supposed to make me feel better about it?" My brain paused there because it was making the connections I didn't want to know about. I was figuring it out, and I didn't want to, so I asked, "And...and how could you know that?"

Ivan reached into the inside pocket of his jacket and pulled out a narrow thing that he threw to me. I reached for it too late. It bounced off of my fingers and landed in the gravel. I knelt down to pick it up; it was a small knife with a leather cover and a simple wooden handle—

I threw it away like it had bit me and tried to get up and run backward at the same time. My heel hit the cement parking space marker, and I hit the gravel ass first, scraping up my palms. I looked up and saw the silver of Ivan's bolo tie glinting in the streetlamp light. I waited for him to swoop down like a bat and pick up the knife. I wondered how far I'd get if I ran. I imagined his weight catching me from behind and pulling me down, the feel of cold metal parting my skin. Does your heart slow to a stop as your blood drains away? Or does it pound until it destroys itself and just blows up in your chest? Not that you're probably conscious long enough to find out, or to care.

Ivan and I stared at each other, me panting and beginning to realize that I should really be running, and him pulling out a cigarette and lighting up. He took a couple drags before gesturing at me with the open pack. I shook my head. Maybe I should've tried going for the knife, instead.

"Well, you're no hero, but I don't know you're a coward, either," Ivan said.

"The murderer had dark hair," I answered.

"I had dark hair once. And I was quite a big man, for my village, at least. But people were all shorter back then."

"So, what, I'm supposed to think you sent your doppelgänger out to save me?"

He shrugged. "I don't see why you shouldn't think it. You saw his knife."

"He was just a bum. He was going to ask for change or something." That's how it always was, anyway, with a dirty look or a "God bless you" if you didn't respond, but no knives, nothing more threatening than aimless cursing.

Ivan took a slow drag and nodded. "You go back to your fantasy world, then, where everything is simple and scientific. It'll be easier once you forget about the man you watched disappear before your eyes."

"You didn't have to kill him."

"It's what I do, Sean. I channel death, or suck away life, however you prefer it. Your life is an hour or two shorter already." He nodded back at the bar. "I come here to feed. So many lives all around, I don't take much from any one."

I looked at the knife still lying in the gravel, small and quiet. "Why are you telling me all of this?" Because villains only gave away their secret plans when they thought it was too late for anyone to stop them.

"I didn't save your life and risk exposure so you could just drink your world and yourself into oblivion."

"Then what *do* you want from me?"

"I want you to pick yourself up, dust yourself off, and go back to living. You were never meant to see any of what you saw, anyway. You were meant to run away like any sane man and go on with your life, maybe with the piss scared out of you for one night, and a story to tell around the bar, but otherwise all right."

"I'm s'posed to believe you just saved me to be *nice*? You killed a man to be *nice*?"

Ivan's cigarette burned bright orange. "I have morals. Death isn't purely evil, just as life isn't purely good."

I shook my head, which made the world spin. All these answers, and I felt empty, stretched. I'd taken a wrong turn somewhere, but going back the way I came just might kill me, or my head, at least, and going forward took me beyond anything I knew and maybe could deal with. But there was Ivan, flicking ash and waiting for my decision, the wide, white brim of his Stetson encasing his head. It was like one of his damned stories, where the devil himself appears with some wager that'll destroy the wayward traveler no matter what.

Well, then I wouldn't choose.

"I'm going home," I said, finding myself on my feet and dusting off my jeans.

Ivan gave no sly smile or shocked exclamation. He only looked me over, like he was translating me before I even knew what I meant exactly. He nodded. "Maybe you'll find more peace there. Take care of yourself."

With my two week's notice given at work, and my brother expecting me as a houseguest, and a pile of stuff to sell or give away already mounting on my coffee table, I keep waiting to feel more at ease. Like maybe my things are all tainted with this place, and getting rid of them will make me clean and light and able to flit away from this old apartment and this dry, dusty city, and I'll leave all the trouble behind. My brain will feel the change and snap back to reality and let me think straight again. Once I've got the place really packed up, it'll start to sink in, and I'll be able to relax, 'cause they've been paving over their folktales for two hundred years back East, so it's got to be quieter.

ABOUT THE AUTHORS

Susan Budavari has written two psychological suspense novels, several award-winning short stories and has co-edited three mystery/suspense anthologies for Red Coyote Press. Prior to that, she worked in chemical research and information management in the Pharmaceutical industry and served as Editor of several editions of THE MERCK INDEX, a best-selling encyclopedia of chemicals, drugs and biologicals. She is an active member of the Desert Sleuths chapter of Sisters in Crime.

Warren Bull is the author of ABRAHAM LINCOLN FOR THE DEFENSE (PublishAmerica, 2003). Warren's award-winning short story, "Beecher's Bibles" is included in MANHATTAN MYSTERIES (KS Publishing, Inc., 2005). He contributed a memoir to GRAB YOUR TIGER, authored by Kathy Schwadel (Keen Publications, 2007). His short story, "A Lady of Quality" won the 2006 Best Short Story of the Year Award from the Missouri Writer's Guild. Warren has published twelve short stories and six non-fiction pieces in a number of places including *Amazon Shorts, Great Mystery and Suspense Magazine, Espressofiction.com, Mysterical-E, Kansas City Voices, Crimeandsuspense.com,* and *Mouth Full of Bullets.*

Howard "Doc" Carron, born in Brooklyn, New York, is currently a Supervisor of Adult Reference in Gilbert, Arizona. His career includes: photographer, musician, teacher, ceramist, silversmith, sculptor, painter, wood block artist, writer, librarian and chef. Howard taught overseas from 1969 to 1993 at the elementary, secondary and college levels in Japan, Okinawa, Korea, Azores, Philippines and Germany. He is married and the father of three daughters.

Diana Catt has three children, a husband, two dogs, three cats and a Ph.D. in Microbiology. She is currently an instructor and postdoctoral research fellow at the IU School of Dentistry. She is also the owner/operator of a private microbiology lab which specializes in the analysis of mold in the environment. Diana's short mystery, "Photo Finish," appeared in a collection of mysteries with an Indy 500 theme, RACING CAN BE MURDER (Blue River Press, 2007.) Her hobbies include writing, reading, racquetball, birding and hiking.

Suzanne Flaig is a writer, editor and publisher from Phoenix, Arizona. Besides writing short stories, several of which have been published, she has completed a mystery novel, TERROR NEAR THREE MILE ISLAND, set in her home state of Pennsylvania. She has published nonfiction articles about music, writing, and roller skating, in various magazines and newsletters. An active member of Sisters in Crime, Suzanne is currently seeking an agent for her mystery series. Learn more about her work at her website: www.authorsden.com/suzanneflaig

S.M. Harding published papers, essays and articles as an academic, and has now turned to writing fiction. Her short stories have appeared in *Detective Mystery Stories, Great Mystery and Suspense Magazine,* and the anthology RACING CAN BE MURDER. She won the 2005 Bill Baker Scholarship to the Antioch Writers' Workshop and belongs to Sisters in Crime and Mystery Writers of America. She currently works as a chef in Indianapolis, Indiana and is working on a novel whose protagonist is neither an investigative reporter nor a chef.

Dr. Gay Toltl Kinman has eight award nominations for her writing, including three Agatha Award nominations. Her publishing credits include several short stories in American and English magazines and anthologies; six children's books; a young adult gothic novel; two adult mysteries; and several short plays. She has written over one hundred and fifty articles for professional journals and newspapers; and co-edited two non-fiction books. She also writes for three book review columns. Kinman has a library degree and a law degree. Website: http://gaykinman.com

Kris Neri's novels include the standalone thriller, NEVER SAY DIE, and the Agatha, Anthony, and Macavity Award-nominated Tracy Eaton mysteries, REVENGE OF THE GYPSY QUEEN and DEM BONES' REVENGE. Her latest publication is THE ROSE IN THE SNOW: TALES OF MISCHIEF AND MAYHEM, a collection of her short stories. She has published nearly sixty stories, and is a two-time Derringer Award winner and a two-time Pushcart Prize nominee for short mystery fiction. She teaches writing online for the Writers' Program of the UCLA Extension School, and is co-owner of The Well Red Coyote bookstore in Sedona, Arizona.

Sarah Parkin began her freelance career in 1999 writing articles and biography essays. In 2007, she became a contributing writer for *View Magazine*. During that time, she has continued to construct novels and short stories. She created Sparkin Productions, LLC to take her writing to a new level and reach new markets around the world. She enjoys reading, walking, swimming, cooking, and baking. She is active in several writing groups, including Sisters in Crime, Romance Writers of America, and the Scottsdale Writers Critique Group.

D.B. Reddick was born and raised in Canada, but has lived in the United States since 1973. He holds master's and Ph.D. degrees from Michigan State University. Reddick is a former newspaperman and college journalism instructor. He is currently Director of Public Policy Research for the National Association of Mutual Insurance Companies, a national property/casualty trade association located in Indianapolis, IN. Besides writing, Reddick is a competitive walker and has completed more than 30 half-marathons. Reddick lives near Indianapolis with his wife, Becky. This is his second published short story featuring Charley O'Brien, an all-night radio talk show host.

Gary Earl Ross is a professor at the University at Buffalo EOC and the award-winning author of more than 170 published short stories, poems, articles, scholarly papers, and public radio essays. His books include THE WHEEL OF DESIRE AND OTHER INTIMATE HAUNTINGS; SHIMMERVILLE: TALES MACABRE AND CURIOUS; and the children's tale DOTS. His produced plays include SLEEPWALKER: THE CABINET OF DR. CALIGARI (based on the classic silent horror film); the courtroom thriller MATTER OF INTENT (winner of the Edgar Award from the Mystery Writers of America); the mystery PICTURE PERFECT; and the political drama THE BEST WOMAN.

Carole Sojka spent two years with the Peace Corps in Africa after obtaining a B.A. in English from Queens College in New York. When she moved to Southern California, she earned a Master's Degree in Public Administration at the University of Southern California and worked for many years as a law office administrator. She began writing fiction about ten years ago and writes both novels and short stories. She now lives in a small town in Southern California with her husband, two dogs and a cat, and writes full time, except for a lot of traveling.

Judy Starbuck, an Arizona teacher, writes a mystery series entitled *Deadly Strokes*, dealing with issues in today's schools. Protagonist, Aimee Dionne, uses her handwriting analysis skills to solve the cases. Ms. Starbuck, an adoptee, found her birth family as part of a search and support organization, and the adoption theme is also woven throughout the series. Her writing credits include "The Sun Also Sets" (MAP OF MURDER, 2007) and "If I Were Serving Books for Dinner" (Arizona Republic, 2005). A graduate of Arizona State University, Ms. Starbuck has taught for over twenty-five years, most recently in the area of gifted education where she received the Golden Bell Award for excellence in teaching. A member of Sisters in Crime and a student of graphology, she lives in Scottsdale with her husband, Mike.

Nancy Streukens is a writer of mysteries and historical fiction with a 30-year career in technical writing and finance. The first chapter of her mystery, DEATH WRITES A CHECK, won third place in the Sacramento Public Library's Mystery Writers' Contest in October 2007. Her short story, "In Search of Millie," was selected for a Sisters in Crime/Capital Crimes Chapter anthology to be published in 2008. She lives with her husband and her dog, Tokie, in northern California.

Gigi Vernon loves all things historical—fiction, ruins, museums, film. Any time period, any place is her personal motto. Originally from the Washington, D.C. area, she now lives in beautiful, often snowy upstate New York where she began writing to avoid her dissertation. Despite her procrastination, she eventually managed to earn a Ph.D. in history. Her mystery short stories—various historical time periods and places—have appeared in *Alfred Hitchcock Mystery Magazine* and elsewhere. She is currently working on more stories and a historical mystery novel set in snowy medieval Russia.

John Randall Williams' short story, "Randy," appeared in the 2007 anthology, MAP OF MURDER. He is a contributing columnist to *The Mendocino Mix*. He is a cartoonist and has appeared in San Francisco's *Bay Area Reporter*. John is currently looking for a publisher for his first novel, THE MALACHITE DICK while working on his next novel, THE TROUBLE WITH GODS. John is an Executive Director of EcoArts of Lake County, a non-profit promoting visual art and ecologic stewardship. He is co-Producer of the Coyote Film Festival. John Randall Williams lives on Cobb Mountain in northern California. His email is jwilli1894@yahoo.com

Rachelle N. Yeaman is teaching English as a foreign language in Europe and gaining inspiration from her travels. She graduated from the University of Arizona with a BA in Creative Writing and German in 2007, and has turned her ambitions toward a novel publication. Previous short story publications include "Eye Strain"

(MEDLEY OF MURDER, 2005) and "Sinfully Sweet" (MAP OF MURDER, 2007), each co-authored with her mother, Sybil Yeaman. Her hobbies beyond writing include reading, avoiding housework, and jewelry making. Her favorite color is purple, and neither the Czechs nor the Germans have convinced her to like beer.

Frank Zafiro served in U.S. Army Intelligence during the end of the Cold War. He became a police officer in 1993. Most of his stories (including "Dead Even") take place in the fictional setting of River City with recurring characters. His second River City novel, HEROES OFTEN FAIL, was published in 2007. Dozens of his short stories have been published in print and online magazines, as well as several different anthologies. Besides writing, Frank enjoys good movies, his three children, and hockey. You can keep up with him at http://frankzafiro.com